Tonight is no different than the rest as I close my eyes and take that rage into the dream with me, still searching for killers who would end another life as easily and painfully as they had those of the ones I've loved. Although this is the task I accepted before I came to earth, to never truly sleep, to always hunt instead of rest, to kill some damaged soul lurking in the corners and shadows of my dreams, I sometimes wish for a reprieve.

PRAISE FOR THE WORKS OF B. HUGHES-MILLMAN

"PURGATORY'S ANGEL is an awesome paranormal romance that fans of Sherrilyn Kenyon and J.R. Ward will really enjoy…No simple angels here."
- Examiner's Women in Horror Author, Danielle DeVor

"PURGATORY'S ANGEL is a must read! From the first chapter to the final chapter it keeps you wanting more. The battle between good and evil in its finest. B Hughes-Millman keeps you guessing to the end."
- Dana Thornock, Book Reviewer

"DARKEST FOREST is constructed properly and the characters developed in a most satisfying way. It turned out to be a compelling story line which I cannot wait to follow into her next novel and the series beyond."
- R. P. McCabe, Mystery Author

"B Hughes-Millman does it again in this installment of her Black Casket series. The execution of the emotional conflicts couldn't have been done better. I'll read this again and recommend it to everyone."
- Nichole Severn, Book Reviewer

"I love RESURRECTION'S ANGEL! The suspense, the plot twists, the characters - great story! – pass the hanky!"
– D. B. Sieders, Urban Fantasy Author

"With compelling characters, interesting subplots and plenty of paranormal action PURGATORY'S ANGEL is the kind of

book that keeps one up at night! Kudos to Ms. Hughes-Millman for some of the most well-written action scenes this reviewer has ever had the pleasure of reading!"
- Chantel Hardge, InD'Tale

"I loved RESURRECTION'S ANGEL. It kept me on the edge of my seat and my mind engrossed. I never knew what was happening next! All through the book I kept waiting for a dull part but it never happened. I read this one in less than a day!"
- MeLisa Holden Bruner, Book Reviewer

"I think it was a combination of what was happening in the story with how well everything was written (how enticing, how fast-paced, how attractive the narration was) with my personal love for the theme, but whatever it was, it kept me reading."
-Misanthropist Book Reviews

B. Hughes-Millman

A Dark Angel Novel

Purgatory's Angel

City Owl
Press

This book is a work of fiction. Names, characters places, and incidents either are products of the author's imagination or are used fictitiously. Any resemblance to actual events or locales or persons, living or dead, is entirely coincidental and not intended by the author.

PURGATORY'S ANGEL
Dark Angel Novels: Book One

CITY OWL PRESS
www.cityowlpress.com

Cover Design by Tina Moss. Cover angel photo by Rafael Mercado Salas. All stock photos licensed appropriately.

Edited by Heather McCorkle.

Second Edition 2018.

For information on subsidiary rights, please contact the publisher at info@cityowlpress.com.

Print Edition ISBN: 978-1-949090-16-1
Digital Edition ISBN: 978-1-5199330-4-1

Printed in the United States of America

For my Mother

Who taught by example, the traits of a Dark Angel

For my Husband and Children

For showing patience with my Dark Angel ways

CHAPTER 1

Why do I find it safer to entertain romantic thoughts of someone I've just killed or one I'm about to? No commitments? No worries he'll turn out to be a bastard when I get to know him better? Probably. Or maybe I don't want to explain who I am and what I do. Luckily, I've never had that conversation. *I'm a dark angel, I kill demons in my sleep. And you? What do you do for fun?* Never imagined it to go over well under any circumstance. Guess that's why I've never tried.

Most people fear death. Many, because they question where they'll go when the cold hand of eternity grips their mortal throats; others, because their final destination is absolute. For me, death is a cool glass of water in the choking heat of an Arizona summer, infused with ice and a tall, inviting straw. Death has always beckoned me to "drink up" from the moment I began killing.

Hushed voices force my heavy eyes open. I'm in a state of confusion while blinking away the haze. How can this be? I've never been so disoriented before.

The room is dim with strategic lighting illuminating crystal vases and glass sculptures. Clear shelves display opulent art pieces; a child with a bucket digging in the sand, a translucent nude woman overcome from behind by a wave of seawater, two elderly men playing checkers. Each is uniquely crafted with accuracy and splendor. I've never seen such intricate glasswork before. My head throbs and vision blurs as I scan my surroundings.

Is this a dream, or am I awake? A room filled with potentially dangerous objects is *not* the best place for anyone if I'm not certain, especially when someone I've never met is advancing on me. Should I fight or hold back?

I step backward to get a better view of the room and feel my arm tilt an unseen glass figure. With the smooth, swift reflex of a ninja (yeah, that's right, *nin-ja*), I spin and reach for the vase about to shatter upon impact. Before it can fall into my grasp, however, he captures it with barely a flinch. My eyes turn up to his and I catch my breath.

His hair is dark with loose, thick waves nearly covering his eyes. He smiles in my direction. *Shit.* He's gorgeous. How can I kill someone *that* insanely handsome?

Hopefully, the flutter of my heart is only noticeable to me as his hand takes mine and his lips brush my cheek, and caress my ear. He whispers, "I'm glad you came," as if he knows me. *Who the hell is he?*

A hint of Ireland rolls on the back of his tongue and I close my eyes momentarily, taking a deep breath. The scent on his throat is musky like the moors outside of Dublin after a rain. No, I've never been there, but somehow I know the fragrance. The alluring aroma captures my attention, seducing my soul. Where am I? More importantly, *am I awake*?

While rising to full height, I run through the events of the day—did I eat breakfast, go to work, drive here—I can't recall the entire time. I remember eating breakfast *and* being at work. There's the moment toward the end of the day when Sarah entered my office and surprised me with a cup of coffee. All of this is fresh in my mind. What I don't remember is how I arrived at this joint. I can't even remember opening the front door. This is an important detail.

If awake, I won't forget the guy standing in front of me. I'd return just to see his penetrating eyes again. If dreaming, though...

The heavy beating of my heart continues as I scan the room, taking in each piece of hand-blown glass and polished crystal vases, colored figurines, and soft lighting. Sarah is standing near a brilliant dish shaped like a half piece of wrapped butterscotch, but her eyes are on me. What is she doing here? There's a sly grin on her face as she watches my reaction to *him*. What does she know that I don't?

My gaze meets his. I'll finally see his eyes, deep green, still framed by those dark tresses. His smile takes my breath away and it is in this moment I see it: the front door has no handle. I close my eyes and grit my teeth at the realization.

Damn! Dream.

Every muscle in my body tightens and my heart races with anticipation. Before the sun breaks the horizon, one of us will be dead. My best calculation guarantees it'll be *him*.

***

I take a deep breath, then another, as if I'm in the middle of a vigorous workout. Why is my heart pounding? What went wrong? Where am I?

There are no sharp objects, no vases or glass figurines, only torn covers as I lay face down in my own bed. The pillowcase is stained. *Crap!* He split my lip.

Why the face? I always hate it when they go for the face. Defensive wounds and bruises on forearms are easier to explain. *I was sparring with my new partner last night. Yes, as a matter of fact he is a master, and much better than me, obviously.* They always believe that one, shake their heads and walk away; the lie that usually works until I get hit in the face. This time: *I'm training for a championship match. My opponent got a bit ambitious.* Hopefully, it'll stave off concerned glances.

If I were married, they'd have my spouse locked up for domestic abuse. If I told anyone the truth—that I hunt in my dreams—they'd lock *me* up. If they only knew the monsters that roam the night, waiting in shadows for their prey. If they understood the demons populating their subconscious, they'd be too afraid to close their eyes.

That hot guy in the corner office, sweet grandmother across the street, they all have something dark lurking beneath the surface. Most times it's a benign grudge they've carried since junior high. Sometimes it's a hidden defect they can't control once they start dreaming. When their minds slip into REM, their inner demons roam. Whatever they kill in the night remains dead in daylight, the cause of death precise to how they died in their dream.

Every muscle in my body aches as I push up from the mattress. The monsters seem to be getting stronger with each new night. I kid myself that splashing water in my face will wash away the filth from the night before. Every morning I try to cleanse hatred from my soul while preparing for my day. Used to work. Not anymore.

The mirror doesn't show my dread over what I've seen and what I've done. I'd buried my emotions many years before. Only determination shows at this stage. I sometimes wonder if others can recognize my growing self-loathing as easily as I? Does it show that I'm getting weary of the evil I encounter? I've begun to fear my growing self-hate more than the killers I meet in my sleep.

The reflection in the mirror shows my split lip is nearly scabbed. Thankful for that. After scrubbing the dried blood trapped between my teeth, I flip my hair into a ponytail, and then pull on loose shorts and a t-shirt. A good workout will clear my thoughts.

As I leave the bedroom, though, my house feels different. There's a lingering scent of someone else. The vibration of a mortal's energy only dark angels can sense. The feeling of another with higher aspirations but low self-esteem clings to the walls and coats the doorknobs. I try the front door. *Unlocked.*

Now I search each room—slowly, carefully—one at a time. The living room, around the central fireplace, kitchen and dining room, twin master bedroom, guest room, bathrooms and workout room; all are empty. But their essence still lingers. How is it possible? This'll bother me all day. I need to punch something.

The next hour I'll spend hitting the bag to release my frustrations and calm my mind. I prefer to work out like I'm training for a boxing match. If my muscles aren't burning, sweat running down my face by the time I'm done, I usually go another hour. That would be a typical training session. Today, however, I'm already feeling beat up. Wish I could remember my dream. Maybe the sore muscles could be explained. I've only felt this worn once after a fight, but that was years ago when I first started hunting. I hate thinking of that time and push the memory away. The lack of clarity is disturbing and this workout isn't improving my lucidity. Maybe a good jog will clear my mind.

During my morning routine, I always run through the events of the previous night. Who did I fight, where did they hide and how did they attack? Are there new techniques I could learn and adapt into my training schedule? Mostly, I remember how they smelled.

Scent is important. Your nose can tell you what kind of demon they are, where they roam. The high-class ones usually smell of money and expensive wines. Sometimes they reek of caviar. The smell *nauseates* me.

The poorer ones smell of cheap fabric, discount stores, and desperation. Periodically, I catch a hint of stale whiskey, rotting trash, sometimes pee. Oddly, I prefer that to the fish eggs.

Funny, no matter how hard I run, my memory still isn't improving. Last night is merely a blur to me. I can recall a room of glass and crystal, tantalizing creations. More like candy to my soul. Shame I had to kill him. If those sculptures were his, he was quite talented. So many brilliant minds with a dark side that sends them straight to hell. Why'd he have to be one of them?

Odd that I still clearly remember his face, the soft lines that sharpened when he smiled, a dimple in his chin like mine. The eyes...I'd only seen eyes that green one other place. The mirror. The one part of me I like are my irises and he had the same.

Why'd it have to be a dream? The story always ends the same when I'm asleep. Maybe I'm growing tired of that, too.

I also remember his hair. Nearly ebony, and his skin. Olive. *Delicious*. I'm sure he's broken a number of hearts. Nearly melted mine with his touch.

Ugh! Enough of that. I'm not the melting kind. I'm far too cynical for a crush. So why can't I get him out of my mind? Shame he had to be a demon. Because he's the best looking I've ever had to exterminate.

Already ran a mile and the only other thing I can remember about last night is how he looked. Nothing else? Am I still in high school? Let's see...there was Sarah, there was the room of glass and there was Irish Eyes, facing off with me. So what happened next? His eyes played with me. Mine narrowed on him. He circled me; then, moved toward the door.

I remember saying, "Let's skip the dance, shall we? You know why I'm here." So cliché. Sounded cool, anyway. I may be a bit melodramatic for my age.

But he didn't say a word. What was he doing at the door? Pulling a knife from behind the front desk? Wrapping his fingers around a heavy vase? I can't see it. Why?

Nocturnal fights have never been blocked from my memory before. I always wake lucid as a matter of fact. Tends to be a family trait. My grandmother shared with me every fight she'd ever had. She'd hoped to give me pointers. At ninety-nine years old she remembered every detail, what they used against her, how they smelled and how badly it hurt when she woke in the morning. Purging darkness from our earth doesn't come without consequences.

She fought until the week before she turned a hundred. That's when my parents found her broken body lying in her bed one morning. Mom said Grandma must've hesitated. I find that hard to believe. She was the best. Taught me that to hesitate was to fail. "Always focus and never shrug," she'd say.

Grandma? Shrug? Didn't happen. But we'll never discover how she was finally bested. Only the monster in her dream would know. Someday I'll meet up with them. And when I do you can count on one thing: I won't shrug.

Mile three. A woman leaving her house stares at me as if she knows my secret. Then, she turns and locks the front door. The front door—*Irish Eyes*. That's what he was doing, locking the door. I was trapped in his shop and so was Sarah.

Sarah!

The last mile is lost as I worry for my coworker and friend. I can't see the trees passing me by, cars cruising down the road, dogs barking at my heels. Nothing captures my attention as I stretch my legs and dash toward the house. I can't remember if she escaped. Only way that could've happened is if I'd tossed her out before an exit was secured. I didn't do that. At least I don't remember removing her. Then again, I don't remember much of anything.

The demon must have been thrilled having two prey. He thought I'd be controlled at the threat of my friend's life. Did he kill her? Did I kill him *first*? I have to know and I left my phone at home.

By the time the door slams behind me, speed dial chimes her number in my head. "Pick up the phone, Sarah, pick up the phone!" No answer, so I hit the shower and scrub myself clean before pulling on slacks and a suit-jacket. Next stop is Sarah's place.

Even after ringing the doorbell five times and pounding like my life is in danger, she doesn't answer. I can't think. How could I allow a fight to happen with an innocent bystander in the mix, especially one I know? I've never fought with the victim in sight. If they saw the demon I'd killed in their sleep on the evening news, there's great risk they'd begin asking questions and end up complicating my life even more.

There's just prey and predator in my type of dreams. The only other occupant would be me and I always separate victim from attacker, send them into a kinder dream or wake them with a cold sweat. Then, I finish the deed.

Last night, however, he locked the door. That meant we were locked in the dream together. No one leaving until a final outcome. The kill-or-be-killed moment had begun. A mortal had to die, victim or perpetrator, before the seal could be broken. I don't remember killing the Irish man. I don't remember.

I won't risk my reputation by acting like a prowler, crawling in through a window. Sarah's neighbors are already paying too much attention to me. With her not answering her door, I can do nothing more than go to work. If she shows, all is well. If not, her mangled body waits to be discovered. If she doesn't come in today, I'll call the police and report her missing. Can I think of a good reason to worry over an employee potentially playing hooky for a day? I may be clever but this will definitely stretch my imagination to the limit. With my mind preoccupied over Sarah's fate, I head to my car and drive straight to work.

When I arrive at the bank, the lamp on my desk is lit. *Let it be Sarah.*

As I walk into my office, the first thing I notice is the surface of my desk. The damned thing is clean and there's Sarah. What is she doing in my office and why'd she clean my desk? I hate when she touches my stuff. I like my working area messy, stacks of papers and files always within reach.

Her smile lights up when I enter. How can I be so relieved she's alive and annoyed at the same time? Hopefully, she has a terrible memory when it comes to dreams. I feel cranky all of the sudden, realizing I didn't even stop for coffee. This'll be a long day.

She glances at her watch as if nothing's wrong. "You're early, aren't you?"

Would still be home if you'd answered your damned phone. Agh! I'm dying to hit something. "Have work to catch up on. Checking status on some loans," I tell her. Better to lie. I throw myself into my chair.

"Burr, it's cold in here." Sarah rubs her arms, breaking into laughter. "I had the oddest dream about you last night. I'll have to tell you one of these times over—"

Abruptly picking up the phone, I start dialing. She might forget by the end of the day.

As luck would have it, I'm left to myself for the bulk of the morning. No one wants to be near me when I'm in a mood. Most of my day is spent making calls, closing open files and messing up the top of my desk again. No interruptions and no Sarah casting confused glances my direction. You might say my Wednesday is ending perfectly with less than an hour 'til close. Of course, that's when someone knocks on my door. *Shit.*

"Go away."

"It's Sarah, we need your help up front."

Sigh. "What is it?"

"Problem with an account. Customer wants to talk to the branch manager. Says he's missing funds."

"Can't you handle it?" I sound too impatient. I don't care.

"I'm not the branch manager, boss."

Hate it when she's right. "I'll be out."

I'd sigh again, but it won't make the problem go away. Could I slip out the back door without being detected? *Probably not.*

The lobby is fairly empty—two tellers, one loan officer, Sarah, and our customer. He's standing near the counter and turns as I near. My gait noticeably falters and I bite down on my aching lower lip. When he reaches for me in concern, I immediately jolt backward. Then, I hear his voice.

"Are you all right?"

The Irish lilt is familiar. His deep green eyes drill into mine like he's never seen me before. Thankfully, he didn't recognize me. At least not now that he's awake.

"You okay, Jaime? You look like you've seen a ghost."

Not funny, Sarah. I *am* seeing a ghost.

I wave her away. "Forgot breakfast, uh, and lunch. Low blood sugar." Returning my attention to the customer, "How may I help you?" I clip my words while holding out my hand to him. I'll finally learn his name.

"Collin Leary. Crystal Creations."

His hand slips into mine as it had in my dream. I'm trembling while wrapping my fingers around his palm. In my mind I see him whispering in my ear, asking my name as his lips strafe my cheek and then my ear. My heart flutters once again. But he doesn't lean in, nor does he whisper, doesn't even ask my name. Not sure why I'm disappointed.

"Jaime Connor," I offer anyway. That's it, I'm a stricken school girl.

My breathing becomes shallow. I swallow deep. He's staring at my mouth. *Why the hell is he staring at my mouth*?

"Your lip's bleeding." He points to his own. I'm having trouble moving my eyes from them. They seem so soft and—*My lip's bleeding. Damn it!* I dab it with my fingertips, realizing the cut from last night must've broken open when I bit my lip.

"Fell in the shower this morning—" *Damn it, damn it!* I forgot my excuse. *I fell in the shower. Stupid.* Sounds too prepared and not prepared at all. "Let's see what's wrong with your account, Mr. Leary."

Moving to the nearest cubby, I push behind the computer as he sits across from me. Knowing he's perched there makes me focus on the screen. If I look into those eyes again, I'll...well, I can't be sure what I'd do. My best guess is I'd throw him down right here, fervently kiss him or slit his throat. *What the hell?* I *never* want to kiss anyone *fervently.* What's *wrong* with me? *Get your mind off of him, now.*

Once my attention is back on the screen in front of me, it takes nearly an hour of searching through records, cross-referencing times and transactions to get the matter figured out. Somehow a deposit of the previous evening ended up being split into several customers' accounts early this morning. Does he know how to manipulate our system? Did he do something intentional to make an excuse to stalk me at work? By the time I'm finished, I want to snap his neck. That is, I'd snap his neck if I hadn't already killed him. Why the hell is he still alive?

"All resolved." *Now I can wash my hands of him.*

Troubling that he's now closer to finding my home. Once he has that information, he'll haunt me every night until one of us is dead. *I'd prefer it be him.*

"You're a miracle worker," he says and hands me one of his cards. "Please come by my gallery on Friday. I'd love to show you what I do."

"I'm sure you would." I sound too flippant, but Sarah snatches the card from my hand with glee.

"We'd *love* to go."

I hate her perkiness.

Poor demon schmuck doesn't realize he'll die one more time before I ever see his gallery in person.

When he takes my hand this time, I notice his fingers are rough with thin scratches and ridges in the cup of his palm. I've suddenly forgotten how handsome he is and wonder what made those marks. Now I'm hungry for the hunt and this rat is on the menu. *Purr.*

Yes, we'll definitely meet again, Mr. Collin Leary. I promise.

CHAPTER 2

In the moments before I go to sleep at night, I think of those who left this earth before me, grateful for all they have done to prepare me for this time and wondering how my life might be different had they not succumbed to the demons in their dreams. Too many years have passed. The many decades I've lived on earth don't show on this near mortal body, this tired angel's face. Too many nights I've studied the textured ceiling above my head, feeling alone and angry. My anger isn't directed at them. I know they did their damnedest to fight for their lives. They had to. Otherwise, why would they have fought so hard to put the skills to survive in me? No, my discontent is not with my fallen parents or grandparents, it's leveled at those who caused their deaths.

Tonight is no different than the rest as I close my eyes and take that rage into the dream with me, still searching for killers who would end another life as easily and painfully as they had those of the ones I've loved. Although this is the task I accepted before I came to earth, to never truly sleep, to always hunt instead of rest, to kill some damaged soul lurking in the corners and shadows of my dreams, I sometimes wish for a reprieve. What I wouldn't give for one night of peace. Perhaps

I will have that when I'm dead.

From the first day I woke in Colorado Springs, I've hated the place. I was young and preferred the trees of Washington State. Colorado was too dry and brown. But a demon had found our Seattle home so I understood why we had to leave. With my father dead and mother severely injured, we had no choice but to move with first light.

For months, I moped around, longing for the thick, lush green I loved. Eventually, I found thick, flowing crimson instead. Now I can't purge Colorado from my soul.

Impatience over our hasty move—not to mention the trauma of seeing my father dead—had caused severe anxiety and resentment. I rebelled against my unusual new surroundings. Soon, however, those emotions were replaced with intrigue as I caught the scent of the indigenous souls. There was something strong and sedate in the aroma. There was a feeling of being settled and a sense of uneasiness lying beneath the surface. I was curious to know what caused the disturbance. There is a deep history here that most never knew. Something about it made me shudder, with fear or anticipation, I wasn't positive. What I knew for sure was the voice of death calling out in the night. That was when I started dreaming and the hunted became the hunter. My turn to play.

Only eleven years old, I hadn't been very big and hadn't developed full strength, so I was led to the weaker monsters, ones who were deadly, but inexperienced. There were a lot of those in the area, punks who thought they were killers, torturing animals and young kids for ritualistic sacrifice. Women who'd sell their souls, even kill their own child, for a shot of poison in the arm. I was afforded an opportunity to sharpen my skills. Slowly and completely.

By the time I started high school, I'd graduated to more vicious demons, ones who lurked in alleyways to surprise you in the shadows of your dreams at night. I drew on my hatred for the one who killed my father, used it to destroy the others, still searching for the one.

Soon, I'd found him, murderer of dark angels. He'd tracked us to Colorado, somehow caught our scent in the air. I'd barely started dreaming the night he appeared in my bedroom. He was leaning beside my window, playing with the curtains.

"Your father never told me you were so beautiful while pleading for your life. Had I known, I'd have come for you long ago." He had lust in his gaze while moving to my bedside. "I've been waiting for you to dream. I'm dying to play. Can we begin?" His eyes digested my body as he licked his lips, impatient to start.

I'd considered this moment, prepared for it since I'd started hunting. I'd imagined him waiting in the shadows for me and knew exactly what to do.

Without comment, I slid from the bed as if I hadn't seen him, so he spoke again. "Aren't you wondering how I found you? Aren't you afraid of me?"

He asked far too many questions, wanting me to give a frightened response. I gave him something else.

I fought the impulse to turn and bludgeon him where he stood, instead, slipping into my bathroom and closing the door. As soon as he breached the room, barely appearing past the doorframe, I impaled him with the shower curtain rod.

"No, I'm not afraid of you."

With all other kills, I'd walked away before they'd taken their last breath. This one I observed. As he slipped to the floor, I crouched in front of him, watching his face turn soft. I knew he was in a darker place for eternity. I also knew I'd never fear a shadow again.

I often think about him as I go hunting. I wonder if I'd

allowed more time to play, would he have killed me? I felt cheated in a way, not having taken more time to make him endure my wrath and know my pain as he slowly drifted into the darkness. There was so much I wanted to say before he gasped his last breath. For starters, why did you kill my father? And do you realize he wasn't the only thing you took from me?

Before he came to my room, I'd imagined the satisfaction of seeing him dead. Now I wish for more. I've craved more of his blood on my hands as he looked into my eyes in fear. I wanted him to know he was going to die and dread the minutes, every second, ticking off in my room. Maybe it was best to take care of him the way I did, create a known outcome. My morbid sense of entertainment, however, dreams of alternative scenarios.

Sometimes I look forward to the deadly dance. I pretend I'm playing with my father's murderer. Some nights I want the monster to know the fear his victims felt. Other nights, I want them to pay for what they've done and what another had done to my family.

I'm asleep early, searching for the next deficient soul to cross my path, for our separate dreams to meld into one, anxious to begin. Tonight I want a good fight to relieve my frustrations. My mind searches the darkness, wondering if I'll see Collin Leary. No doubt, Green Eyes also searches for me. He showed his intent when he walked into my territory.

After a moment of darkness, I find myself following an effervescent stream; mountain water with natural fizz. I'm meant to trace the flow. Any body of water typically leads to my target.

This stream draws me to a park surrounding a small pond. Several Aspen line the perimeter. On the edge of the dream, formation is an area I refer to as the shadows. It's the darkness that cloaks whatever lies within and beyond.

Usually, the shadows separate the real world from that of the sleeping. At times, the shadows serve to separate one dreamer from another, forming the intersection where dreams and dreamers cross over and the realm of somnolence becomes shared by more than one. When that happens, each person can take some amount of control of the dream. Whoever changes it first is the sole one who can change that aspect and no one else can alter it but that dreamer.

Here, a young girl sits on a bench, waiting. She appears to be crying. There are no others around as I search the park. There's a bubbling pond fed by the percolating stream. A nearby gazebo has benches circling the exterior. I'm hesitant, yet I move across the grass to sit with the girl. When I reach her side, I can tell that she's frightened, so I kneel beside her.

In the dream state, I have the ability to read the thoughts of most everyone I meet, killer or victim. Paired with an angel's extraordinary sense of smell, I learn all I need to know of the souls populating my sleep. The closer I am to children, the more they can catch my scent as well.

"You smell nice," the girl whispers and smiles, her eyes still filled with tears.

To innocent souls, I smell of the place they've nearly forgotten. The memory brings back the feeling of love and comfort, something we all desire. The smell of an angel reminds them of home. Not home on earth but the one they knew before coming here.

Darker souls sense death when they near us. They can't smell love or comfort anymore. If they could, maybe they wouldn't kill. If their subconscious could remember where they came from, perhaps they would think twice before sending another on to the after-life in such a devastating way.

"Are you alright?" I ask, continuing to search the area.

"I'm lost," she answers in a weak voice and takes a deep, shuddering breath.

"You're not lost, Princess." Taking her hand, I draw her to her feet, leading her up the steps of the gazebo. "Here's your castle, waiting for you."

Her smile grows as the wooden structure magically forms stone turrets and fortified walls.

"What a lovely dress you're wearing today." Her pajamas transform into a full satin dress with flowers and ribbons. A silver crown appears on the messy toss of hair on her head. The grass turns to a field of purple flowers as she creates a kinder dream for herself.

"Did you make this?" Her innocent eyes reflect the moonlight when she turns her face toward mine.

"No, Sweetie, you did." At that moment, something catches my attention. Has the demon joined our dream? If it is, they'll take control and change it to a new scenario, one where the girl becomes his victim.

From the corner of my eye, I see someone in the shadows, moving toward us. "Let's see if we can find the Queen Mum." I tilt my head toward her and she smiles back, all traces of tears diminished.

When she grabs hold of my hand, I lead her across a field of violets to the edge of the pond. Kneeling beside her, I take hold of her shoulders. "Do you trust me when I say I won't hurt you?" I ask and she hesitates for a moment then nods. "Good. Because I wouldn't ever dream of harming you, do you understand?"

She nods again.

"The Queen Mum is in there." I point to the water and her eyes grow wide with fear. Flowers crush beneath a set of rushing feet behind us and I know there's no time to explain. "You'll see her as soon as you wake, I promise."

Before she can run, I throw her backward, her body careening toward the water. In her fear, she tries to grab my sleeve, but the momentum carries her under. Within seconds, the girl and her purple satin dress can't be seen and I know she awoke in her bed, although I'm still asleep in mine and continuing the dream with another.

The crunch of stiff blades of grass grows nearer as the intruder swiftly approaches. Their sense of the dream we're in has changed the landscape to a barren field. Without hesitating, I spin and kick legs out from under them. The resonance of a young male voice cursing me as his jaw hits the ground brings a satisfied smile to my face. Now I can circle him like a hawk zeroing in on my prey.

"Son of a—"

"Don't say it." Before he speaks again, I stop and lift his chin for a look.

Damn. He's only a boy, fifteen at most, initiated into a gang, so below my league. The scent of fear on his clothing tells me the frightened little girl was intended for his first kill.

After knocking my hand away, he claws at the ground until he pulls himself to his feet. I'm nearly a foot taller. He couldn't be more than thirteen. I'd overestimated his age.

"You're just a kid," I tell him and shake my head. "What're you doing? You don't belong out here."

He reaches into his pocket. "What do *you* know, you mother—"

"Stop! Don't open your mouth and don't pull your hand out of your pocket." I stare him down with a look he's seen before, one his mother would give to show the severity of the situation.

He hesitates. "What're you gonna do? Nothin'!" He lifts his shoulders, trying to appear taller.

"What I'm *gonna* do is make you wish you'd kept your

hands in your pockets, that's what. You don't want this. And if you decide to do it anyway, I'll kill you right here. You pull out that knife and I'll have no choice but to slit your throat with it."

His dilated eyes drift down his arm, his expression showing he can't figure out how I knew. If he realized who he was talking to, it wouldn't surprise him that I can read his mind and his emotions.

"If you kill, in your sleep or while you're awake, I'll find you. I promise you that."

He stares back at me with wide eyes, trying to decide if I'm bluffing. "You some kinda cop?" His voice falters.

A song from the eighties creeps into my mind and I laugh aloud. "Yeah, I'm the dream police. Go home." Shoving him into the same pond as the young girl, I know he'll wake in a cold sweat in his bed. There's no doubt he won't forget the dream. Hopefully, he doesn't forget the message.

Since there has been no kill as of yet this evening, I'm still caught in the world of nightmares. My body still prone in my bed, my soul searches the plane where all dreams materialize. The barren fields dissipate and I'm led to the slumber of the next killer.

As I turn away, a whimper stirs my senses. The gurgling continues, but I'm no longer beside a brook. Instead, I'm in an office building on the expensive side of town. The new dreamer has changed my surroundings.

The room is tastefully decorated with stuffed bookshelves and soft chairs placed around polished cherry office furniture. On a corner of the desk is a small, bronze statue. Beside it, there's a brass clock with the inscription, *Boss of the Year*. A placard sits at the top of the desk. *Phillip P. Bradley*. In the adjacent wall, a hidden closet with the door slightly ajar contains two pressed suits and several rows of royal blue ties.

Why would any man need that many neckties, all the same color?

A rustling in the next room perks up my ears. The door is open and the lone light in the building is in the outer office. The continued sound of gurgling fills the air, but it doesn't seem like water anymore.

I'm careful not to make a sound while entering the lobby. To my left is a smaller desk nearly masking a montage of personal photos taped to the wall. One of the pictures shows a young woman kneeling next to her dog. She's cute, but her clothes are a bit too snug and her top far too revealing. Not appropriate in a prestigious office. *Out of place.*

Kneeling on the floor in front of the desk is a man in a suit, leaning over a woman with a necktie around her throat, pulling it tighter. Fear dilates her eyes while she chokes and fights to get free. I'm paralyzed for a moment, remembering a night long ago when *my* screams were muffled. The voices of two laughing boys had drowned out snapping embers in a mountain campfire.

The stifled cries of a frightened woman return me to the room with lavish office furniture and professional literature. I can still save her. She hasn't expired yet. As I move toward them, however, something slips around my neck and pulls me backward against a warm body. The stubbly bristles of a late afternoon beard catches my hair when he draws me into his chest. No matter how hard I tear at the binding, I can't work myself free. The constriction of my windpipe limits the air passing through, but doesn't cut off my breathing completely. He's toying with me, unprepared to kill me…yet.

"I've been waiting for you. I have your favorite tie." His hot breath brushes my cheek and I wonder if it's *him.*

I gather my strength in anticipation, waiting for the scent of Ireland to fill my mind. When I'm sure the bastard is Green

Eyes, I won't take my time with him. Once I've extracted the answer as to what happened last night, he'll meet the ending he deserves; swift justice. As I attempt to draw a deep breath, I realize there's no fresh scent of moorlands to calm my senses and simultaneously stoke the killer in me. All I smell is expensive cologne. *Damn.* It isn't him. My breathing becomes heavy. Suddenly, I'm disappointed he didn't show.

Trembling with anticipation, I continue surveying my surroundings, desperately hoping to calm my fear. Small lamp on corner table. More filled bookshelves. Several other small bronze statues.

The noose around my neck loosens slightly as he slips in front of me, shoving my back against the wall with his palm pressing firmly into my chest. Finally, I get to see his eyes. Not green. Blue. The pressure of his body pins me securely. I'm still surveying the scene, wondering at the relationship between the two killers in this dream with identical hair, height and build. As soon as the thought crosses my mind, the one still hovering over the woman turns to glance back at me and the one who has hold of me. They're the same person.

The degenerate is recalling a previous kill and the memory is exciting him into a repeat performance. *With me.* The feeling of his body pressed into mine makes me shudder and I grit my teeth. His well-manicured hand slides up the back of my thigh. In his mind he has me in a tight skirt and low-cut shirt. *Great.* The bastard's imagining me as his sexy secretary. *Jerk.*

One more look over his shoulder and I recognize something about his kill-site. There's a scent of salty fish and a hint of rotted wood. He hadn't killed here in Colorado. She was near the ocean. Probably the West. I can feel the flutter of seagulls in the distance. Cold, not warm. Maybe somewhere along the Oregon/Washington coast.

"How do ya like it, huh?" The strong smell of mint breath

spray infuses with the aroma of garlic chicken when he speaks. "Do ya like it rough? Ever beg your lover to spank you hard?" As he pulls my thigh upward until my knee is against his hip, the grin on his thin lips spreads before he slaps the side of my ass. My eyes narrow as I allow him to drive my anger to the edge. *Keep going, asshole, I'm nearly there.*

His accent is definitely Midwest. This man is a serial killer. She wasn't his first. Unless I end him tonight, he'll kill again. In his sleep and while he's awake. He doesn't care. There's no conscience to reason with. The thought makes my heart beat faster and my blood turn hot.

My attention is drawn immediately on him when his free hand slips under my skirt again; then, gently rubs before slapping my ass once more. He keeps staring me in the eyes, waiting for fear to show in them. His touch makes me sick, sparking my fury over a terrible event many decades ago, when I was still young and innocent, one in which he hadn't participated. I'll use that memory to enjoy the kill that much more while savoring every moment.

With teeth still clenched, I lower my foot to the floor and then bring my knee up to connect with his groin. This time *I* watch *his* eyes. When bone meets flesh, he flinches slightly, but he's not as fazed as I'd hoped. He's obviously been kneed before and I didn't use full force. If I'd given all I had, though, he'd be dead. That wouldn't be very fun now, would it? Why do I love this game that'll just make me hate myself later? Am I no better than the scum I hunt in my sleep?

"Is that all you got, Baby?" He's prodding me on, licking his lips as his fingers slide around my thigh and into me. My body lurches with repulsion at his invasion and I knock his hand away. I'll give him what he's asking for. The asshole has no idea that, if I had wanted a swift kill tonight, he would already be dead. But, I'm reveling in the control I have over his life and his death. I'll let this play on for a little while longer.

He shakes the sting in his hand from my smack, shoving his groin into mine so I can feel his erection as he tightens the fabric around my throat once again. Then, he nudges the neck of my shirt to the side with his mouth. The sting of his teeth penetrating my shoulder is followed by the smell of iron. My eyes close and my anger deepens. This has gone far enough.

"Come on, *Phillip*. Let's play," I tell him and he lifts his head in surprise, my blood coating his lips. *My opportunity.*

Bringing my forehead down hard into his face causes his nose to crack and splatter blood on my white shirt. Grabbing hold of a finger beneath my skirt, I bend it backward until he sinks to his knees.

With his middle finger tight in my grasp, I slowly increase my grip. "You won't be using this anymore, *Phil,*" I say through gritted teeth as the bone snaps and shatters. He screams in agony.

As he lowers his head to cradle the shattered finger, my knee cracks his chin hard enough to send him backward. Pulling the necktie from my throat, I toss it to the ground beside him. I return to his office, leaving him writhing on the floor.

My stride is slow and tantalizing, enticing him to follow if he wants me. And he will. He's addicted to the chase, the melee of another human fighting for survival. The greater the struggle, the more invested he becomes. Much like me, he enjoys allowing his victim enough room to think they might win, and then pulls them back to finish the deal. *Sick bastard.*

By the time I reach his desk he's standing in the doorway, leering at me with fury and lust in his eyes, blood running down his chin. Reaching for the lamp on a nearby table, I flick it on to illuminate a nicely framed photo in the glow. The picture of Philip was taken in front of a large brick house with tall windows, surrounded by lush landscaping. I know the neighborhood. *Very* upscale.

"You're rich. Congratulations, *asshole*." Picking up the picture to study it, I see the smile on his face as if there's nothing wrong with him. He's standing next to a woman, the two of them flanked by a pair of teenage boys and a young girl. Poor woman probably has no idea what he's been up to and why they've had to move so many times.

"Nice family. They know you're a rapist? Does your wife have any idea you hire single women with no one to worry when they go missing?"

His jaw tightens and his eyes narrow on me. "Put that down."

Blankly staring back at him, I slam the picture flat on his desk, enjoying the sound of shattering glass. "Pretty room you have here. Kill all your women at work?"

"Just the ones who ask for it." The dim light illuminates a gleam in his eyes. His hatred for me is obvious, but he's enjoying the chase as much as I am.

"Let's make this epic, then. Shall we?"

At my invitation, he moves forward with the tie dangling from his hand. I stand still, noticing everything around me without taking my eyes from him. I'm only able to use the objects from his mind to defend myself, that is unless I've prepared in advance of the dream; planted the idea in his mind before he slept. Since I never know the demon I'm led to, the idea is virtually impossible. The lamp is too light. The plant beside it—still not enough to bash in his brains. Books, table, chairs. Drawer… Gently opening it a matter of inches, my hand slips inside to search for a weapon. Top of desk; name placard, Day-Timer, clock, statue, shattered glass. Perhaps I could wrap my fingers around the bronze. Might break some bones, smash his skull, but there should be something more, a backup. I hate to leave it to chance. After all, he does have as much control over this dream as I do.

As the thought enters my mind, my hand slips across something sharp. That'll do. I pull it behind my back while keeping his attention on the hand reaching for the bronze. Impatient to begin again, he throws a punch, but his fist blows past my cheek when I turn my head. "Is that all you got, *Phil*?" I taunt him back.

The hand with the statue swings forward and he catches it with the necktie. His strength is unusual and surprises me by the move. I'm taken off guard and the bronze is yanked from my grip as he pulls me toward him before flipping the tie around my neck once again. He's very talented at this. The asshole should have his own freak show in Vegas. *Or, maybe not.*

With my back against the desk, he leans his body over mine and pulls the ends tight. The breath is caught in my lungs until they burn and I allow it. For some reason, I enjoy the feeling of almost suffocating. Near hypoxia excites my rage and makes the kill more satisfying. A smile of accomplishment slips across his lips as he leans over to kiss my mouth, his tongue still rancid with garlic and his jaw covered in blood from us both. My hand reaches up to push his pugnacious face away. The stench of his breath assaults me as he opens his mouth to speak. "You're mine, now. I'll own you for all eternity," he nearly whispers.

I don't think so.

Pulling his head to the side, I bring the other hand up. The shard between my fingers plunges deep into his neck. The tie around my throat loosens when he reaches for the red-soaked glass. His fingers try to plug the hole in his artery, but blood still flows. After pulling the noose free, I wrap it around his neck, drawing him to sit on the floor in front of his desk. Almost immediately, the fabric is soaked red as I lean over with my lips to his ear.

"How does it feel now, *Baby*? Are you having *fun*?"

His pupils dilate as I crouch in front of him. Staring into his irises, I see the wild eyes of two deranged boys who tried to end my life many years ago. No matter how many times I try to kill it, the memory won't die. The death of Phillip P. Bradley won't cleanse those demons from my soul.

"Are you scared?" I ask.

He nods. Why am I still discontent, watching the fear in his eyes turning to terror? Studying his expression for another moment, reveling in the kill, I finally stand and walk away. Saliva gurgles in his throat. I close my eyes in disgust, hating myself for wanting more satisfaction.

As I reach the office door, something seems out of place. I smell the presence of another. But, before I can turn, I'm hit from behind. With a hand to my head, I spin to face my attacker. They're gone. The smell, the feeling of another breathing soul, surrounds me, but my vision is blurred. The pain grows unmanageable. I sink to the floor as Phillip takes his last breath.

CHAPTER 3

Sunlight glares through the curtains surrounding my bedroom window. My skull aches. There's a deep scar in the wood of my headboard from last night's fight, stained with fresh blood. What the *hell* happened last night? Reaching for the back of my head, I notice my hair is wet and I'm dizzy. The red-stained pillow doesn't help settle my stomach, either. Think I'm gonna vomit.

Damn. Damn. *Damn!* A concussion. How'd I get so sloppy?

I'm gonna need stitches. Better call Sarah, tell her I won't be in. Then, shower the filth from my body. I can still feel his hands on me and in me.

Staring at my face in the mirror, I wonder how I've allowed myself to sink so low. Instead of going into the dream, taking out the degenerate soul, and waking like I did when I was younger, I play with him. I want to drag out the inevitable, let him think he can win *then* take him out. Sometimes, I have a hidden yearning to be killed by one of the demons I meet at night. If only pride would get out of the way to allow the desired ending to my existence here. Too bad that same pride doesn't notice the self-loathing permitting me to let a serial killer soil my body with his touch. The game, the yearning to mind-fuck someone who's already sick beyond repair, it's the obsession I can't exorcize from my perverted soul.

Decades have passed since I've felt anyone gently caress my shoulder or stroke my hair in a moment of kindness. I crave the touch of another but fear the commitment of a relationship. *Oh, God,* I'm so *fucked up*. Why is it I've settled for trading the warm comfort of tenderness for a fierce thrill from a killer's hands? Some angel I've turned out to be.

My greatest fear is I'll someday become one of them. I fear the idea of giving in to the darkness, becoming a rogue angel. The thought makes me cringe. Can I find something to make me want to live again before that happens?

Thankfully, I'm able to make an early appointment with a doctor who's fairly new to this area. The clinic isn't far from my home so I have time to clean up as best I can before leaving.

When I arrive, the nurse scrubs my cut and disinfects the surrounding area with iodine. She regards me as if I'm a weak woman, battered, victimized by a man I profess to love while making excuses for his crime. I let her patronize me. This wouldn't be the first time someone assumed they understood my troubles.

Nearly half an hour passes before the doctor walks in and takes a look at me, shaking his head. I'm surprised at how handsome he is, but mostly at how familiar he seems. I'd expected someone older and more weathered. His hair is light brown with a touch of gray peppering his temples. Soft blue eyes peer down at me, smiling even though he's frowning, like someone I once knew, long before I came here. But it is a ghost of a memory, one I can't grasp.

"How'd it happen?" His voice is emotionless while he examines the torn flesh.

"I fell, hit the corner of the counter."

He stops touching my scalp and sits on a stool in front of me with the expression of a parent who knows they've been lied to. "A blunt object cracked your skull."

I can only stare back at him with little more to say. "Blunt counter," I defiantly replied, anyway.

He had me. Questions about my husband and his occupation.

Does he drink?

"I'm single."

Am I in a relationship?

"No. I live alone. I'm completely alone." *Pathetic.*

He regards me as if I'm lying.

"Come home with me if you don't believe me."

He's good looking, but that's not the point. It's not like I want to have sex with him. Just want to prove my point.

"Much more of this, young lady, and soon they'll pick you up in a body bag." As if I didn't already know. Surprisingly, he isn't impressed by the sarcastic rise of my brow. *Hm.*

The whole time he's stitching my head, I think about Collin Leary, wondering if he's the type to ambush someone while hiding in the shadows. But then again, cowardice didn't seem his style. I remember the night in his gallery, how he smiled as he circled me. The confident grin on his face, the way his eyes tracked mine, showed he knew fighting me was a risk and he was willing to carry through regardless of the consequences. No doubt, he saw the challenge in my eyes as well while I stared him down, waiting for the first throw. But then, I don't remember what he did after that. All I know is he locked the door. The rest is gone, not even a blur. Why can't I remember? Even with a skull injury, I recall everything from last night, right up to the point where I was cold-cocked. At least I think I remember everything. Did anything else happen last night—

between the time I went down and the instant Phillip took his last breath—the moment before waking? Did the second attacker—Collin Leery, maybe—take advantage of me? If he did, I'll be sure he suffers before he dies.

Then, I begin to wonder if there's a correlation between the one who hit me last night and why I can't remember the fight at the crystal boutique? The sole person who recalls the dream is Sarah. Hopefully, she still remembers. She did yesterday morning. I'll need an excuse to get her alone and find out what she knows.

Fifteen stitches and a prescription for painkillers and I'm finally on my way. The crumpled script is tossed in the trash on the way out. I stopped allowing pain to control me long ago. Figured I deserved every aching moment I've experienced in this life.

I'm home long enough to call Sarah and pull on a clean pair of jeans. The white scoop-neck top is easier to sneak over my head. My face is pale, dark circles under my eyes. I'd lost a bit of blood, which reminds me. I have to take care of my bedding.

Torn sheets, bloody pillow and pillowcase, all tossed into the fireplace. Something I've done since that night in the mountains. I was only fifteen and still traumatized. Couldn't bring myself to wash my blood out of the sheets, so I burned them instead.

Watching the blaze devouring 600-thread Egyptian cotton reminds me of that hidden campsite and two boys pulling me from their car, throwing me to the ground in front of the glare of headlights. Closing my eyes, I push the thought from my mind once again. Why must I remember them every time I burn my sheets? Why can't I get beyond that night?

Soon the evidence of last night's fight is purified. As the flames flicker down, I conclude no amount of fire could purify my soul.

After putting my hair in a ponytail, I grab my purse and car keys and head out to meet Sarah at the mall. The drive is too long with my head still aching. Passing cars are a mere blur in my peripheral vision. Maybe I should've kept that script for painkillers after all. Might be a good reason to go back and see that handsome doc. What in the hell is wrong with me? First a demon, now my doctor. I may be losing my mind.

Since it's Thursday, the place is fairly empty, exactly what I was shooting for. Sarah is late as usual, so I wait, ignoring the different scents of those around me, thinking only of Phillip Bradley. Remembering the scenario, the office, his appearance, I ponder more on what happened afterward. What I smelled last night was familiar but brief. There was no opportunity to discern the origin. They waited until I'd finished the kill. My mind was preoccupied with Phil and the tie I'd wrapped around his throat, turning from blue to purple with his blood. I was imagining his wife finding him in the morning with a deep hole in his neck, the one I gave him in his sleep. Of course she would cry and try to shake him awake, never realizing he'd intended to kill his secretary. He'd hired her for solely that purpose. *Boss of the Year.*

When I turned away, there was the new scent and something more. The feeling was of a breeze rushing through a thick section of trees, pine, and ferns. Whoever it was had been in the state of Washington. Had they followed me from there? Was it Collin Leary? Doesn't seem likely, but there are many unknowns about this man.

Sarah suddenly plops down on the bench beside me and I'm immediately assaulted by the sickly strong odor of cologne. "Run out of perfume yet?" *Choke.*

"No, silly. Still have plenty. Why? You *liiike* it?" She swipes a strand of hair from her eyes and waves her wrist in front of my nose. I usually like her perkiness, but lately, it seems to grate on my nerves. Maybe I'm getting too old for her nonsense.

"Hate it. Makes me sick." The only way to repel the nausea is to breathe solely from my mouth. If she just understood the repugnance of her scent, she'd destroy the bottle to save us all.

Sarah laughs at me as if I'm joking. She'll never get me. "Why'd you wanna meet anyway? I thought you were sick."

"I need your help." As expected, her eyes center on me like she's interested. "I need a dress."

"What kind of dress?" She finally becomes serious.

"The kind you wear to an art gallery event."

I hadn't expected her to bounce up and down on the bench, clapping her hands. *Chagrin*. Serious moment ended. I don't remember her ever being this perky. Something's up.

After grabbing hold of her hands, I hold them tightly together. "Stop. You didn't just win the lottery."

"I knew you'd change your mind. He's so hot, isn't he? I had a feeling you liked him, too."

"What d'you mean, *too*?"

She scoffs at me. *Annoying*. "You mean to tell me you didn't notice him staring at you? I thought he was gonna drool on the desk while you were looking into his account." Abruptly standing, she puts her hands on her hips. "You'll need something black."

Hmm, perfect metaphor, I think.

"And sensual. Short and tight," she adds, reaching for my hand, pulling me to my feet.

"Not tight or short. Nothing sensual." *Maybe this was a big mistake.*

"Low cut is a definite."

What? "No."

"Do you want to get his attention or are you planning to bore him to death, hmm?"

Hmm, hadn't thought of that tactic. One of these times, I'll try boring my demons to death. Maybe I can get them to kill *themselves* out of pure desperation.

She grabs my arm. "Leave it to me." I may have lost control of this situation.

With a death-grip on my bicep, she pulls me down the corridors of the mall. My head is still aching, partly Sarah's fault with her incessant chattering and the gag-inducing perfume. Reconsidering my decision to meet with her, I begin to think I should've taken the doctor's advice and stayed in bed. My curiosity could have waited another day. I may regret this.

Once we reach the upper floor, Sarah stops in front of a store obviously geared for teenagers.

"No." My expression of distaste isn't enough.

"Why not?"

Without saying a word, I give her *the look.*

She narrows her eyes in contemplation and a show of disapproval.

"Sarah, I'm a woman, not a child."

Reminiscent of a sixth grader, she heaves a sigh and rolls her eyes as if to say *whatever.*

Turning in place, I start surveying the stores in my general area. Cooking supplies, cheap jewelry, sporty shoes, fine jewelry, department store. I stop in place. Department store. Ladies fashions. Looks classy. That's the one.

Reacting as if she's my teenaged daughter, Sarah scrunches her nose at me. "No way. That's for old ladies. Are you an old lady, yet?"

If she only knew. "Yes."

"No, you're not. Come on."

My voice is nearly pleading as I try to convince her. "It's a classy store. Look, they have designer clothes." When I move toward the entrance, she grabs my arm. I had no idea Sarah was so strong.

"I can't let you do it, James. You're dressing hot for Mr. Hottie or you'll embarrass me." This time *I* sigh and roll my eyes. My response doesn't stop her from grabbing my hand and dragging me away from the one viable store I can see in this mall.

For more than an hour, we rummage through several boutiques and small chain stores, searching for the perfect dress. Sarah and I have very different tastes in clothing I've come to realize. In fact, there are few things we have in common. I wonder how we became friends. Perhaps I was looking for something sunny to accent my dark side.

Eventually, we find the right dress, back at the department store I'd wanted to try in the first place. We compromise on one with long sleeves to hide my scars, slightly snug, but not breathlessly tight and above the knee, but not too high. A slight amount of cleavage is visible, more if I bend over. The only time I'll bend over Collin Leary, though, is to check his pulse, ensuring there's none.

Sarah chooses one for herself that is slightly less revealing; long sleeves because she's always cold and a high neckline because she doesn't like her chest. Ah, I see her game. She's trying to look frumpy so I'll be the most interesting choice in Mr. Glassblower's gallery tomorrow night. She's setting me up, the little vixen. If Sarah knew the truth about Irish Eyes, she might reconsider her plan.

Before leaving the store, I replenish my dwindling supply of bedding. Four pillows, five sets of sheets. This should get me by for another week.

"Starting a boarding house?" Sarah is growing curious

about my personal business. Not a good sign.

"Yes."

She recognizes my sarcasm and laughs at me. I should consider purchasing in bulk.

When we're done spending our money, we migrate to a quiet restaurant and I sit across from her in the booth. Sarah orders a daiquiri while I stick with water. Normally, I'd go for Tanqueray and tonic, but with as much blood as I'd lost last night, I can't afford to thin what I have left with alcohol.

Taking a sip from my glass, I lean forward on the table. Sarah does the same. Her expression turns sly, almost devious. I'm curious what that means, but my focus is elsewhere. I'll store this visual information for later.

"So, we're alone, now. Tell me about your dream." I look her in the eyes as she sips from her drink again.

"What dream?" She stops and looks at me oddly, like she's keeping something from me.

Am I overly suspicious of everyone in my life? Rather than start any drama, I ignore it, realizing it's just flaky Sarah. "The dream you had about me. You said you wanted to tell me about it, now's your chance."

Her eyes suddenly light up. "Yeah…Yeah, that's right. Oh, my gosh, it was incredible. You were with me and we went to this place. I can't really remember much about it except there was this guy and he was so hot you could barely move, kinda like that glass guy in the bank yesterday. Then, it got weird." She takes a sip of her drink and smiles at me.

"What do you mean it got weird?" Growing curious over her comment, I lean closer, knowing this is what I was waiting for.

"He hit you. I was shocked and was about to jump on him like a wolf spider. Didn't see *that* coming. Guy hitting a girl for no reason doesn't happen every day."

Our server interrupts with a plate of mozzarella sticks. Sarah seizes one with her fingers and starts nibbling on the end, crumbs falling in her lap and clinging to her lips and chin. She's already forgotten our conversation. I want to reach over and smack the crumbs off her face and the food from her grasp. My impatience grows beyond any harried moment in my past and I wonder why.

Watching her chew like a starving rodent causes a repulsive reaction within me. I don't think I've ever eaten with her before. Suddenly, I'm grateful for that. Can I get her mind off that cheese nugget and back to our conversation before my stomach weakens again?

"And then?" I prod.

She's still distracted by the food, causing me to roll my eyes again.

Why'd I pick Sarah to be my sole confidant? Because she usually doesn't ask too many questions about my private life, I guess. She doesn't get overly inquisitive about my scars, either. Most people pretend they're concerned and dig deeper to try to save you. What they don't realize is I'm saving *them*. I have a job to do. That's all. I go to sleep, go in, kill, and get out. No trouble at all. I can't explain to them what I'm doing and I can't tell them why I don't share my *deepest secrets* with them. Makes friendships awkward if they're attentive and emotionally involved. Most people can't move beyond the idea I don't have the same troubles they do and they'll never be able to understand the ones I have.

Sarah, well, it's simpler with her. She worries about everything in her own little world so she hasn't the time for *my* problems. And, I prefer it that way. I have a chance at a relationship with someone who isn't trying to kill me *or* save me. *Refreshing*. So, although I may get annoyed with her lack of attention, it's the attribute I need most from her.

"Sarah!"

"What? I'm eating. You could use some food, too. Size one-half? Really?"

"Sarah, you were telling me about your dream." I sound too impatient, too anxious.

"Why are you so interested in my dreams all of a sudden?"

I had to think of something. The last thing I need is to stoke any suspicions in her. Good excuse… Thinking… Got it.

"Sarah. You left off with some hot guy hitting me. Wouldn't *you* be interested, too?" Yeah, that's it. An eyebrow raises a smidge. The other follows.

"Oh, yeah." She leans forward. "I was about to throw something at him when all of a sudden you swing back and you totally kicked his ass."

"And then…"

"That's pretty much it."

What? Not possible.

"Did I kill him?" *Crap*. Why did I ask that?

"I swear, James. Sometimes you're so morbid." She laughs at me and I feel my jaw tighten.

Now I'm furious because I can't ask the question again without looking suspicious. Or psychotic. Unless she offers, I won't know if I killed him without asking again. Not knowing the answer will drive me crazy. Can I reach across the table and shake her without drawing unwanted attention to myself? But I have a thought.

I may be a respected branch manager of a small bank, but I'm also human. At least they see me as human and I *am* part mortal. Wouldn't I want to kill someone if they attacked me first? Isn't that a normal reaction? Maybe not normal for normal people, but Sarah knows me as a super-tough martial arts expert. That would make me a force to be reckoned with, wouldn't it?

"Sarah, I have skills that would make me a dangerous person when challenged or attacked. Wouldn't it make sense that I'd rip out someone's trachea if they hit me?" I'm making sense to her without being morbid. I. Am. Clever.

"Okay." She's eating again.

I wait, impatiently drumming my fingers beneath the table where she can't see them. "So?"

"What?"

"Did I kill him?" I'm waiting, watching her trachea, gritting my teeth.

"I don't remember."

"You don't remember?"

She shakes her head.

"You remember me beating the shit out of him, but you don't remember if he's dead?"

"Why does it matter? I told you the most important part. You kicked his trash."

True. It *was* important to know I fought back. If I hadn't killed him, Sarah and I wouldn't be here to discuss this right now. Somebody died that night. I'd be safe in assuming it was him since he punched me and I took him to town. No demons have ever hit me in the mouth and lived to laugh about it. So why was he in my bank yesterday? Is there another one of him? Did Collin Leary have a twin who died in his sleep two days ago? There's only one way to tell. I'll be at his gallery on Friday. Perfect opportunity to find out what he knows and if *his* inner demon has any plans for retribution.

Chapter 4

Unlike most people, I have no aversion to dark streets or narrow alleyways. I do some of my best hunting in these places. I love the feeling of a change in pulse when my heart rate quickens, the sole thing that lets me know I'm alive on nights like this. I suppose it's why I'm always so aware of what my heart is doing from one moment to the next. Slowing, fluttering, pounding like a drum. Seems more like an indicator of how much danger I'm facing or how bored I am. Otherwise, I'd kill without noticing the subtle innuendos of fear or excitement.

In my wakened life, I usually don't have the luxury of elevated blood pressure. There's little about working at a bank that pumps me up. Typically, banking is a normal, safe environment. *Dull.* I prefer the thrill of blood racing through my veins to a safe and moderate life. I love confrontation, but on *my* terms.

In my dreams, I have control over the outcome. At least, for the most part. I'm strong. In fact, I was born with the ability to achieve the strength of five men, or two male angels, as long as I train. And I do, every day, for every possible scenario. The predator has no idea what he's up against. Basically, he thinks he's got it all figured out. He sees a vulnerable woman and feels assured his dream will end *his* way. Me? I create a new narrative, one he's not expecting. I change the story to allow an escape plan for his prey. Then, I turn his anger back on him. Most times, he destroys himself by trying to eliminate me. If I stay calm, become totally aware of my surroundings, in most cases it all comes together beautifully.

As I walk the empty streets in the realm of my dreams tonight, I'm enjoying the quiet moments before the fight. My mind clears as I breathe in the scent of emptiness surrounding the early formation of my nightmare. This space is devoid of hatred and anger, allowing the desperation of the hunter and the hunted souls to incubate. The scent alters and I catch a glimpse of a shadow scurrying into an alleyway ahead. I'm not sure if they're victim or perpetrator. There's only one way to know for sure.

When I round the corner, I notice the sleeve of a coat pull behind a barrel. Could be a trap. I know better than to wander up to them without checking their scent. My eyes closed, I wait for their subconscious to reach out to me. Soon the smell of rubbing alcohol, translucent tape, and latex gloves infuses the vacant air. Their sound emanates the soft hiss of a respirator, lightly puffing while a child quietly moans. An unexpected tear rolling down my cheek startles me and I draw a quick breath.

How did that happen? I never cry. At least, I haven't cried in decades.

The soul behind the barrel has a daughter wasting away with cancer. The young girl awaits the surgery to remove her brain tumor. No insurance. Inching toward the frightened woman, my eyes burn with the tears I'm fighting.

Cautiously approaching the barrel, I crouch and peer

around the side to see her wild eyes. "Are you okay?" She doesn't answer although she knows I won't hurt her. She can smell kindness on me. "Come with me. I know a safe way out."

When she places her hand in mine, I pull her to her feet. "Your name is Julia, isn't it?" She nods. "Julia Lyster?" She nods again. "I have a message for you, Julia. When you wake tomorrow, go to the Bank of Colorado Springs on Academy Boulevard. Don't forget. A grant was set up in your name to help pay your bills. I'm sure it'll be more than enough to take care of your needs."

When I smile at her, she smiles back. As tears fill her eyes, she flings her arms around my shoulders and surrenders a grateful hug. I'm hesitant to hug her, not fond of displaying emotions, so I rub her back to comfort her instead. "Everything's going to be okay. But you need to be at your daughter's side right now, all right?" She wipes away a tear and nods. "Let's go."

I need to get her to safety and there's no water in the general area of this dream. My only other chance is to find another surface that will reflect her image. There are no mirrors, but there could be glass. Yes. That's it.

After taking her out to the main road, I lead her down the street. Not far from the alley we've exited is a building with a large, unbroken window. Once there, I turn her until her back is to the glass.

"When you wake, go to the bank as soon as it opens. Speak with the branch manager, Jaime Connor, or her assistant, Sarah Maxfield. They'll have the money for you, okay?" She nods, sniffling and wiping tears from her cheek with the back of her arm.

Her body jolts when I grab her by the shoulders of her jacket and throw her backward into her image. The minute her body hits, she disappears and I'm comforted that she awoke. Staring into the glass, I imagine her waking in the chair at her daughter's side, resurrected from her nightmare. Another tear escapes my eye and I quickly wipe it away. I can't afford to be weak. Time to move on.

The call of the demon leads me down a quiet back street, whispering in my mind like a haunting dirge. My senses are heightened. There are no mortal sounds in this dank existence but the clap of my bare feet on dry pavement. In this dream, my clothing is the same I'd worn to bed. Their expectations of me are low, making me realize this planned kill is unemotional, no more than a contract.

As my presence echoes past empty warehouses and shuttered buildings, my heart begins to quicken its pace. Tension builds in the air, but it isn't my tension. The monster senses me, thinking I'm Julia.

Suddenly, my footsteps aren't the only echoes I hear. Another set of feet duplicate my pace. Intentionally hesitating, I give them time to catch up. Their gait slows as well, like they're toying with me, hoping to intensify the expectant fear.

I'm unsure how much I want to invest in this evening. I'm still not healed from last night's ambush. Still, a part of me wants to play with this predator, for Julia's sake more than mine. She deserves to sleep well knowing he won't bother her anymore. Maybe I'll wait to see how aggressive they become before determining how painful their death will be.

There are no weapons at my disposal here. Brick exteriors and boarded windows form a bleak backdrop for my nightmare. I'll have to use strength to remove this demon from existence. After sauntering for five barren blocks, I duck around the next corner. Leaning against the wall, I patiently wait for the demon.

They slow, taking their time, wondering if I'll ambush

them. When he rounds the building and finds me there, fear stirs his anger. Soon, a knife appears in his hand and he's shoving me flat against the bricks. I could have dodged, taken him out before he even saw me, but what would the fun in that be? With the blade to my throat, he tries to hide the panic in his eyes, working to stoke his fury, but I see more than he can feel.

His sense of the monster he's become has numbed him to all other reality. He uses self-pity to reconcile the violence. I don't care what he has endured or how bad he feels about himself, there's no reasonable explanation of murder for pleasure.

The scent of dirty money coats his soul. He works for a loan shark. His job is to settle up with the debtor, sometimes make an example of them. The type of example he prefers is terror, even death.

At the smell of demise on me, he begins to sweat. "Where've ya been?"

"Oh, you know, around." Staring flatly into his eyes, I intentionally push him toward the line of anger. I'm not sure why.

His teeth grind behind tight lips, a thin mustache moves back and forth in frustration. "Where's the money?"

"Uh, *what* money?"

A twitching eye betrays his mounting dread. "The money you owe Larry. Where is it? You're suppose ta have it by last week and then you disappear. You know, Larry's pretty mad. I'd of spoke up for ya again, but then I'd look bad. I already told Larry you'd have it for him once before. He thinks I lied. I don't like Larry thinkin' I'm a liar. That's bad for business. You understand that, don't ya?" The stench of stale cigarettes assaults my senses as he speaks.

"Well… Maybe. But you're a liar because you've never told

Larry any such thing for *anyone*." His fingers shift nervously on the handle of his knife as I continue. "You're a selfish man. You wouldn't move your lips a millimeter to help another."

This life he professes to despise is the life he relishes. When he kills a desperate person, he thinks he's destroying the part of him he loathes. Yet, no matter how many destitute souls he brings to their knees, he's never satisfied. He will *never* be satisfied.

The truthfulness of my revelation causes him to fear me more, which just increases his anger. I wonder why he hasn't already tried to kill me.

"Shut up! You don't know anything 'bout me." Fear is replaced with rage as his facial gestures become animated.

But I merely shrug my shoulders, triggering his fury and causing him to slap me. Part of me thrills at stirring his anger. When the sting of his blow wears off, I shoot a disapproving glare at him and slowly shake my head.

"Yer stallin'. Gimme the money or ya know what I'll do."

"Paint my nails? I'm desperately in need of a manicure." My expression doesn't change as his jaw tightens.

Growing impatient with my insolence, he presses the blade into my neck. "Ya wanna manicure? D'ya realize I can kill ya? Larry gave me the choice, ya know. Yer life's mine, now. An' seein' I'm the one who's controllin' your ability ta keep breathin', maybe you should ask yourself: will he kill me tonight or will he let me live? I'm known for bein' reas'nable, though, if you beg real nice, I might find it in my heart to give you some time even though you've greatly disrespected me. What d'ya think?" Suddenly, he becomes annoyingly condescending. "D'ya need more time? Huh? Can you get down on your knees and ask for one more week?"

"How about another month?"

The fool doesn't realize I'm unfazed by his lack of control.

Instead of reassessing the situation, he grits his teeth and swings his fist at me, not even considering I might be able to kill him with a simple head-butt to the nose. Rather than defend myself, I decide to accept the blow and see what happens. The disaffected look in my eyes infuriates him even more.

"I wanna hear ya beg," he growls, grinding his teeth as he speaks. "Makes me feel like I've accomplished somethin' today when someone's cryin' on their knees. Don't ya agree?"

"Nope." I smile. "I prefer a manicure. Just look at these nails." My eyes narrow as I raise my fingers to his line of sight.

No matter what his victim does, regardless of how sincerely they beg, he kills them anyway. This punk followed me, believing I was Julia, with intent of taking me out even if Larry already had the money she owed. He doesn't care she has a daughter dying in the hospital. This guy revels in the power of making someone cry, pleading for their life. And just as they think he'll show mercy, *bam*! He kills them. *Bastard*.

When he slaps my face again, I feel the bite of his blow linger on my flesh. "You better feel like begging for yer life, bitch."

Sigh. I hate when they call names. Thusly, I feel a sarcastic wave coming over me. Oh, wait, I was already drowning in sarcasm. *Never mind*. "Can't we talk about this?"

He grabs my shirt in his fists and slams me against the brick wall again. Guess he doesn't appreciate my sense of humor, but I laugh in his face anyway. "You enjoy this *far* too much."

The knife to my throat again, his words shower me with spit. *Great! A spitter*. "I said beg! I wanna hear ya cryin'!"

"I lack experience in begging. And yet, something tells me you've been on your knees before. So, how about it, can you show me how you did that? A simple demonstration." My voice is flat to show the absence of fear.

Before he can answer my belligerence, I reach my hand over the top of his, the one holding the blade, and grab him by the pinkie. While I'm bending it backward, he growls in pain as I stare into his eyes and snap the bone. Grabbing the next finger, I break it at the knuckle until it bends in the shape of a "u." His screams echo between the buildings as I reach for another and crush the bones with my index finger and thumb. Finally, he drops the knife, but catches it in his other fist.

Cool move.

Turns out he's ambidextrous, too, as he slashes the blade across my abdomen. Damn, I hadn't anticipated that. Anger burns through me. These are my favorite pajamas. No doubt I'm bleeding all over them *and my bed* and will probably need more stitches when I wake.

After examining my stomach, I lift my eyes to his. He's stunned at my reaction, cradling his hand in his arm. Playtime is over. With one swift movement, I knock the knife from his grasp and jam the heel of my hand into his nose with near deadly force, knocking him to the ground. I hear the distinctive snap of his collarbone. Blood pours from his face and I'm reminded of Phillip Bradley. Two different people, both poisoned with black souls.

As I'm about to pick up his knife, I'm hit in the left side with something solid and long. *Shit!* It can't be the same asshole who blindsided me last night. I fall to my knees, holding myself while reaching for the blade and trying to catch my breath. My eyes search my surroundings, but there's no one. The killer is writhing on the ground before me, groaning loudly over his broken fingers, nose, and clavicle. He couldn't have been the one to hit me. This scenario is almost familiar. But I haven't killed him, yet. They didn't even wait for the kill, *bastards*!

The demon debt collector screams out, "You broke my nose, you—"

"Shut up!"

I'm listening for their footsteps, but there are none. They're here. I can smell them nearby. The sound of wind filtering through pine boughs fills the air. Whoever it is has the sound of the forest in their essence.

As I rise to my feet, holding my wound, another blow comes at me from the right and I barely reach my free hand out in time to block. I can't see anything but a cloaked shadow moving in the darkness. I grit my teeth to keep from crying out in pain, unwilling to show weakness. Waiting for them to move, I hold both of my aching sides. Blood loss and pain slow my reaction as the shadow darts at me again. I'm struck by something hard and flat, a board maybe, across my back, sides, abdomen, all in rapid succession. Letting go of my wounds, my hands shoot up to block the board from striking me in the head. This devil is talented and fast. If it had connected, that blow would have knocked me out.

The world sways. Damn, I'm losing too much blood. My hand clamps back onto the wound. Another strike comes at me, hitting me square across the ribs. I hear the crack and know something is broken. I can't withstand much more. This has to end now.

Still holding the knife, the blade facing away, I hunch over, waiting. I close my eyes and let my senses take over. A rush of wind whispers in the shadows and I smell wintergreen. My arm strikes out and I feel the blade connect. A groan confirms it. I've wounded them.

Before I lose consciousness, I fall to my knees beside the still twitching demon I was meant to exterminate—the debt collector—and plunge his knife deep into his sternum. His body goes limp and I fall to the pavement.

CHAPTER 5

The birds aren't singing this morning as I wake. A sharp pain shoots through my abdomen as I roll to my side to see the clock. My breathing is shallow. For the first time in my life, I feel like I'd rather die than endure this pain. My hands tremble uncontrollably. *Damn*! I can't believe I became too focused on the demon and didn't keep an eye on the shadows. *Sloppy*!

This wound is too deep to ignore and too suspicious for any self-respecting doctor to overlook, either. This time, I must do something I've never done before—confide in someone. It's the only way to protect myself. But who could I trust?

There's Sarah. I've known her for several years now. Can't even remember how long it's been. And, to my knowledge, she's never revealed anything personal about me to anyone else. As if there was ever anything personal shared between us. But, there are my scars. Come to think of it, why *doesn't* she ever discuss me with her friends? Am I that boring to her? *Sigh*, I'm getting off track. And the bleeding isn't subsiding. Being insecure won't close this damned wound.

So what about Sarah? Could I trust her with this? Nah. She

would never understand what I'm trying to say. After our conversation yesterday, there's no doubt in my mind I'd end up having to save her life more than once because she was too foolish to purge me from her mind before falling asleep. Sarah is definitely out. So, who else?

The doctor. The one I saw yesterday. I remembered him from my past. Who was he to me? I wasn't able to see too deep into his eyes. Would've been great if I could read his past. Then, I would know for sure if he's the one. But, he never stared into mine long enough. So how do I know? And how do I know *him*? I dig deep into memories locked away for too long. The sound of his soul, so familiar…

Oh, my God. That's it. Doctor Stanton was my captain in the great war, in the pre-existence. My captain! God sent him to watch over me and help protect me when I needed him most. But, he doesn't seem to remember me. It's often that way with memories of the pre-existence. And it would be best not to flood him with information until he's ready to hear it. Just telling him who I am could force him to deny everything he feels to be true and have me committed. I need to find a way to convince him without alarming him. Obviously, he was sent down without a memory of me for a reason.

Reaching into a drawer, I remove the video camera. I think I may be able to find an ally in him. But I have to be careful how much I let on about who he really is and what he once meant to me. Best to let him pull the information from me. His mind will accept it more easily and not block the truth if he's the one searching for it.

Slipping the device into the large compartment of my purse, I limp to the door and head to the car. On my cell, I'm explaining to Sarah I'll have to skip work again *and* the event at the gallery. Relapse of a vicious stomach flu. She cries and pleads with me. Why didn't I anticipate her emotional reaction? So glad I didn't decide to make her my confident for my true identity. What would she do with that nugget of information? She's still rambling. Should've sent a text.

"Please, please, puleeasse... Rest until evening. You'll be fine once you get out of the house."

"We'll discuss it after I see the doc. Oh, and before I forget, I need you to set up a grant for a Julia Lyster. She'll be in today to sign the paperwork. The grant amount is $750,000. Take it from my CD that matured last week."

"Who do I say sponsored the grant?"

"Tell her the bank has a Healing Angels Fund and the donations are anonymous. Okay? Thanks."

Something in her voice sounds tired. I wonder if I've put too much work on her over the past couple days. A twinge of guilt bites at my conscience. I'll figure it out later, though, once I've seen the doc.

Fortunately, they are able to fit me in between appointments. Waiting in the patient room, I'm feeling anything but patient. My shoulders are hunched in pain and I can barely breathe. After what seems like an eternity, the doctor comes into the room. When he sees me, he sighs deeply, closes his eyes, and shakes his head.

Remembering who he is, my heart leaps with joy for a moment. If I can convince him of who I am, I'll have an ally. God, I'd love to have him as my ally. But I have to play it cool. Lose the smile and turn on my disaffected with society charm.

"Jaime Connor."

"Dr. Stanton, please...don't assume."

Reading my chart on the computer, he eventually turns to me and sighs again. "When did this start happening to you, these *accidents*?" He accents the word as if it's a fallacy. Well, in a way it is.

"I'll explain it all to you. I need you to tell me you can open your mind and keep it open to what I have to say."

Part of him should be open, because of who he is, or was. I just hope it's a big enough part not to send me packing to the padded room.

"Let me see, first..." He nods toward me.

I lift my shirt and show him the dark bruising across my torso. He palpates the skin next to the slice on my abdomen and shakes his head. "You need stitches. You know I have to report this."

"Please... hear me out first."

"I can't let—"

Abruptly slipping off the table, I start for the door.

"Wait."

Stopping in place for a moment, I listen to him with my hand still on the knob.

"If you stay..." he hesitates briefly before speaking again. " I'll do my best to keep an open mind."

I turn back to him, holding the video camera in hand. "Watch this and I'll explain." I open the view-screen and push play. "I sat a camera up in my room to capture this in the event I'd need to convince someone someday that I'm not crazy. I guess this is someday."

He watches hesitantly and within moments, his eyes grow large as he shifts his attention from the screen to my face then back to the video. "What is this, some sort of stigmata?"

"No."

"I don't understand. Seems like you're being attacked by some...invisible...what is it? Ghosts?"

"Not that either. Please, let me explain." Taking a deep breath, I take a moment to collect my thoughts before beginning again. "Everyone has a conscience. Some are tuned for kindness. Others are weak or fearful. But there are some who are pure evil."

"So you're saying evil spirits attack you at night?" His voice shows disbelief, almost sarcasm.

"Sort of, but not really. This'll sound cracked, but hear me out before signing the papers to send me off." I try to think of the perfect wording, but none will come to me. I have no choice but to jump in anyway.

"I'm one of very few who come to earth with a unique purpose. I'm called a dark angel." Pausing for a bit, I give him time, allowing my words to sink in. He stares back at me with his eyes narrowed and a raised brow. I can see part of him is trying to believe me; another is contemplating his safety in the room alone with me. "Basically, we're sent here to fight demons who hunt in the night, in their dreams. You must've heard about an elderly woman who was attacked in her sleep a couple weeks ago." He slowly nods so I go on. "What no one reported, what they didn't know, was that her attacker was also asleep when he murdered her. That's why there was no forced-entry into her home, no fingerprints left behind, no murder weapon, nothing stolen. She was killed only because she was vulnerable and he wanted blood. The one way for me to find them and stop them is through my dreams. I'm led to killers and they fight me to the death. Well, so far, to their death."

He's shaking his head and I'm worried he won't believe anything I'm saying. "You can't prove anything you said. It's too ludicrous to—"

"Look at the video again. That isn't some scene in a movie. That's me. Unedited, unscripted. If you took this to a professional, they'd tell you it's authentic. But then, there would be too many questions that I can't answer and the world is unprepared to hear. In this segment I'm fighting her killer. He was found in his bed, his throat slit. Police called it a drug deal gone wrong. Only thing is, at this crime scene there were, also, no fingerprints, no forced entry, and no murder weapon." I point to the screen again. "See that, he cut my arm. No one around me and suddenly I'm bleeding. How can that be? And here, I take away his knife. Watch…right…there. I've just finished him off." I slip the shirt over my shoulder to show him my scar.

"You're what, a dream vigilante?" He looks at me with accusing eyes.

"No. I'm a mediator. I intercede to stop another killing, sometimes deter a first kill."

"But you do more than mediate, you kill them."

"I have no choice. If I don't, they'll get rid of me. They kill in the night, in their sleep, and because there's no evidence of their crime, they'll continue to kill. I'm the sole intervention to save others from becoming their victims."

His eyes grow wider with recognition, not of me, but of the idea that I may be telling the truth. My heart wants to dance, but it's too premature for that. I don't have him fully hooked yet.

"How do I know you didn't see the news—"

"Today they'll find the body of a former murder suspect, acquitted on a technicality, dead from a deep wound in his chest. The murder weapon, his knife, will never be found because it happened in his mind, in his sleep. The knife doesn't exist except in REM, but the wound still remains. If they were capable of finding the weapon they'd also find my blood on it." I lift my shirt high enough to show him the deep slash again. "When you listen to the news tonight, you still won't know for sure if I'm telling you the truth, or if I'm insane. You may always wonder if you're doctoring up a lunatic or someone with abilities you don't understand. But at least you'll be doctoring me up."

His face pales. He closes his eyes and waves away the

camera. "I can't watch this anymore. It's too gruesome."

Noticing the scene displayed on the camera, I press the pause button. "Uh, sorry, that one was, um, pretty brutal. Should've seen the other guy." I close the viewer and slip the camera into my purse.

He hesitates, pondering what he's heard. "He did this to you? The one they'll find today?"

I stare him straight in the eyes. "If he hadn't, there'd be a report of another woman found dead this morning. At least I'm still alive."

"You call this being alive? How can anyone live doing something like this? I don't know what I can do for you. How do I even begin to help with…with this?"

"Fix me when I'm broken. Understand I have no way to stop it. I have to sleep and I'll always dream. When I dream, there will always be someone there. I have no choice but to kill before they kill me. That's my life. I've come to terms with it. I need you to patch me when the fight's over. When the killer is done with me. When I'm done with him."

He stares at me from beneath furrowed brows, but I can see his eyes beginning to soften. "I'll do what I can." His hands shake as he reaches for a post-it on a nearby counter. "I'm giving you my cell number. Call me any time of day, weekends, whenever." Then he mutters under his breath, "Sure hope you're not crazy."

I smile at him. "Watch the news tonight. You'll see. No forced entry, no fingerprints."

He shakes his head. "You'll need stitches." He lifts my shirt and touches the bruising on my side, making me wince in pain. "And x-rays."

"I have a hot date tonight, Doc. Any chance you can have me patched up by then?"

His expression changes to incredulity. "Not a chance. You

need rest."

Attempting a flirtatious smile, I tell him, "You know what they say about the wicked."

"Not in this case, young lady. No outings for you. If what you're saying is true, you have another dream to prepare for. You can't fight killers in this condition."

"You'd be astonished at how fast I heal."

He raises his eyebrows at me. "What did I say?"

"All right. All right. I'll stay home. Hope Sarah will understand."

"She your date?"

"Yeah." I said it without considering his insinuation. When I see the smile cross his lips, I realize he thinks *Sarah* is my *hot date*. "No, not *that* kind of date. She's a friend, sort of, not really. A friend, but," *Sigh*. "I'm not real good at friendships."

"Can't imagine why. Well, if she doesn't understand, she isn't much of a friend."

"Yeah. Could be *I'm* not much of a friend to *her*." Hesitating on this thought, I wonder if I should end our friendship. The danger to Sarah might be greater than she deserves. "Dr. Stanton…"

He smiles at me like a father to a young girl. I find it almost patronizing, but I know he means well. "Call me Rick."

Rick, his earth name. I feel the smile on my lips. I can't believe I'm together with my captain once again. But I need to remain cool. He doesn't know me, I mean, *really* know me, from our distant past.

"Okay…*Rick,* it might be best if you didn't share this. I mean, I don't know how safe it is for anyone who knows about me and, well, you know. I can't promise anything. And whatever you do, don't dream about what I've told you. Do everything you can to put it out of your mind well before you go to sleep, all right?" Felt it best not to share the night Sarah entered one of my dreams. No reason to frighten him, yet.

"How do I do that, keep from dreaming about you?" He looks concerned, like he just learned he was the personal doctor to a serial killer. In a way, he is. And, in a matter of moments I changed his life from secure to treacherously unpredictable.

"Watch an engaging movie before going to bed, especially the first few days. After a while, I'll fade in importance in your memory." Not very comforting, but it's all I have.

He nods, but doesn't say a word. The rest of the visit is mostly silence. I've put a heavy weight on his shoulders. Wasn't fair. Unavoidable though.

X-rays show two broken ribs. Thirty-seven stitches and a brace for my ribcage, more painkillers and I'm on my way. As I leave the doctor's office I shove the slip of paper with his phone number *and* the prescription into my purse, this time feeling more confident about my future. Now I have an ally I didn't have before. One I knew and adored in a previous world. And I won't have to worry about his safety as long as he doesn't dream about my dilemma. Last thing I need is my doctor caught in the middle of a fight.

CHAPTER 6

"Doctor said I have to stay home and rest." Of course Sarah would show up at my door to try and convince me to go.

"James, you can't back out now. You said you'd go with me." She pushes her way past me and into the living room.

The desire to resist leaves me in a rush of pain at her touch as she passes. Simply getting dressed and enduring an evening of snobbery at a gallery would be less painful than trying to convince Sarah I must stay home without revealing the true reason. She's becoming quite a drain. I'm not sure how much longer I can continue this. The risk is too high she'll appear in another dream, anyway. She's unpredictable and I can't ensure she'll survive next time. Sarah isn't overly intelligent either, I've come to realize over the years. The point becomes ever more evident by her incessant idle chatter on the hue of makeup I should wear to cover the dark circles under my eyes. No recognition that I'm in pain. What kind of negligent parents did she have? She's great with computers, numbers, and everything having to do with a bank. With people, that's a different story. I've had to intervene on different occasions while she dealt unreasonably, even irresponsibly, with customers. There's little in the way of common sense where her personality and private matters are concerned. She can never hold together a relationship of any kind for more than a week or two. I often wonder how she made it so far in her career.

After half an hour of her prodding, I finally acquiesce. The fact remains, I'm interested in meeting the man behind the green eyes. I want to get into his head and find out if he's the one beating the hell out me at night or if he's merely some harmless sap I don't have to worry about. If he's safe, I might consider getting to know him better. If not, well, you know. I might make out with him before snapping his neck. Perhaps I'll consider allowing him a taste more. He is drop-dead gorgeous after all and smells beyond fantastic.

The squeeing that emits from Sarah upon my agreement to go burns my ears and nearly the last of my patience. Had I known she'd energetically hug me around the waist and pat me on the back to show her appreciation, I probably wouldn't have agreed or would've at least waited until I was safely locked behind my bathroom door before notifying her of my intentions. Nonetheless, I begin the painful task of getting ready, unable to exterminate Sarah from the premises. She probably worries I'll back out if she leaves me for a second.

Putting on makeup and fixing hair is torture with broken ribs. At the end of the evening I'll take those painkillers Dr. Stanton prescribed. Heh, *Rick*. I feel like a mob boss with my own personal doctor. My incredibly handsome doctor who was so much more to me so long ago. *Damn it!* Pining over two men in a matter of minutes. Am I going through puberty again? I need to stop thinking about them and concentrate on getting ready.

While sitting on the edge of my bed and chattering, Sarah,

thankfully, doesn't notice last night's blood on the edge of my headboard. I'd burned the covers but missed that. *Stupid.* In my weakened state, I'm making too many mistakes.

Thinking quickly, I grab my robe and hang it over the corner post to cover the bloody fingerprints. You never know when she might make a synaptic connection and notice something other than the glaringly obvious. I'm grateful she's not overly observant. Luckily, she also doesn't notice the pain on my face as I strain to breathe while struggling into my dress. This is a bad idea. I can already sense it.

I've never taken so long to get ready for *anything*. Two hours? *Ugh!* I feel like such a *girl*. But at last, the prep time is over and we're finally on our way. Thankfully, talking Sarah into driving took no effort at all. We zipped off toward the city and soon she was pulling up to the gallery. As luck would have it, someone was leaving as we arrived, providing a prime parking spot right in front of the building. Fortuitous?

This time, I notice the front entry. An older building, the exterior walls are dark brown brick. The door has leaded-glass framed in heavy, American white oak. The brass handle is fairly new. Barely a scratch in the satin finish. Just inside the entry is a small reception desk where a young woman sits, taking names of all who enter. She wears a nametag. Mandy. The walls, pedestals, glass and crystal figurines, a variety of vases; all are unnervingly accurate to my dream. The difference is the varying people scattered around the room.

In front of a crystal statue, a young mother scolds her curious son. An elderly couple saunters by. A well-dressed man examines a vase. There's a blond woman draped on the shoulder of a dark-haired man. I can't see his face. Five other participants crowd around them. I have yet to see Mr. Leary and his piercing green eyes.

Out of habit, I search for finer details in the room. A small, green banker's lamp illuminates the reception desk, a pen and guestbook on top. A nearby pedestal displays a glass figure of a woman draped in thin cloth, showing fine details of her naked form. Beside it sits a crystal vase crowned with raised tulips to accent the rim. I remember them from the dream. What's the significance? Multi-level shelves display brilliantly colored glass pieces. Another colorful creation is perched on a pedestal, a brilliant yellow dish shaped like a piece of cellophane-wrapped candy, also from that night. Sarah stood near it in my dream, watching me grow speechless over a clever man. Speaking of *him,* he doesn't seem to be anywhere in the room.

As the thought presents in my mind, I feel the presence of someone other than Sarah at my side. The smell of wet moorland grass relaxes my shoulders as I turn to see those gorgeous green eyes staring into mine. He reaches for my hand and leans forward, nearly brushing my cheek with his lips as he whispers, "I'm glad you came."

Crap. This *is* my dream.

I'm suddenly confused. My heart is thumping and it isn't because I'm in danger. My thighs feel warm and I want him to whisper in my ear again. And at the same time, I want to know how I'm reliving my nightmare.

At that moment, I realize Sarah is no longer at my side. She's moved to the far wall, standing beside that same pedestal with the deliciously colorful glasswork and the same sly grin on her face. What does she see that I don't? *Wait.* I asked myself this same question in the dream.

My eyes search the room. The woman with the young boy has moved on to other pieces. The elderly couple is heading toward the door. The blond is standing in the group, no longer clinging to anyone, talking while watching me and Collin Leary. The well-dressed man is speaking with the receptionist about the tulip-crowned vase. His sleeve rises up his wrist as he leans over her desk. He's wearing an expensive watch. I think it's a Breitling. She nods at his question. He sets the vase down and walks away. Collin Leary is looking dreamily into my eyes. What am I missing?

I need to say something before I look stupid. "Thank you for inviting me." *That was lame.*

I'm such a rake. Why am I so cool in my dreams, fighting monsters who want to kill me, but in real life I can't do anything but clean up debris? Here's this really hot guy and I can't think of an intelligent word to say. Maybe if I imagine he's a killer and this is only a dream, I could say something witty, brilliant even, tempting him to make a move; assault me or seduce me. For the love of God, let him stop studying me in that sensual, I-want-to-run-my-fingers-up-your-thigh, kind of way. It scatters my thoughts too much. I swallow deeply and part my lips to speak.

Before I can turn on my dark angel charm, Blondie has grabbed hold of Collin Leary's arm and is dragging him away. "I'm dying to know more about this beautiful *vaaz* over here." So pretentious. It's a *vase,* not a *vaaz.*

They stand in the corner and she wraps her arms around his like she owns him. Why does this bother me? I barely know him. I've lost all focus of the room. As much as I try to turn away, I can only see them, hovering near a shelf with a deep, tanzanite-colored vessel filled with hand-blown greenery and delicate white blossoms. She rubs the small of his back and then cackles loudly. Her hand trails up to his shoulder and she kisses him on the cheek.

With the breath caught in my throat, I realize I can't watch any longer. My eyes direct downward instead, searching my thoughts, trying to reconcile my inner turmoil.

A quick glance back at the two makes my heart begin to

race even faster. She's turned his chin toward her and is pressing her lips against his. I'm struggling to control the urge to pull every bleached strand of hair out of her head. Why such a violent reaction? Isn't he the man I want to destroy? I'm more controlled while carefully and methodically killing a murderer. I have to get out of here before I do something impulsive.

"Come on, Sarah, let's go."

She's suddenly interested in a glass figurine. "I wanna stay. These things are amazing."

Sigh. Perky. I'm beginning to *abhor* perky.

"I know, but I'm tired and I want to go home, now." I try asserting myself, but it goes over her head. I should've known it was a mistake asking her to drive. I need air.

In a panic, I make my escape through the leaded-glass door. My body leans gingerly against the building as I catch the breath I'd been holding for some time. Something is happening I can't explain. Something about this place, the blond, Collin Leary, even Sarah; an event they all seem to know or understand that I've lost. The key is in my dream, which I can't remember. There's something about this shared dream that Sarah knows subconsciously but can't express. Maybe it's the same with Mr. Leary, possibly his receptionist, too, but I'm completely missing it every time I'm in that room. Why can't I see it?

The door suddenly opens and I endure the pain of lifting my fractured ribcage to stand straighter. When I raise my eyes, Collin Leary is staring back at me, his gaze penetrating my soul. My heart leaps and I can barely breathe again.

"What happened? Are you all right?"

He seems so sincere. Why do I want to shout at him like I caught him cheating? I want to hate him as if he's a demon I hunt at night, but for some reason I can't do either. Something inside me reacts differently to him. Am I losing my ability to recognize evil?

Then, he runs his hand down my arm and my skin tingles. Soon he's holding my hand. I have to speak, but I don't know what to say. Be cool, think of him as one of *them*. Hell, it's highly likely he is.

"I needed air. Been battling the flu." *Real smooth*. I sound so weak. How could I let him see me as feeble? "I should go home."

"I wish you wouldn't. I… I'm not sure how to say this without sounding desperate, but I was really glad to see you. You made my evening when you walked through the door."

I'm taken aback at his humility. And thrilled he's as awkward as me. I might have misjudged him. But even his lack of pretention isn't enough. "I really should go."

"Please don't." He grasps my hand tighter.

"But I thought you were with the…I saw you in there with *her*. She was clinging to you and she kissed you. I…I don't know what I'm saying or why I'm saying this. Damn! You whispered in my ear and I want you to whisper to me again and I want your lips to touch me, but not my cheek. And I…" *What the hell am I doing?* I've lost my mind. "I don't even know you and I'm making a fool of myself. I *really* should g—"

Before the last breath can escape my throat, he grabs me by the shoulders and presses his warm lips against mine. My whole body would collapse in his arms if it wasn't for the pain in my torso. Then, his mouth slowly releases me and I'm waiting for more.

"I'm not *with* her. She's a client. I may humor her, but she's not the one I'm interested in."

The feel of his breath on my lips when he speaks makes the muscles in my legs turn to rubber. He reaches his hand around my back and pulls me closer, kissing me again. My breath is stolen, but not in a good way. I try not to grimace, wanting to forget I was beaten last night, but his touch on my back is torture. There's no way I can tell him how agonizing his hand feels against my broken body. I can't say that I was attacked from behind before I killed a murderer in my sleep. He would think I'm a nut, or a serial killer. So I endure the torture, hoping I'll grow numb soon so I can enjoy the feel of his kiss. As my neurons at last start losing the sharp stab of agony, the door swings open and Green Eyes loosens his grasp on me as Sarah exits the building.

"I see you two are getting along. Don't let me interfere. Just wanted to let you know I'm going. Been a long day and I worked hard while you were home playing hooky, James."

What? Where is she coming from? This isn't like her. Confused at Sarah's newest bout with crazy, I start to pull away from Collin. "I have to go—"

"Coll, would you be a dear and give James a ride home?" She winks at me and I'm not sure what game she's playing.

"No, Sarah, I said I'll—"

Before I can finish, she waves at me while I'm still walking toward her. She slides into her car and starts the ignition. "Sarah, don't you dare leave—"

Her car pulls away from the curb before I can reach the door handle. "…me."

I'm gonna kill her.

"That was your friend?"

I watch her taillights fade. "Not anymore."

As much as I love entertaining this heady feeling he causes, the fact still remains: Collin Leary may be trying to kill me. The last thing I need is to lead him to my door.

"I'll call a cab."

"I can't let you do that. I promise I'm safe." I must have shot a confused glance his way because he begins to fumble over his next words. "I drive very safe. And, and I'm benign. I assure you, I'll be a complete gentleman."

"Benign?"

He stares back at me with an uncomfortable grin on his lips, redness shading the fullness of his cheeks. "Heh, yeah, I guess that's what you call it. Won't kill you, you know…"

My body stiffens at his reply. "What an unusual choice of words." My minuscule level of comfort has just diminished.

"No, no, that's not what I meant. I'll stop before I make it worse." He hesitates for a moment. Then, his eyes soften. "If you're sure you want to call a cab, I understand. But I'd really like to take you home."

I'm too weak to fight if he turns out to be the killer I believe he could be, yet, I'd rather take my chances with him than a cab. Unsure why. *Hello, intuition*? Where have *you* been?

"I'm okay. I'd love for you to take me home." My tone isn't convincing, but it doesn't matter. I'm sensing he attributes it to Sarah's abrupt departure.

The corners of his mouth crease upward as he places a hand on my back and leads me into his gallery. Inside the door, he leans over and whispers in the receptionist's ear; then, he moves through the room to each person. The mother has left with her boy. The well-dressed man is still hovering near the tulip vase, turned so I can't see his face. The group of five pulls Collin aside to ask questions and engage in conversation. The receptionist moves to the door and locks it, standing nearby to avail departures. My skin prickles and my body tells me there's something I need to understand.

The blond woman reaches for Collin and he walks away from her. Did he do that for my benefit? He approaches the man with the tulip vase and they briefly discuss the piece. He seems more focused on me than the customer. I don't think he's even looked the buyer in the eyes. The man plunges his hands in his pockets as Collin lifts the vase and brings it to the receptionist. He points out a brown smudge on the rim. Asks her to clean and wrap it. The smudge appears to be dried blood. My blood? Something I missed earlier. I'm losing my touch.

My body shudders again, telling me danger isn't far away. But who? The man buying the vase? The blond? Collin Leary? Will I see either of them again in one of my dreams? Will I have to kill one of them, all of them, at some point in the not too distant future? I have the feeling of being smothered again. I haven't felt this way since I was a child. What about this place is making me so reactive?

A claustrophobic panic comes over me and I want to leave again. My eyes scan the room once more, searching for signs of blood or anything out of place. The tile floor gleams with wax. A small section not far from me has a dulled surface in an oval pattern. No stain. No wax either. Someone scrubbed it clean.

A glass shelf affixed to the wall is chipped on one corner. An adjacent section is obtrusively empty. There was a shelf there at one time. The figurine of a child is missing a hand. The struggle took place here, not in my mind, not in my dream. Not possible. My dreams never have a physical location in the real world. Why was this one different?

The five guests saunter to the door, discussing the pieces they intend to purchase. One of the men lingers in front of me, studying my face. I smile back at him, but he doesn't return the pleasantry. Collin's receptionist unlocks the door and holds it open for them. Then, she closes and locks it again. Why do I cringe at the sound? The lone man in the suit gathers his treasure and departs also. I just realized, I never saw his face. Odd. How did he get by me without at least one opportunity for a glance?

One person left.

Collin is patient with the woman who wants more of his attention than he's prepared to give. Her hands strafe his chest and then slip down the inside of his arms. His posture turns stiff as he politely smiles. I find her desperate advances too awkward to watch and turn to the girl beside me.

"You work here long?" Pathetic question, but I'm not in the mood to be creative.

"Little over a week." She answers as if hoping to find something better.

"What do you plan to do, your dream career?"

She rolls her eyes and looks over her glasses at me. It's late and she doesn't want to answer my silly questions. Even a fool knows, I could care less about her dream career. *Point made.*

Soon Blondie is walking toward us, eyes fixed on me. Her pupils constrict with anger. Apparently, she suspects my presence for his change in attitude. I can't deny her impression. She's right.

Approaching the exit, she reaches for the deadbolt mechanism and flips it. The door is flung open and she storms out of the building.

"You can go now, Mandy. Thanks for everything." Collin approaches the two of us and holds the door for his employee to depart. She doesn't answer as she slips into the night. She doesn't seem to have a positive impression of her employer. Is it him, or is it her own bad attitude? Something to ponder, for sure.

As her foot passes the threshold, the door closes. Collin reaches for the lock and turns it until I hear the haunting click once again. Suddenly, I'm feeling a recurrent sense of déjà vu. There's no Sarah standing near the far wall, however. Only the two of us. What is his plan? My hands tremble as I scan the room again. There are too many weapons to leave here unscathed. The glass shelves would make a perfect tool, though.

As I search for the deadliest item in the room, the lights go out and I startle again. His hands slip over my shoulders. "This way."

Once again, I can barely breathe. The unknown in Collin Leary's world is more frightening than the monsters in mine. Best to assume he's intent on killing me. Will I end up slitting his throat before learning his true nature?

His hand glides down my arm and into my palm. I'm tingling all over as his fingers lock in mine. The confusion is making a wreck of me. Is this his way of lowering my defenses?

"I parked out back. I'll guide you through the dark. Stay close."

Will you? Is there anyone in this world who can guide me through the dark?

Instead, he leads me into deeper blackness. I can't see a thing, not even him. If it wasn't for his palm pressed against mine, I'd think he'd left me here. He must've noticed my hand trembling because he pulls me closer and wraps his arms around me. I've never been in total darkness before. There's always been some form of illumination, no matter how dim, lighting my way. I'm frightened of this unknown realm with a person I don't trust leading the way. I can feel the blood drain from my face as I inch forward.

"We're almost there. Having electrical troubles back here. Dumb lights went out yesterday. Can't get anyone in to check it out until Monday."

Electrical trouble the day before a gallery event? *Convenient.*

Colliding with what feels like a two-by-four, I hear the resonant clash of several boards falling to a concrete floor.

Collin throws his arms around me again to protect me from the avalanche of wood.

"Still doing all right?" I nod, but he can't see my response, so I guess it was more to encourage *me*. "I'm so sorry. I should've had you wait out front while I drove around. I hate to leave you there alone at night." If he only knew how I'm more at home on a dark street than in a blind backroom.

Then, he stops and his hands leave my body, making me feel cold and empty. The sound of steel grinding against steel gives me hope as a sliver of light breaks the darkness. We've reached the door. As he directs me outside, the panic I'd held in check grows viral and I'm shaking all over. While I'm trying to recover, he turns to lock the door with an old, brass key, then back to me with an expression of relief. The look in my eyes must be telling because he reaches for my arms and pulls me to his chest. This time I don't feel the ache in my sides. I'm quivering so hard I just want it to stop.

"Oh, my God, you're so pale. I had no idea you were so scared."

Neither did I.

Considering my body's unusual response, I'm beginning to wonder if I'm reacting to something else. I hate this feeling. I'm not weak and I don't need a man to save me. Only my doctor to stitch me up.

"I'm deathly afraid of the dark." *A total lie*. I'm just afraid of pitch-black spaces where I can't see anything at all. But I'm not in the mood to explain or elaborate.

He apologizes again and strokes my face. The feel of his hand on my cheek is comforting. And at the same time, I hate that he's being so sensitive. My mixed feelings may be the result of a concern that this same hand that consoles me tonight will someday betray me. Maybe I don't want to learn to enjoy the way he treats me and how wonderful this feels. If he's the demon in my dreams, I'll have to kill him. I know I shouldn't get attached. But…

Finally, I'm able to relax in his arms, enjoying the way his hand strokes my hair to the curve of my bottom. To my disappointment, after mere seconds he releases me and looks into my eyes with genuine concern. How do I resolve this to my lack of trust? He seems so caring. How can he be a demon? Yet, there are too many signs around his gallery telling me he's anything but gentle.

"Are you sure you're all right?"

Why do you keep asking that question? Do you hope for me *not* to be all right, expecting to weaken me? I fake a smile and nod.

"Okay. Let's get you home."

Let's get me home? Oh. Now I wish I'd told him *no, I need you to hold me longer.* It has suddenly become crystal clear, he's gifted at confounding me.

Placing his hand on my back, between the shoulder blades, he directs me to his car. *A silver hybrid*? I'm almost disappointed, expecting something sportier, sexier, and less green-energy. He must be making decent money from the look of the furnishings in his gallery, the white Armani shirt and gray Evan Picone slacks, Bulova watch he wears. Well, the watch isn't that expensive, but it's pretty neat, one with a pendulum that swings, winding it when he moves. I'd pegged him to be nearly as pretentious as the blond woman he'd called his client, but I've been known to be wrong. At least the car is clean. If I die at his hands, it'll be in an immaculate, economical vehicle. My DNA will be caught up in the wristband of his self-winding watch. *Minor consolation*.

When he slides into the driver's seat, I realize I've given total control of my life over to him. Hate to beat the same drum, yet, I can't help but wonder if my decision will prove me foolish. Or dead. Is he one of those killers everyone will say, *He seemed like such a nice guy*?

1. Ted Bundy – a handsome young man who worked at a suicide hotline around the same time he was murdering girls on the side of the highway. He would always see female volunteers safely to their cars at night before heading out to kill and bring home some of the heads as trophies.

2. Eddie Gein – the sweet, harmless old guy who regularly bought ice cream for children in the neighborhood while women in the area were disappearing. Everyone trusted him enough to kid sweet little Eddie that maybe *he* was the perpetrator. Quite a funny joke, until they found a woman hung like a deer in his garage and a lampshade crafted from human skin in his house, among other very creepy items.

If I went to Green Eyes' home, would I find ashtrays made of human skulls? Will there be brains and severed body parts in his fridge next to the Chianti?

He reaches over to touch my hand as he drives, bringing my focus back to him and away from the possibilities of the sicko he could be. The feeling is intoxicating; his fingers gliding up the silky black sleeve of my dress to my elbow, tickling the skin beneath. Am I falling for a serial killer, one I should've taken care of less than a week ago? I'm trembling at the sense of him stroking my arm and instead of withdrawing, I want more. My apprehension makes his touch more exciting than I'd ever imagined.

While giving my address and brief directions, I grow hesitant once again. A nagging feeling tells me it might be a mistake. I've decided to take the risk anyway. If he's trying to kill me, we might as well get it over with sooner rather than later. If my past is any indication of my future, I may not be strong enough for a good fight in another day or two.

"So who is this friend of yours? Sarah?"

You don't need to know anything about her. "Just an employee."

"She seems to be interested in your personal life. Had an impression she was trying to play matchmaker tonight."

Forget about her. She's off limits to you. "I get that a lot. I don't go out much."

He raises his eyebrows at me then looks in his rearview mirror. "Someone as gorgeous as you? Hard to believe."

Does he think I'm a simpleton? "One of your favorite pickup lines?" My tone is flat with displeasure at his failed attempt to flatter me.

He smiles, slightly chuckles. "Fair enough. So your friend brought you to my gallery to meet someone?"

Oh, God, back to this line of query again? "Can we talk about something else?"

He chuckles at me again. His mannerisms are so subtle. He's so controlled. And here I am, out of control. How did that happen? Something inside me is afraid if he *is* normal, he'll lose all interest in me real fast. What man wants a relationship with a woman who kills monsters in her sleep, but shudders at subtle innuendos?

"Why do I make you so nervous?"

Aagh. I was hoping he wouldn't notice. What can I say that won't sound like I think he wants to skin me and make lampshades?

"I don't know. I guess because I don't know you, I was deserted by my ride and we're stuck in this awkward situation. Perhaps I'm not yet convinced you won't try to kill me after all. Wasn't what I'd planned for this evening. And I'm a big fan of predictability." That sounded good.

"Yeah? Me too." He smiles, his lips pressing lightly together before they part to show his teeth and I suddenly wonder what he means by agreeing with me. He didn't even attempt to deny the argument that I believe he might kill me. Has he made *predictable* arrangements and this evening has gone exactly as he'd planned? *God*, I'm so paranoid.

Shortly after rounding the corner at the end of my block, his car drifts smoothly into the driveway and I close my eyes, unsure what to do next. Do I wait for him to kiss me good night and then dart from the car? Do I let him walk me to the door? Invite him in? I wonder if it's obvious I've never been on a date. Not that this is in any way a date, but it sure seems to be ending like one. Before I can talk or move, he takes my hand again.

"Can I walk you to the door?"

My danger meter starts sputtering to life, shrieking in my head while my trembling fingers wrap around his. "Yes."

By the time we've reached the porch, I already have keys in hand. Stopping at the door, I turn to him and look up into his intense gaze. Who can think with those beautiful green eyes staring deeply, raptly, like this? Definitely his other secret weapon.

"Would you like to come in?" *Crap!* Why did I ask that?

"No. I don't think I should."

I'm relieved and also confused once again. How many times will my assessment shift between serial killer and sexy man who thinks I'm nuts?

He takes both my hands and a shock of excitement shoots through my legs to the tops of my thighs. "I might not be able to keep my promise."

Bewildered, I shake my head. I don't understand what he's getting at and he's searching for words for the second time since I've met him.

"I can't lie. I'm unusually attracted to you. Right now I want to go in that house and kiss you in a way I've never kissed anyone. But I respect you too much. So I think it's best I say goodnight right here."

His restrained desire is a turn-on and I feel a strange and stimulating heat creeping through me. Now I want him to stay and kiss me like he's never kissed another woman.

This time, when his hand reaches for my face, I don't flinch. The feel of his touch on my skin is a sedative. I may not need a pain pill to sleep tonight.

As he leans into me, I meet him half way. The warmth of his lips and his tongue lightly brushing against my teeth makes me breathless. Although I don't want to let go, I have no choice. I have to sleep. The monsters are calling me.

"I really should go." My breathing is heavy.

"I know." His also.

His face is flushed and I have no doubt mine is, too. When I reach for his cheek and stroke it with the tips of my fingers, I wonder how it would feel to have him biting my neck, his nose brushing against my ear and his body pressing into mine.

"Will you go out with me tomorrow?"

I'm taken aback at his invitation. He's confident. I like that.

"I think I may be busy." *Regretful, but safe.*

"Are you brushing me off?"

"No. I just think I may be busy." Truthfully, I'd rather heal before he wraps his arms around me again. Besides, there's no telling what tonight's monsters have in store for me.

"Then, go out with me. Please."

What *is* this with everyone begging me to do things with them these days? I'm not a rock star.

"Under one condition."

"Anything."

"You promise to stay benign. You won't kill me."

He grins at my request, his perfect white teeth glaring in the moonlight. "What an unusual choice of words."

Now all I can think about is his beautiful smile. "What

time?" *To hell with safe.*

"Seven-ish?"

Smiling back at him, I nod my agreement. Bringing my hand to his lips, he kisses it lightly and then backs away as I grit my teeth. *Was hoping for another kiss, elsewhere*. Before he drives off, I go inside. With my back against the door, I recall the highlights of the evening. Mostly it entails anything having to do with his lips and the heat developing in parts of my body I'd forgotten existed.

Although I'm distracted like a lovesick girl, I remember to lock and bolt the door before heading off to bed. Unfortunately, my ribs still ache badly and I've decided to take that painkiller after all. I'm hoping my demon is weaker than me this night.

CHAPTER 7

Before falling asleep, I spend an hour purging Collin from my mind for fear I may conjure him into a dangerous dream. Hopefully, he's distracted enough by something other than me to keep him from materializing through his own cognitive desires. When all thoughts of him are erased, I'm finally able to sleep. My eyes won't stay open anyway and I'm soon wandering a darkened path in the mountains above my home. My favorite trail is tonight's hunting ground. Gold Camp Road. I know this area as if I was born here. Spent many days biking into the backside of Seven Falls. In the day, it's a beautiful and serene place to clear your mind of demons. Tonight, I'll be searching for them instead. The venue for the battle is not by my choice. I'm led to where the demon's mind dwells until our dreams meld into one.

Looking up at the moonlit trees on the side of the steep incline causes me to chill. Several years have passed since I've had any desire to visit the mountains at night. This is the first time since I was fifteen. Lingering memories of that devastating night still find a path to the frightened girl deep within my soul. My preferred way to fight back is to drown those memories in neglect, pretend they don't exist, although I know my efforts are temporary. Tomorrow, there'll be another unsuspected stimulus to bring it all back again. To take my mind off tortured bodies and scarred souls, I think about the history of this area instead.

Gold Camp Road was once a short line railroad. They delivered packages to miners and their families who lived in the side of the mountains. They'd toss their provisions onto a dock beside the tracks as it slowly passed. At times, the sacks of sugar or flour would burst open from the impact.

There are several railroad tunnels along the track. Eventually, the railway was shut down and the tracks covered in dirt and gravel to make way for a road. Cars traveled Gold Camp Road for a time before aging tunnels made it unsafe. The passage was blocked off and years later, opened to hikers and mountain bikers. Unsafe tunnels are completely blocked to traffic.

Reaching the first railroad tunnel, I notice the entrance and exit are blocked off. The one way through is to take the path to the right over the mound once you've crossed a small creek. On the other side, the trail soon widens, making it easier to travel if you're on a bike.

Within moments I'm on the back side, searching the shadows for anything unusual. I've grown more cautious after my previous experiences, leaving nothing to chance.

As I reach the mouth of the tunnel, a rock falls at my feet. To think it fell on its own would be irresponsible. I know better. My instincts tell me to hide in the shadows near the opening of the tunnel. Someone will show soon enough.

Before long, I hear huffing and puffing, coughing and moaning as someone stumbles down the side of the mound. *For God's sake.* Am I tracking some buffoon in a bad comedy? Obviously, they're strangers to hiking or climbing, maybe even exercise. And they have taken that physical trait with them into this dream. Odd.

Chuckling to myself, I can just shake my head. Maybe it's some overweight city punk, preying too far from his turf. Perhaps I won't need to hide after all. This should be an easy night.

In the dim light, I see a tall, lanky figure fumbling down the face of the tunnel. This demon seems so out of place and I can't help but wonder if he realizes what he's doing. When he reaches the ground, I can see him more clearly in the glare of a full, ethereal moon.

A man in his middle to late thirties is searching the trail, looking for something, but not in a threatening way. This scenario doesn't seem right. He should be searching the dark for his prey, stalking by the scent of fear, but that doesn't appear to be his intent.

As he turns in the filtered light, something about him feels familiar. He isn't dressed like a punk in his well-tailored suit. Another serial killer? When he faces me, I recognize his hair and the thin scar on his chin.

Crap. Dr. Stanton. This *is* a bad comedy. Oh, my hell.

"Dr… Rick? What're you doing here?" As I move closer, he appears stunned.

"I don't know, I—Jaime? Are you all right?"

"I'm fine, but you're not safe here. What happened?"

He shakes his head and runs his hands through his hair. "I don't know, I was thinking about all you told me and the next thing I know I'm here. Am I dreaming?"

Realizing he made himself the demon's prey, I heave a deep sigh to show my frustration. "Yes! You're dreaming and you're in one of my nightmares. I told you to clear your mind of me. How could you let this happen?"

"I didn't believe you." He takes a deep breath. "I thought—

I don't know what I thought. I guess I thought there was no way I could end up in any of your dreams."

"I repeat: *you're not safe here.* You know the subconscious mind can be more dangerous than a conscious one. You've seen the video. These are not cub scouts I'm fighting. They're killers. And there's no telling when we'll meet up with—"

Something moving in the brush several yards away interrupts my rant and captures my attention. "Shh."

I hope it's only a harmless animal Rick conjured in fear, but there's a greater possibility it's Homo-sapien. Realizing the implications, I grab Rick's arm and speak in a hushed tone. "You're in danger now, do you understand that?"

"I'm such a fool…"

"Shh." I shoot a frustrated glance at him and whisper back. "Yes, you are." I can't be too mad at him, though. I knew he wouldn't believe me. He hasn't changed a bit since the pre-life.

He whispers, "I should have listened."

"Yeah. You should've. Now, you either do as I say or you won't wake up tomorrow." Then, I hear the sound again but closer. "We have to move. Now. Run!"

Taking his arm, I start full kick, down the dirt road. Steep mountainsides rise like skyscrapers up one side of the trail and down the other, causing him to be disoriented on the dimly lit path. My escape plan is to make the intersecting trail five miles ahead. I can only hope this dream still has that feature, and that this doctor is in good enough shape for his mind to allow him to make it. Somehow, I doubt he is.

The sound of him panting is disconcerting since we've barely gone a quarter mile. "You a runner?"

"No. Why?"

"I can tell. You need to start if you're planning to jump into my dreams."

"I doubt I'll let this happen again."

The look on his face indicates he wants to slow down. He keeps turning to see what's behind. The demon in the shadow is still chasing after us, but we're well ahead of him so far. It won't remain so if Doc slows his pace.

"You have to keep going! Don't stop! Don't look back!"

"I'm trying! How do we get out of here?"

"*We* can't. There are two ways to remove *you* from the dream. The best way is to throw you in a body of water." I'm looking over my shoulder to him as we run, hoping he can keep up.

"What did you say?"

"Throw you in water! It's the easiest and most effective way when you're dream takes you to the wilderness."

"What does that do?"

"Wakes you immediately."

"And the second way out?"

"Someone dies. Hurry up. I know a stream. Might be big enough this time of year. Let's go."

He's trying to keep up with me, but I can tell he's having trouble. If he isn't used to exercising, forcing him to go all out the full five miles without a rest could kill him as quickly as any demon. Fear is difficult enough, but to throw in an extraneous workout he's not accustomed to which his mind is reacting, as well as the added elevation that any doctor would consider detrimental. In his mind, all these factors could be fatal. I'm taking a chance pushing him so hard. He may go into heart failure. Last thing I need is to kill my doctor and sole ally with a heart attack in his sleep.

By the time that thought enters my mind, we've nearly made it to the second tunnel. Three miles left to go and Rick is breathing heavily. I'll have to do something soon before he collapses. I'm sincerely worried about him.

"You all right?" I shout over my shoulder.

He nods but doesn't answer. His bronchial tubes are constricting. I can hear it in his wheezing. Suddenly, I see him lurch forward and stumble to the ground. I'm almost positive he tripped over a rut in the road. Did the demon put that damned thing there, or did Rick conjure it unwittingly? Sliding to a stop in the gravel, I turn and rush back to protect him from whoever is chasing us down. My body between him and the monster that pursues us, I'm anxious to confront.

Doc gasps for air and waves me on. "Go! Leave me here!" He shakes as he struggles to rise.

"No! Get up and start running!" The press of the encroaching demon's power is growing stronger, meaning it's gaining on us. "Take the first side path you see! It's off to your right! If I'm not with you, throw yourself in the river! Make sure your whole body's submerged. Do it now! Go!"

I send him on and hope to hell that trail is there as it is in real life. No sense in letting Rick know it might not be. If he believes in it strongly enough, he might take control of the dream and make it so himself.

An impressive silhouette of a man in his thirties lumbers toward me as I rush him, head down. Firmly connecting with his torso, I throw him over my back. With a loud grunt, he lands flat on the ground behind me. After turning toward him and preparing for another attack, I see he's taking his time rising to his feet. This fight's been pretty easy so far and I hope I'm not foolish in thinking I'll be awake before I know it. As I rush him again, he kicks my feet out from beneath me and I crash into the gravel. *Road rash.* I *hate* road rash. Hardest cut to heal. At least I can't feel my broken ribs and slashed abdomen in the dream state. Only the new wounds I receive will affect me, and this scrape is stinging like hell as I brush the grit from my forearm. When I turn to get my bearings, picking gravel from the gash, I notice Rick is still watching in astonishment.

What is he waiting for?

"Get out of here! Now!"

The predator notices my interest in protecting my companion and it doesn't take a genius to realize Rick is easier prey.

"Go! Run!" I scream while scrambling to my feet.

This one may be fast, but he's no match for me. The main reason I train nearly every day is to ensure there's no one faster, stronger, or more agile. No doubt, this one won't be brilliant enough to outsmart me either.

As he closes in on Rick, I leap forward and take him to the ground again.

"Leave him alone! It's me you want!"

With my arms locked around his throat, he elbows me in the chin. My jaw aches, but I easily shake it off. Luckily, this one has long hair and I'll pull every strand out of his head to stop him if I have to. With a thick handful of locks tangled in my fist, I throw his face into the ground. Rick should be nearing the two-mile mark if he's still running as fast as he can. One mile left.

After rushing to my feet, I kick my opponent hard in the face. A quick check tells me I've knocked him unconscious, but he's not dead. If he was, Rick and I would be safe in our beds by now. I don't have time to finish him off yet, can't snap his humungous neck and I don't have a weapon to effectively kill him. His death will take more than a quick resolution. My first priority has to be getting Rick to safety. If we're lucky, I'll catch up with him and we'll make it to the stream before the demon wakes.

Within a matter of minutes, I've caught him. He looks over at me with wide eyes while limping along as fast as he can. "Is he dead?"

"No. Keep running."

Obeying my command, he picks up his pace, breathing heavily. Another landmark appears ahead, the notched rock. Thank God! The dream is accurate to the waking landscape. A layer of clouds has drifted overhead, dimming the light, and blurring the path.

"A half mile left. You can do it."

He nods again, concentrating on his breathing and running. The side trail is up ahead, but I can barely make it out in the shaded moonlight. Slowing my pace to match Rick's, I decide to run beside him for encouragement.

"We're almost there. I can see it."

A smile finally crosses his worried face. There's a sense of relief as he lengthens his stride, knowing he'll make the last fraction of a mile. When I turn back to see if we're being followed, I don't notice any shadows pursuing us and I'm encouraged.

As we make the smaller trail, I reach for his arm and pull him off to the side. "The stream follows the trail. The deeper water is right…here. Luckily, we've had a lot of spring runoff this year. Remember, make sure to allow your whole body to be submerged. I'll call you when I wake."

Grabbing him by the shoulders, I move him until he's facing me, his back to the water. Then, I give him a hefty shove and he goes flying backward. Before his body hits the water, however, he calls out my name and points over my shoulder. When I turn, I don't see whatever he's pointing to. Still, I can feel someone there, not far away.

A sudden rush of wind and footsteps in the path behind me cause me to turn in a circle to see from where the sensation is coming. Before I can react, a cloth is pulled over my eyes and I'm taken by surprise as I'm pulled of balance and immediately yanked to the ground. For some reason, this asshole knows how to catch me off guard. I swing furiously, missing my attacker. I reach above my head to catch their arms and end their attacks once and for all. Before I can catch hold of any flesh, however, I feel a sharp pain split the upper quadrant of my abdomen and scream out in the night.

Reaching for my side, I feel a long, cylindrical shaft of metal protruding from my flesh. An aluminum pole? *Unbelievable.* Grasping tightly to the cool metal, I carefully twist while tugging it from me, before rolling to my side. The pain is the worst I've felt in a hunt.

The attacker wasn't the demon of this dream. I would have sensed his presence before he could see me. The one who did this more than probably was the one who attacked me last night. I felt the same sense of air moving through the trees. That seems to be their calling card. What's more disturbing is the sense that they weren't acting alone. How could someone hold me down and impale me at the same time? Not possible.

And through the agony, I realize I've forgotten the demon I left on the main trail. He's bound to be awake and searching by now. My scream will have led him right to me.

Now I have double the concern. Someone is waiting in the shadows and an enormous demon is barreling down on me. I haven't the strength to battle both. Is this how my life will end?

As I push up from the ground and crawl on my right elbow and both knees, I search the shadows and listen for their signature sound of movement. Sweat streams down both sides of my face. I hold my side with my left arm and drag the pole beside me as I go. Breathing is difficult. Each minuscule inhalation is torture and I'm still in the dream so I have a monster yet to vanquish before I can wake. Honestly, I wonder if I can kill anything before the pain takes over my central nervous system and I end up passing out. If I lose consciousness, he'll find me and end me without any resistance. Or, the ones who put me in this condition will kill me before he arrives. I'm surprised they haven't already taken advantage of my weakened state. Why haven't they finished me off?

The midriff of my shirt is soaked dark with my blood and I'm rapidly losing my strength. Thankfully, I see a shadow ahead. He looks like a monolith in the moonlight, lumbering slowly toward me. Then, he stops a few yards from me and grins.

"Heh, you don't look so tough, now." But I don't say a word in reply. He doesn't deserve to hear the pain in my voice.

Trying to control my shuddering is a tremendously difficult task. The furious firing of severed nerves feels like shards of glass tearing my abdomen. Taking a deep breath, I force myself to face him, still listening for the ones in the shadows, knowing I may lose this battle. The aluminum pole helps me straighten and remain upright despite the trembling in my body. Bent over and supported by the post in my hands, I stare down the defective man on the path. At one and a half times my size, he towers over me.

"I'm gonna break you in two for what you did to me back there." His voice is confident as he smirks with delight. But, when he reaches for me, I swing the pole and catch his fingers.

Immediately upon the crack of aluminum against bone and flesh, the monster shrieks and I hope it won't be the worst he'll know from my hand before this is over. Regardless of the final outcome, I'll show him pain.

Waiting for the right moment, I watch patiently so as not to miss an opportunity, still paying attention to the shadows surrounding me. I may only get one. Trickling blood and sweat tickle my flesh as I remain still. His nostrils flare and his fist tightens. I can see he's almost there. Then, he lunges.

Using his forward momentum and his weight, I shove the post into his chest. As he falls on the weapon, the crack of his ribs echoes around me while the pole tears through his heart and part of a lung. He's killed instantly and I collapse to the ground beside him, never feeling its impact as I fall deeper, deeper, back into my own bed.

CHAPTER 8

When I wake in my bed, my sheets are wet with sweat and blood. A sharp pain in my side radiates through the rest of my body. Moving is torture. Will this be the injury that'll end my life?

Even in my agony, the slight tug at my throat when I lift my head becomes more concerning. Reaching up, I feel a smooth strip of silk and pull it from around my neck. Examining the familiar fabric in the morning light, a frightening realization bears down on me. A royal blue necktie. *Not possible.*

The cloth used to blind me, pulling me to the ground to be impaled. Someone was in my room last night, interfering with my dreams, helping the monster. That's what Rick saw, the person in my room.

Rick!

Hopefully, he made it out all right and didn't have a heart attack while falling toward the water. If he's safe, he'll be waiting for my call. Thankfully, I had the forethought to program his number into my cell before leaving for the gallery with Sarah. Pressing speed dial, he picks up on the first ring.

"Jaime?"

"You're okay."

"Give me your address. I'm coming over." He must hear the pain in my voice. "Make sure the door's unlocked. I'm on my way."

I'm unsure if I can roll out of bed, let alone make it to the door to unlock it. As excruciating as this is, I'm ultimately able to slide to the floor and crawl across the room, each movement sending shocks of pain from torn nerves, like lightning flashing through me. As soon as the door is unlocked, my mind grows hazy. I can't feel my side anymore, nor my body, as everything in front of me goes black.

As I slip into early REM sleep, I feel I'm being lifted and carried through the air. The movement causes fresh pain that forces me awake. My eyes barely open to see the curve of a man's broad shoulder covered in a clean, white t-shirt. Instinctually, I nestle my face into his strong arm. I'm reminded of the night I fell asleep in front of the fireplace downstairs and father lifted me in his arms and carried me upstairs to my bedroom. I was eight years old and life hadn't become so complicated, yet. The memory brings me comfort and a moment of solace.

After laying me on the bed, he lifts my soaked shirt. "Oh, my God." The voice is Rick's, not father's and I'm instantly brought back to the present where life is cruel and people kill for pleasure.

"Leave Him out of it," I barely choke out. "He didn't do this to me." My voice is so weak and hoarse I barely recognize it myself.

"Well, *He* didn't do anything to stop it. If I believed in Him, He and I would have a serious discussion about this."

"I don't *believe* in Him, Rick," I whisper and he smiles knowingly. "I know Him."

At my revelation, he stares back at me oddly. I doubt he trusts I'm in control of my faculties. Perhaps he thinks I'm a bit off.

"He sent me here, remember?"

Rick grins and nods as if placating a child, as if he's patronizing me again.

"I sometimes forget. When those like you are sent here, those who are not designated dark angels, you don't remember. But *we* do. Remember." I swallow and draw a deep breath as he uses alcohol swabs to clean my wound.

"This looks bad. What'd they beat you with this time? A pole?" He shakes his head.

"You were there. What did you see? I was blinded." As he separates the skin to see how deep the wound goes, I can't help but gasp.

"I don't…remember…before you shoved me in there were two people, larger than you. One behind you with a strip of cloth."

"Like this?" I reach for the necktie.

"That's it. But how? You said weapons used in dreams are left there."

Closing my eyes to control the pain, I can just shake my head. My mouth is dry and my lips feel cracked. Although I'm craving water, I know my stomach is too weak to hold it. After a deep, shuddered breath I try again.

"What was the other one doing?"

"They were holding something in their hands, something long. I couldn't make out what it was. Almost looked like a…shower curtain rod. Does that sound ridiculous?"

No. That's impossible. The shock of what he'd said turns me mute and I slowly shake my head. My mind is reeling at the idea. The one who killed my father, died in my bathroom, pierced through the heart by my shower curtain rod. There were only two people who knew. One of us is dead.

"What was He like?" Rick breaks into my thoughts.

"Who?" I'm startled, thinking he may have been reading my mind.

"God." He looks me in the eyes, appearing as if I'm about to tell him something epic. "What was He like when you were up there?" He points to the ceiling.

Relieved. "Oh."

Thankful he brought up a topic to take my mind off a killer who should be dead, I search my mind for an explanation he'll interpret correctly. I'm unsure what to say, but decide to answer him simply. "Just."

He seems confused. "I don't understand. How could He be 'just' sending someone here to endure this at the hands of beasts?" He gestures toward my torso.

"I chose to come here. I knew what I'd be doing before I agreed."

"Still doesn't sound fair to me."

"The situation is as fair as it can get. Wouldn't you jump into raging rapids to save a drowning child?"

He hesitated, possibly considering my response before answering defiantly. "Yes, *I* would jump into raging rapids to save a child, but I wouldn't throw another person in for me."

"He didn't throw me in, I volunteered. God tries to keep humanity from destroying itself. He gave me the opportunity to help. You know, He didn't just send one to save you."

His brows pinch together in confusion and he shakes his head.

"Jesus. Most people think God only sent Him and then forgot about them. Jesus was the greatest God sent, but not the last. Still, seems like no matter how many God sends, humanity is determined to rebel, determined to self-destruct. When I think about what Jesus endured to save you—save me too, I guess... This is nothing considering what He went through." The memory of his suffering causes me to cringe. "Painful to imagine. I've never known *that* kind of agony. And yet, it's still never enough."

"There are others like you?"

"I don't know anymore." I take a deep breath and wince at his touch. "Used to be. I may be the last."

He peers down at me, silent, seems to be trying hard to form a question in his mind, but unsure how to ask. "What happens if... if you're the last one...What happens when you're, you know, gone?"

"If I'm the last one? When they take the last dark angel from this earth, the world will be in the hands of Lucifer and we'll see the beginning of the end."

"The beginning of the end?"

"The apocalypse. Armageddon."

He's still for a while. I guess he's considering what I've said. Then, he takes a deep breath. "Sorry. This wound is too deep. I have to get you to a hospital. They'll need to open you up, find out if they nicked any organs."

"I can't." The pain is unbearable, but I'm resolute.

"If you don't—"

"Don't start with me, Rick. First of all, take a look at me. Don't you think they'll wonder how I was impaled by a pole no one can find? Second, and most important, if you put me to sleep on the table I'll dream and I'll fight, thrashing around until they can't do a thing."

He thinks for a second before answering again. "They can paralyze your muscles so you won't move during surgery."

"You do that and I won't be able to fight the demon in my sleep either. I'll die on the operating table and the agony I'll endure when I do will be much worse."

"What do we do? If you have internal injuries, you could

bleed to death."

"Pray. I'd rather die from internal injuries than at the hands of a serial killer with a sick sense of entertainment."

He shakes his head and sighs again before turning to my wounds.

"Can you stitch me up?"

"I can try, but this'll take a long time and you'll be in a lot of pain."

"Then, unless you've given up on me, you should probably get started."

"I have sutures in my bag, some Lidocaine…" He hesitates, staring in his black med bag. "I'll need more gauze."

"What you have will work." A sharp pain causes me to gasp.

"You're bleeding too heavily. I need something to blot the blood while I'm sewing."

"Clean towels. Bathroom cabinet," I answer between quick, short breaths.

Rising hesitantly to his feet, Rick leaves the room and returns with an armful of towels. After cleaning the skin around the damaged section with some liquid solution I've never smelled before, he lays four of the smaller towels in a square around the wound in my abdomen.

"The Lidocaine has epinephrine. It'll slow the bleeding, help me see what I'm doing." Pulling out a syringe, he fills it with the anesthetic. When he pierces my torn flesh, it feels like a dull knife tearing my skin. My head grows light and my sight turns dark again.

"Don't leave me now, Jaime." His fingers pat my hand and then my cheek. "I need you to stay awake."

"I'm here." My eyes flutter, but I can't open them completely.

"Do you have family that lives nearby?"

I shake my head.

"Parents, anyone who can watch over you?"

With my eyes closed, I shake my head again.

His voice sounds so far away. My mind wants me to sleep. "Keep talking to me, Jaime."

When I open my eyes again, I search the room, making sure I'm not dreaming. I take a deep breath to answer him. "Gone."

"Gone where, Jaime?" He pats my hand again. "Where are your parents, Jaime?"

"Died. Both."

He's quiet for a moment, contemplating, I suppose. "Were they…Did they also fight, like you?"

Unable to speak for a moment, I nod instead and lick my lips, wanting water so badly. Somehow, I'm able to find my voice. "They're with *Him* now."

I can tell he understands as he returns to closing my wound. "What do you remember about it? Heaven."

"We don't call it heaven; we call it the pre-existence." By keeping me talking, Rick has helped keep me from falling into a deep sleep, making me more alert. I'm thankful one of us knows what they're doing.

"The pre-existence, then, what was it like?"

"Amazing. Indescribable. Think of the most beautiful color you've ever seen and imagine its brilliance even more enhanced." I try to think of another example, but my mind isn't completely clear yet. "Remember…hmm…the best feeling you can recall, deep love, greatest accomplishment…then imagine that feeling magnified by one hundred. You feel…pure love, confidence as if you've never been hurt. That's what the pre-existence was like for me."

"Huh." He ponders quietly for a while before speaking again. "I have a question." He pulls a stitch tight and ties it off to snip the ends. I can feel the tug on my skin, but the pain is much less now. "If He loves us so much then how can he allow such evil to happen to us?"

"He doesn't really *allow* it. People on earth invite it." Rick shakes his head like he doesn't comprehend so I try to think of a way to explain it more clearly. I've come to trust him enough to share the past he's forgotten. "You know there was the big battle in heaven, right?"

He cocks his head, staring back at me. "Never heard that."

"It was big. Huge. Lucifer, you know, Satan, wanted control, wanted to force us all to be alike when we came down to earth. His plan was to force us to be good. There would be no challenge, no danger, no pain, no hate, and no free will. But we'd all make it to heaven when we died."

"Doesn't sound too bad to me," he replies, pulling another stitch.

"I guess…if you want someone else making decisions for you. You wouldn't learn from your mistakes. No way to find out for yourself why you're directed to do it one way instead of another. We wouldn't know what it was like to really live, make choices. Everyone would be perfect, at least Lucifer's idea of perfect, and there would be no reason to come down here. With such stringent constraints we wouldn't know what excellence was."

Another sharp pain from Rick's needle makes me flinch. I bite the inside of my cheek. I release the breath I've been holding and he stops stitching for a moment and caresses my hand. I nod to him and he continues stitching.

"Okay. So, Lucifer wanted to be the jerk boss of the earth. Is that what you're telling me? So what's new?"

"And… he wanted to be seated at God's throne so we'd worship him instead. That was really his plan."

"Ah, Lucifer didn't just want to be boss of the earth, he

wanted to be a celebrity amongst the Gods. Kind of like those, what do they call them, reality TV stars?" he asks and I smile at his over simplified reference and nod. "And that wouldn't fly?"

I chuckle then flinch again, cautious not to strain the muscles in my abdomen. "No. It wouldn't fly. There were some who wanted the same as Lucifer, but most didn't. No one who has a body on this planet wanted his plan. You didn't. But, so many have forgotten what they fought for and want more than they agreed to. Their unwillingness to love and take care of each other causes Lucifer to become stronger. People full of pride, greed, hatefulness, each negative thought invites him into our world and builds him up."

He looks up at me, his eyes deep with questions. "Did…you know me back then?" Smiling at his innocence, I nod my answer in the affirmative. He smiles back, his blue eyes sparkling. "So what happened? In this battle?"

"It was enormous. Greater than all the wars this planet has had put together. The pre-existence was on fire. We fought side by side, you know. You were always there. Do you remember?"

His eyes go distant as he searches his memory. "Yeah…I think I actually do remember. I can't believe I… had forgotten. It's becoming so clear, now. Did you know that when we first met, I mean on earth, that is, that I was, you know…did you recognize me back then?"

"No. Not at first. I knew we had met, but I wasn't sure when or where. The more I thought about it, I realized it was you. I was convinced before I took the leap and showed you the video yesterday. When I realized who you were, I knew I could trust you."

"How is it that I never even considered it before, but the memory is becoming clearer to me now?"

"When you tell people about the battle they always seem to recall that one event in the pre-existence. Only that one, though. Guess it was a great enough moment God couldn't hide it from us."

"Lucifer was cast out, right?"

"Mm hmm. By the dark angels, archangels. I was always beside the archangel Michael. We cast him out together, you know. You were there, too."

"I remember now. You were one of *them.* You and Michael were almost always together, leading us into battle. I can…I can see it. You were like generals."

"And you were my captain."

"You played such an important role in heaven…I mean, pre-existence. How could they demean you with the title dark angel?"

"Dark angel isn't demeaning. It's what I am. When Lucifer came to earth there was no one here to protect anyone. That's where we come in. Other angels are there for comfort or to fulfill peaceful missions, clean and pure souls. Our role isn't peaceful and there's no comfort. There's nothing clean or pure about what we do. Mostly, there's pain, but it's necessary. You need someone who's willing to get the dirty jobs done. I always think about what I do in those terms."

He's quiet for a while as he stitches. Then, he speaks again without looking up at me. "Do you know *all* the dark angels?"

"Not all of them. I was pretty busy."

He clears his throat and grows quiet again.

I see the realization weighing more heavily on him, now. Yesterday, I was some nutty girl who thought she was a warrior. Today, he has the life of his commander in his hands.

Suddenly, he shakes his head in disgust. "This is my fault. If I'd listened to you in the first place I…I wouldn't have shown up in your dream. You'd have killed that awful man and been safe in bed before this happened to you."

"Guilt won't heal me. I need you to be strong. Whatever happened last night would've probably happened anyway."

"I distracted you."

"You understand me more, now, so it was a good thing. Let's move on."

He's speechless for a while. I wonder what he's thinking and allow him time to find the words. Soon enough, he does. "Why do you hunt in your dreams? Why not allow the police to handle this? After all, they *are* murderers."

"First, and most important, I made the deal before I was born. I agreed to come here and do this. I consider it a privilege."

I'm taken aback at the sparkle in his eyes as he watches me intently and it causes me to hesitate for a moment, studying his expression. I wonder what could be going through his mind. Is he remembering how close we were? Was telling him about his past a mistake I'll regret?

Shaking the thought from my mind, I continue on. "Second, if we let these demons kill as they wish…what if the one they choose was meant to cure Small Pox, or AIDS? We can't protect everyone, but we do what we can. For this purpose alone, it's worth having a hit squad from heaven. Most demons start out killing in their sleep. They're murderers all the same. The ones they meet in their dreams still die. Their heart is no different. As I told you yesterday, there's no waking evidence of their crime. They can go on killing without retribution. Eventually, they'll murder in the light as well. They always do. That's why we're sent here. To help more of humanity fulfill their destinies, keep Lucifer from getting all the good ones out of his way. I may hate having to do it, but I understand the reason why. Someday, I hope to stand next to God, to his left side where all the archangels gather…I hope…I want to know I did my best while here on earth."

He digests what I've said, taking a deep breath. "What about the ones who murder during the day? Can't you leave those to the police?"

"If they murder in the day, they'll always murder in their sleep. There's no way for anyone but a dark angel to stop a nocturnal kill. And if there's no murder weapon, there's no evidence of their crime, no way to bring them to justice."

"Sometimes the murder weapon is left behind." He glances at the blue tie on my bed.

I note the glistening blue fabric on the pillow beside me, unwilling to touch it again. "Yeah…Sometimes things aren't what they're supposed to be."

"How is that possible? The necktie, here, in your room, I mean."

"I have my suspicions, but I'm not exactly sure." I think about it for a minute, knowing he's waiting for me to explain. "A demon from my past."

"One you've already killed?"

I close my eyes and nod affirmatively.

"They can come back to life?"

"Sure hope not." After confronting Collin Leary or someone who looks a lot like him, in a dream, only to find him alive the following day, I'm not so sure any more about anything I thought I knew.

Now all I can think about is last night. The battle with the giant. The ambush at the stream. There were two. Were they gang members? Thinking of the thirteen-year-old I'd tossed in the pond, I know it couldn't be him. He was shorter than me.

Is it possible Collin Leary was one of them? He knows where I live, now. If he's the one attacking me in my sleep, he doesn't seem to want me dead. At least not yet. He could've finished me off already. Instead, he's playing with me, as if he wants me to suffer, but why? And how did he know about my father's murderer and the necktie killer? If he's the one who's been following me in my dreams since that day, does he know what happened to me that night long ago; about the one who held my wrists to assist my attackers when I was only a teenager? Whoever this is, they seem to know what frightens me, insistent on using it against me. For what purpose?

Suddenly, Rick stops pulling the needle through my flesh and lets out a deep breath. "Jaime," he seems frustrated, "your muscles are torn beneath. They did some real damage this time."

"Can you sew me up?"

"Not easily." He stares me in the eyes. "You have to stop hunting until you're better."

"Not possible."

"You're stubborn."

"Yes. But that has nothing to do with this. I hunt the minute I fall asleep. If I don't, they'll hunt *me* and kill me before I wake."

Frustration creases his face while he thinks. "You won't live to see thirty this way."

I laugh and then wince.

"What? What's so funny?"

"Heh, I'm seventy."

"That's not…that's not possible."

"Not bad for an old lady?"

He's speechless, shaking his head. He turns back to working on stitching me up. "I need to start working out."

I chuckle and wince again, unable to stop laughing through the pain. "Stop. That hurts."

"Then stop laughing at me," he teases and smiles warmly. The respect shows in his blue eyes. "I'm serious, if I want to keep up with you I'll need to start working out, for real."

"Yeah. You might think about doing it for yourself, too." He rolls his eyes at me while tugging on another stitch. "Can't promise you'll look like you're in your twenties, though."

"Funny. You're such a funny girl, lying here with half your stomach stitched up."

"Frankenstein's bride?"

"Almost." He's silent for a moment. Then, he takes a deep breath. "Jaime, what are you hoping for? What do you want from this life?"

I've never had anyone ask me this before. I had to think hard, really look inside my soul to answer his question. Is it appropriate to tell him that most of the time I just want to die?

"I don't think I want anything from this life except to leave when I'm done. Problem is, when that day comes I'm afraid there'll be no place for someone like me, at least not in heaven, not anymore. I don't really feel like there's a place for me anywhere, not here *or* there."

"Haven't you tried to ask God if you're worthy to go back? You still talk to Him, don't you?"

"Oh, no, He hasn't spoken to me since I left."

"Why? You were one of His generals, a favored warrior one would think."

"I don't know. I want to think He broke contact so I wouldn't desire to return more than I already do. Sometimes, I wonder if it's because I don't deserve His presence or if He has better things to do than worry about an angel like me."

He closes his eyes and shakes his head. "Keep this up and you may have that conversation anyway, real soon."

He's right. "Until I figure out who's blindsiding me, or how to find them before they find me, this'll keep happening."

"Until they kill you."

"Until they kill me."

Rick is silent for a long time. Thinking, I suppose. Not sure what's on his mind. I know it has to do with me and everything I've told him today. He has a lot to think about. I won't tell him I have a date tonight. He wouldn't approve. Considering what happened last night, I'd rather go and stay out all night. I can't help being apprehensive about going to sleep. Besides, I'll heal a little more before I have to fight again, if I can have more time.

"I don't think I've ever sewn so many stitches. There's at least sixty, Jaime. Your new personal best." He wraps the syringe, the needle, and half-empty Lidocaine bottle in plastic and shoves them into his bag. "You need to rest. No dancing tonight, okay?" He grabs my arm and shakes it, attempting a smile. "You'll start bleeding if you're not careful so stay in bed as much as possible, nothing to raise your blood pressure."

He shakes his head again. He's done it so many times since he's been in my house, I wonder if he has a headache by now. "Hate to leave you, almost wish I could stay here with you. When you sleep tonight you'll probably end up tearing them out with all the thrashing and kicking. Keep the brace on your ribs, okay? It'll help your bandages stay put when you fight."

He's struggling with his thoughts, guilt painting his expression. There's nothing I can say to relieve his mind. Obviously, he worries he'll walk in tomorrow and I won't be breathing. I wonder the same.

Without looking up at me, he places all of the medical supplies in his bag. Seems like he can't look me in the eyes, either.

"Rick?" He stops, but doesn't turn to face me. "In my kitchen, there's a key holder. The only one hanging there is a spare. Front door. You can take it."

He nods and heads for the bedroom door. As he reaches for the knob, he wavers, speaking without turning. "Every night you're saving *us* from evil that stalks us in our dreams."

His back is to me, he still faces the door. "Even though in so doing, you'll probably die a violent death." He takes a deep breath, hovering on the words he wants to say. "Where's *your* angel?" he whispers.

"God sent you."

Releasing the air from his lungs, his shoulders slump and he opens the door. "I'll check on you in the morning."

"Thanks." As I lie in my bed, I hope he won't know the pain of finding my bloody corpse tomorrow. I can say from experience, the effect on your soul is devastating.

CHAPTER 9

Before he left, Rick set a glass of ice water on my nightstand. I suppose he thought it would keep me in bed longer. He advised against eating anything, only clear liquids; broth or tea. Then, he left the rest to me. He said he'd return tomorrow and advise me what I can eat depending on how bad I look. The sorrowful curve of his brow as he said goodbye showed he's taking this much harder than me. Poor guy looked a wreck.

I see these attacks as an indication that my day of return is sooner than I'd thought. The idea of my impending death brings mixed feelings. My greatest worry is what will happen once I ascend, not just to the people of this planet but to my soul. I'm afraid I won't be able to answer for what I've done on earth. How do I explain why I'm a vengeful angel? Vengeance isn't supposed to be a heavenly attribute. I find it hard to believe God will understand my desire for retribution over an event that happened so many years ago. How do I tell Him that no matter how many demons I've killed, I still can't wash self-loathing from my soul?

Still, I'll fight the demons He leads me to until the day I

die. I've lived with the knowledge that this has been my destiny since the day I was born. There wasn't a period of adjustment. As for Dr. Rick Stanton, he's only begun to understand about someone like me. He's still learning how to cope.

When humans finally know who they are and realize they haven't come near to fulfilling their purpose, the realization becomes a heavy burden for them to bear. I see this in Doc. He's aware there's some function he isn't fulfilling and he's torn between what he wants and what he should do. It's not fair for him to judge himself so harshly, though. Until today, he had no idea.

As my eyes grow heavy and I'm about to drift off to sleep, the cell phone on my nightstand rings. The number isn't familiar so I answer it apprehensively. I'm not in the mood for a sales call today. Instead, I'm pleasantly surprised by the near-Irish accent on the other end.

"Thank you for allowing me to drive you home last night."

I feel a smile cross my face until I remember the necktie on my bed. "How did you get my number?" Filtered light reflects the gleaming pattern of blue silk in the bunched fabric beside my pillow.

He doesn't answer immediately and I can imagine his face as he searches for an answer that doesn't sound like he's stalking me. "Well, to be honest, I found it in the guest book from last night."

"She didn't ask for my number."

"She asked everyone for their number. They're all in the book."

"Not mine." I'm insistent. I have more than a personal interest in finding out how my unlisted number became imprinted in his book, if, in fact, it is.

"You just don't remember."

"I remember everything."

"Everything?"

I want to lie. "Almost everything." But I don't.

"Uh, I'm really embarrassed now."

"As well you should be."

"No. I mean, I realized the handwriting for your name is different than the handwriting for your number. Someone must've added it after you signed in. Huh. Maybe your friend?"

Remembering back to last night, there are many things I noticed in that gallery. Sarah lingering near the desk after I signed in wasn't one of them. I suppose she could've done it before she left, when I was outside being distracted by the crystal carver. That would make sense.

"Maybe..."

"You sound tired. Did I keep you out too late?"

I imagine him smiling, remembering the touch of his lips, also his comment that he would kiss me much differently if he came into my house. The heat, the electricity. *Damn*. The pain shooting through my abdomen.

"Jaime? Are you there?"

"Uh, I had a rough night last night. Didn't sleep well. Still feeling effects of the flu."

"Please tell me you're not cancelling."

I sigh, and then grimace.

"I know this sounds desperate, but I have to see you again. I really want to see you tonight. Promise I won't keep you out late. We can even make it earlier than planned."

Suddenly, I'm curious. He *does* sound desperate. What does he have planned? Does it include the use of a blue necktie?

Ugh! This is stupid. I'm being paranoid. *Right?* So why does my skin tingle whenever I think about what deadly plans he may have for me? Can't believe I want to share more than a kiss with someone I think may be trying to kill me. I'm too close to ignoring Rick's warning and going out anyway.

I can't take a shower to wash my hair. Can't even bend over the sink. I'll have to go on a date with dirty hair. *Classy.*

"Are you still there?" He sounds worried.

"Haven't hung up yet. How about five?"

"Perfect. I'll be there at five—"

"What should I wear?"

"Something… as nice as you wore last night. I'll see you at five."

Mmm. Why do I feel like I've been asked to prom? This giddy feeling is infectious. If I'm not careful, I may find myself on the phone with Sarah, dishing about my *totally groovy date. Yuck!*

By *nice* I wonder what he's shooting for. Dressy? Black? Somewhat, but not overly, revealing? Sexy? In my mind, I run through the dresses in my closet. Most are appropriate for working in an office or a bank, not a date with a sexy could-be-killer.

Wait.

The red dress I wore to the Valentine's charity auction. Curve-hugging, above the knee and low-cut enough to create a stir without showing any cleavage. *Perfect.* There's a cropped jacket to match. Covers my arms. Problem is, I won't be able to zip without…Mmm. The glass blower could help. Brings a smile to my face.

If Doc knew what was going through my mind, he'd slap me awake. If Green Eyes had any idea, he'd cancel the arrangements and plan a home cooked meal. My stalker. My killer? *Shit.* I'll probably die at the hands of a man I'm desperately obsessed with. I'm hopeless.

Thankfully, I have three hours to get ready. I'll put enough gel and spray in my hair to make it presentable. I can do most of the preparation in bed, makeup, hair, but I'll have to get up to put on my clothes and shoes. Then, I'll be up the rest of the time so I'll wait until the last minute to dress.

When the doorbell rings hours later, it feels like I've been resting for a short while. Oh well, I've saved my strength for the evening ahead. So much for having three hours to get ready. It's a good thing I put on my makeup and did my hair before falling asleep.

"The door's open!"

Slipping out of bed, I slowly and carefully pull on my dress while he becomes familiar with my kitchen and living room.

"Help yourself to anything you like." I meant the double entendre.

"Made reservations."

"Where?"

"It's a secret." *Mmm, Collin Leary, you* are *full of surprises.*

When I try to pull up a clean pair of panties, I realize it's impossible. There's no way I can bend over. Trying everything feasible to get them on doesn't bring success, either. *Unbelievable.* I can kill a monster with a shower curtain rod, two as a matter of fact, but I'm not clever enough to pull on my own underwear with broken ribs and a hundred stitches in my belly. I can only shake my head. Stockings? The same. Would it be too assumptive to ask Green Eyes to help? *Hmm.* Taking a tender breath, I decide against it, better simply to go without. My dress is long enough. No one will notice.

Slipped into my shoes, naked legs, jacket pulled over my shoulders and dress zipped above the brace on my ribs, I saunter out to meet my date. The anticipation is practically killing me. *Excuse the pun.*

When I enter the room, he's leaning against the counter in a crisp, white shirt unbuttoned to his sternum. His sleeves are rolled to below his elbows. I find that hot as hell, and I have no idea why. Between that and his half-open shirt, it's clear he's cut like an athlete. His slacks are charcoal gray. Well pressed.

I can't swallow. If I don't do something quick, I'll start to drool.

Gulp. "Will you zip me?"

He's staring back at me, eyes silently caressing my body, as if he hadn't heard what I'd said. *Try again*.

"Zip?" I turn to show the back of my dress and then face him again.

"Huh? Oh…yeah, I'd love to."

Without hesitating, he moves behind me and his hands slide up my arms to the shoulder. My skin comes alive at the feel of him carefully gathering my hair and placing it on my shoulder. He grasps the fabric at the base of the zipper, causing me to catch my breath. Holding the material with one hand, just above the rise of my bottom, he slowly pulls the zipper the rest of the way to the top with his other. I'm still holding my breath, feeling his hand resting on my behind, waiting for him to finish. He seems to be taking an awfully long time to pull his hand to the top of my dress. I get the feeling he's enjoying this.

When he's done, I feel him gather my hair again and pull it further to the side to lightly kiss the back of my neck. The blood flushes hot through my body as I close my eyes, pretending I'm not wearing this dress and we're not standing in my kitchen. I've never had a man do this to me. At least not in a way I found alluring. Oh, man, I find this *very sensual*.

"You look stunning." He's breathless.

So am I.

Glad I wore makeup. Hopefully, he won't be able to tell how pale I'm sure I've become. If I stand much longer, I may pass out on the floor. It would be an annoying end to an evening that has so much promise.

"We should probably go," I tell him, but he doesn't answer. "You made reservations."

Sudden recognition. "Oh, yeah. We should go."

His hand trails down the back of my arm while he stares into my eyes. I hold my breath again. When his fingers reach my hand, they slip into my palm and he squeezes gently.

"Let's go," he says and directs me to the door.

This time, there's no hybrid car sitting in my driveway. Instead, there's a sleek, black Mercedes. *Wait.* It's an E-series. *Hybrid.* I'm certainly amazed at his obsession with green. Wonder what other obsessions I should be searching for.

The drive to the restaurant isn't as painful as I thought it would be. The ride of this car is unbelievably smooth. If I live through the week, I'll *have* to consider getting one.

When he pulls in front of the Penrose Room, I'm thoroughly impressed. I can tell it was his intent as he stares at me with a silly boyish grin. Instead of waiting for valet to open his door he steps out and moves immediately to my side of the car.

I decide to allow him the moment. Seems important for him to be the gentleman. Besides, it's much easier if he opens the door and helps me out of the car. His assistance takes more strain off the parts of my body trying to heal. Also gives me the opportunity to hold his hand longer, look into his eyes more intensely. There's definitely more than a smolder between us.

As we wait for the hostess to seat us, he pulls me close and slides his hand up my back. The brace around my ribs makes me self-conscious and tense my muscles at the brush of his fingers. He has to feel it beneath the fabric of my dress. Still, I enjoy the feel of him so near. The thrill of his breath on me, combined with the pain of my wounds, causes a shock of pleasure to shoot through my body. There are others milling around us, but I can't focus on any of them. Only Collin captures my attention with his sedating scent and stimulating energy. Has anyone ever died of excitement?

The short wait seems like forever, though, since my head becomes light and my vision begins to blur. When the hostess returns, I'm relieved to see her as she grabs two menus and directs us toward our table. Collin Leary follows behind me with one hand in mine and the other at the small of my back. I still feel weak although his hands on my body make me crave him more. Not sure I'll make it through this evening.

We're seated near the window and handed the menus. He sits across from me, his menu lying over his plate. When I peer up at him, I notice he's studying me as if he's amused.

"What?"

His smile grows to a mischievous grin. "Just watching."

I raise my eyebrow. "You aren't planning to order?"

"I already know what I want." He raises *his* eyebrow.

My cheeks flush and I raise the menu to hide my face.

"Their *foie gras* is excellent."

Even while making a pretentious observation he's sweltering hot. Collin's radiant heat rises up the hem of my dress and I cross my legs. Is there any act he can't steam up? I feel him staring through the menu in my hands.

"I'm taking a sabbatical from duck liver." I lower the menu enough to see his eyes. "Thanks for the suggestion, though."

The playful banter makes him more excited. I can feel his longing from here. He slides his feet further under the table until they're nearly touching mine. I unfold my legs and move my toes to meet his ankle and wonder if he's noticed I'm not wearing panties. Would explain his reaction.

"What looks good?"

I can still feel his eyes on me. Lowering the menu, I raise

my eyebrow again, a playful grin on my lips, hesitating for a moment. "The roasted salsify and green apple soup sounds,"—lowering the menu to my plate, I slip my tongue across my lower lip before lightly biting the flesh—"Delicious."

He's staring at my lips, dumbstruck. "How do you make an appetizer sound erotic?"

I don't say a word; only stare into his deep eyes with a subtle smirk on my face. This could go on all night. And I must admit, I kind of wish it would. Something about this carefree, flirtatious side of him is very attractive. Unfortunately, the waiter shows at our table to discuss the specials. He assumes we're celebrating an anniversary. Must be the look in our eyes since neither of us is wearing a ring. I order the soup and Collin orders Ahi tuna. He encourages me to order more, but doesn't press too hard.

When the waiter leaves with our menus, Collin reaches across the table for my hand and lightly strokes my palm with his fingertips. I can't push the thought from my mind, if he kills me, I'd probably die in some deliciously erotic way. I don't want him to stop touching me, but my head is suddenly light again and I won't last leaning forward against the hard surface. To preserve myself the embarrassment of passing out on the table, I slip my hand from his and lean back in my chair.

"Are you all right? Your face suddenly went pale."

"I'm fine." I smile at him, feeling the blood returning to my extremities. "Felt dizzy for a moment."

"I can take you home."

"For heaven's sake, no. I didn't eat much earlier, tender stomach." All of it true.

"Well, then don't you want more than soup?"

I shake my head. "Tender stomach." I lightly touch my

abdomen.

The realization shows in his eyes. "Oh, I'm sorry. I shouldn't have talked you into going out. I should've made you dinner at home. Kept you in bed all night." I raise my brow and cock my head at his comment. "I mean…take care of you. Let you rest."

We both chuckle, our eyes still playing with each other. "I'm fine. The soup will feel good in my tummy." I wish they had a long straw so I could sip it to me as I lean back in the chair. But this is a nice restaurant, not a soda shop like I knew when I was young. Right now I miss those for more reasons than one.

Recalling the day he came into my bank, I suddenly remember the unusual scar in the cup of his palm when he took my hand. My curiosity won't wait so I lean forward again and reach for his right hand. He slips it into mine and I notice the ridges aren't as deep. I turn his hand over to see the healing scars.

"What happened?"

The look in his eyes drastically changes. "Sharp vase."

He pulls his hand from me and sits back in his chair. Suddenly, his eyes won't meet mine. An unusual reaction.

I don't understand. The feeling is as if I walked from a hot kitchen into a deep-freeze locker. My body shivers at his reaction as I sit back in my chair and ponder. What did I say? Did I give him those scars? I can't help but wonder if he's intent on exacting revenge. Might've been a huge mistake to entertain going out with him this evening after all.

When the waiter returns with our meal, we eat in awkward silence. Collin doesn't finish his and notices I've barely touched mine.

"Is it okay?" His voice is flat and emotionless.

The soup grows cold in a delicate ceramic bowl as I search

for the proper answer. "It was great. I just can't…" I shake my head and crinkle my nose.

"Let's go." He stands, pulls two hundred dollar bills from his wallet, and throws them on the table. Then, reaches for my hand. His fingers are pressed in the small of my back again, but it isn't as tender as it was earlier.

The waiter notices us passing him on the way out. "Was everything okay?" he asks, concern evident in his voice.

"It was great." Collin's voice is cold, causing me to shiver.

The whole way home he remains silent. A shudder travels through my body as I wonder what will happen when we get there. I'm practically incapable of protecting myself. Maybe he already knows this. Perhaps tonight was all a test to see how badly I've been wounded and how capable I am of being fighting back. Damn, I should have faked it better. In letting him come right to my door, I'm giving him the chance to try and kill me in person. What was I thinking? Will Rick find a horrible mess when he visits tomorrow? Why didn't I listen to him?

My mind races with the possibilities of how this evening will end. Collin Leary could merely pull up to my house and let me find my way to the door alone. Or he could walk me to the porch, say goodbye, and leave.

There's a great possibility he might help me inside, muffle my cries, and then kill me before I can put up much of a fight. I can't help but obsess over his reaction to my question. My curiosity created a sudden unexpected turn. Did he believe I was mocking him and that I should already know what happened?

Is it reasonable that I expect him to exact his revenge tonight? Maybe he'll walk me inside my home and torture me until my body can take it no longer. Or, possibly kiss me, seduce me, until the right moment when I'm in the throes of ecstasy and not expecting it, he'll slit my throat.

I don't think I've ever thought so much about my death than I have since meeting Collin Leary. In the past, for the most part, I've contained my emotions, didn't think much about the killer or who his victims were and how they died. Didn't think of how they would kill me, either, if they were able to catch me on an off day. Now, I find myself obsessing over my own potential mortality. I wonder how many people Collin has murdered, how he's killed them, and how he might end me. Maybe my obsession is brought on by the desire for my earthly existence to be over. Part of me hopes Collin Leary will end my life tonight. My sole fear at this point originates from what is still undefined. What will it feel like and how terrible will it look when he's done?

My body is trembling with pain and anticipation. I feel as if I'm wading through his back room without the lights. The blackness, the unknown, is worse than a familiar danger.

When we finally arrive at my house, Collin pulls his Mercedes up the driveway and parks. I get out of the car without his help. The stress of worrying over what will happen causes me to feel weak and sick to my stomach. Moving cautiously, I make it to the porch and up the steps to my front door without collapsing. With the key slipped into the lock, I open it a crack before turning. He's standing directly behind me, staring down at me. His eyes aren't as hard as they were at the restaurant, but they're much less than warm. Swallowing back my fear, I turn and lead the way into the house as he follows. If we're going to do this, we might as well get it over with, now.

Barely past the threshold, he closes the door behind him and shoves my body against the wall. I bite the inside of my cheek to keep from crying out in pain.

His eyes nearly glow in the dark as he stares deep into

mine, his breathing growing heavy. "Is this what you wanted?"

His question confuses me and I can't answer. Does he think I want this? *Do I want this*? His hand goes to my throat and I don't know if I should fight or let him get it over with, quickly and without resistance. And in my confusion, I hesitate, frozen like a child to this spot. Why am I not fighting? My heart is racing faster than before while I stare back at him, more frightened than I've ever been. Then, he leans forward with his lips spread open, but before reaching my lips, he stops.

A peculiar look crosses his face as his eyes move back down the front of my dress, stopping at the midriff. When I peer down I see a growing circle of dark red forming on the fabric.

"I'm calling an ambulance—"

"No. No ambulance. No hospital."

My head is light, but I have nowhere to sit. My body goes numb and I can see nothing but blackness, the blackest color of darkness, the greatest depth of nothingness that I fear and have only known in the back room of Collin's gallery until now. His disembodied voice—panicked but far away—calls my name. I can barely hear myself pleading with him. "Don't call…"

My last thought is that Collin Leary won't have to kill me now.

CHAPTER 10

The floor is cool beneath my bare feet as I drift into consciousness in the subtle darkness of the unknown. The dress soaked in deep, arterial red no longer covers my form. The cloth now draped on my body is a white men's dress shirt, sleeves folded to the forearms. Lifting the bottom hem, I discover I'm now wearing panties. *Relief*. But who pulled them on me? Then, I notice I'm not in my own home.

The scent is familiar, like wet moorland grass. Is this Collin's house? Am I hunting on *his* turf, expected to kill him tonight? Being here and remembering his sudden coldness at dinner stirs my pride and makes me seethe. Was he toying with me a mere night ago while speaking sweetly of wanting to kiss me like he has no other, a comment that made my body catch fire? Was it an act when he chuckled casually at my awkwardness? He wasn't so subtle or gentle when pinning me to the wall, his hand to my throat, inside my doorway. My life was in his sultry grasp. Why didn't he kill me? Is he getting a thrill out of watching me suffer like this? I feared him and desired him all in one breath. Was that his plan?

The rat foolishly played with the cat, like he was equal to

my strength, as if I couldn't destroy him with a swipe of my claws. Now I despise him. Why didn't he end this, get it over with while he had the chance? Shall I take his life in this dream as I should? Or will I let him finish seducing me and then kill me in my sleep? No. He's the one who dies tonight. I would never give him the satisfaction. I'd rather suffer at the hands of a rogue angel than a bastard like him.

This is the first dream where I ache from my waking injuries. If I were conscious, the sensation would be closer to excruciating. But here, the pain isn't so great I can't fight. The best part of being a dark angel? I don't feel too much agony until the fight is over and I wake. It's a way of protecting me during the hunt, I guess. Since I spend more time awake than asleep, I'm not sure in which span of time I'd rather feel numb.

As I progress through the house, exploring the new terrain, I feel a set of eyes in the shadows, watching me. I turn to them and they're gone.

Before long, I come upon a number of rooms to which I merely glance inside; a formal sitting room, a tastefully decorated living room and a nicely furnished guest bedroom, all empty of souls. His taste for décor imitates his personality—subtle, but elegant. I hesitate to move toward the kitchen. My mind hasn't prepared me yet for a room with sharp objects. Not in my current condition. Wherever there's a weapon, the demon will have access to them, also.

Moving upstairs, I check the master bedroom, walk around the heavy, oak sleigh bed with a raked headboard. I can't help but wonder if he's ever tied his victim to one of the rungs and held her throat as he did mine. This is where Green Eyes, no doubt, lays his head at night. I smell him on the covers. Does he ever find the need to burn his sheets once he's finished killing his prey? A tall, picture window overlooks the bustling city below. I reach out and feel the thick window coverings.

Silk. He has expensive taste. I wander into the bath. The large, tiled, walk-in shower with a clear glass enclosure and separate garden tub are empty as well. The next two bedrooms and bathrooms are exactly the same. I resolve myself to fate and head to the kitchen. The setting of the battle is not of my choosing.

When I enter the room, there's someone standing near the sink. A man is washing his hands in a stream of water pouring from the faucet. His hair is thick and dark; familiar. A bloody knife sits on the counter to his right.

The floor is a beige tile. The walls are dark blue with a tan and brown mosaic tile border. Alder wood cabinets accent the azure walls. One with a glass pane exposes ceramic plates and bowls, heavy hand-blown drinking glasses. Granite counters, tall center island, also with granite and alder. There's a knife set to the side of a large butcher block cutting board. One of them is missing. A metal rack above my head holds iron pots and frying pans suspended from the ceiling. Many potential weapons at my disposal.

This time I wait for the demon to turn on me.

Soon enough, he does. His eyes are dark. Not Collin's. The face is more rugged but nearly as handsome. I don't understand. Why is this demon hunting on another's turf? The expression on his face remains emotionless as he picks up the knife and moves toward me.

"Wasn't expecting *you* tonight, but I can be flexible, how about you?" He smiles at me, his eyes appreciating the shirt that barely covers my thighs.

Fury burns through me. Did Collin lead him into this dream to have another kill me instead? Has he sent someone else to weaken me some more? *Bastard.*

I stand in place with my eyes narrowed, waiting for him to reach me. When he does, he brings his free hand to my throat and throws me back against the refrigerator as Collin had. I'm finally numb and can't feel the impact shift my broken ribs. Why am I not fighting?

The monster starts to kiss me, his lips hungrily covering mine. His tongue invades my mouth with a deep swipe, making me cringe when he bites into my flesh as if he's starving. In my state of shock, I can't respond to his touch. I can only stare ahead, studying the room as if I hadn't yet seen him, as if he isn't holding a bloody knife at his side while pressing his hardened groin into me.

The thought of the one in the shadows causes my body to shudder. I find myself hoping the eyes watching me belong to Collin Leary, wishing he was the one preparing to spill my blood. A tear trickles down my cheek as the mouth of a monster moves to my neck and his hands slide up my body to my breasts. The lips and fingers don't belong to Collin and I'm disgusted. I hate the feeling of him clinging to me, pressing against me as if I should enjoy it. So why haven't I ended him yet? He's already had a kill this evening. I know I'm meant to be his next victim.

In a moment, my stunned silence turns to fury and I pull the rage from deep inside me. With the force of my ire, I reach for his chest and shove. As he flies backward I scream out in pain, my voice echoing throughout the house. While I move toward him, his knife cuts the air, tearing the sleeve of my shirt. Reaching above my head, my fingers make contact with the handle of a cast iron skillet and I pull it from the hanging rack. Wrath reaches outside of my body as I swing my hand backward. The might of my blow snaps his head sideways and he crumbles to the floor, dead before his face connects with the clean ceramic tile. The frying pan slips from my hand, falling to the floor beside him.

At the same time, I see another and I turn on him with

treacherous intent. The one who watches from the shadows lunges for me. I swing my fist to protect myself, but they're faster. He grabs my shoulders and shouts my name.

Collin Leary. *How did I know?*

Rage still robs my mind of the side of me that's human. My dark angel ferocity presses me to destroy him as the adrenaline quickens my heart rate. Turning back on Collin, I knock him easily to the floor. When I fall on top of him, I wrap my fingers tightly around his throat.

"No!" There's fear in his eyes and I hesitate.

At that moment he gains the advantage and throws me onto my back, shifting my ribs even more. I scream out in pain again then feel his hands pin my wrists to the floor.

"Jaime! Wake up! Look around you! Your dream, it's over, Jaime, he's dead!" He let's go of my hands, gathering me into his arms. Stroking my hair, he gently rocks me until I recognize my bedcovers with spots of fresh blood. Collin is topless. I'm still wearing his shirt with a torn sleeve, blood trickling down my arm, also coloring the mid-section. Why is he in my room, watching me hunt?

Earlier thoughts invade my mind; the killer with his fingers kneading my breasts, his acrid tongue grazing my teeth. And Collin saw every shameful moment. Bile rises up my throat as the pain plaguing my body reaches heights I've never before known. I push him away and scramble to my feet. My breathing is labored and my body is racked with agony. The center of Collin's white shirt has a growing circle of red. I'm still bleeding. My head is light and my stomach is weak again. Should I call Doc? First, I rush into the bathroom and fall to the floor in front of the toilet, vomiting. Collin wets a washcloth and crouches beside me, wiping my forehead and cheeks. For some reason, the feeling comforts me.

"Are you done?" He tilts his chin toward the commode

and I nod back.

He rises to his feet and flushes, gathering me into his arms. Bringing me from the bathroom to the bedroom, he lays me on the bed. Then, he lifts my shirt.

"I don't know how to stop the bleeding."

"My purse."

He shakes his head like he doesn't understand.

"Need my purse."

Recognition sets in his eyes and he leaves the room. When he returns, he offers me the handbag and I rummage through. "What're you looking for? Let me help."

Taking a deep breath, I whisper to him. "Cell phone." My breathing is growing more labored. Each gasp is agony.

He reaches inside and finds it first swipe. He hands it to me. I press the number two button and hold until it dials. Doc Stanton is my only speed dial. *Sad.*

"Jaime!"

"Rick…" My voice is shaky.

"I'm on my way."

I end the call and hand the phone to Collin.

"Jaime, I'm sorry. I didn't mean to…" He sighs. Either my sight is blurred or his whole body is shaking. His eyes appear red. Had he been crying? That doesn't seem consistent with my impression of him.

Lifting the collar of the shirt, his eyes turn downward then to the ceiling knowingly at the question in my eyes. "I changed your clothes. Tried rinsing out your dress, but…think I may have ruined it." I pull up the bottom of the shirt. "Yeah." He hesitates and looks away again. "Put those on, too."

I swallow and close my eyes. Practically panting, I want to take a deep breath, but it hurts too badly. My ribs already ache with the shallow ones I'm taking.

"Do you want some shorts before this…Doc, gets here?" He's still kneeling at my bedside like a nervous child.

I shake my head. It hurts too much to move. To hell with privacy.

In a matter of minutes, Rick is in my room, hovering over me like a mother hen. His eyes are serious in spite of the glint in his blue irises that tells me how much he's come to care about me. The handsome curve of his strong chin has grown taught as he grits his teeth and tightens his jaw.

"What happened? What did you do to her, you monster?" He says over his shoulder, while unbuttoning my shirt and unfastening the red-soaked brace around my ribs.

"She was asleep."

Collin doesn't say he took me to a restaurant and became angry with me for some reason. He doesn't tell him how he shoved me against a wall when he brought me home, maybe intending to kill me. I don't tell him either. Let him think I hurt myself in the fight. If I told Rick I thought Collin was a demon, he wouldn't understand why I haven't killed him already. Hell, I don't understand why, myself.

Rick looks at me disapprovingly. He already suspects something. I *am* wearing Collin's shirt, after all.

When he pulls up the soaked bandage, he releases his breath. "You moved around too much. I told you to stay in bed. Stitches pulled, but not torn through. Oozing, but not too badly. My biggest fear is you're bleeding internally." He pulls a bottle of alcohol and a package of gauze from his bag. He was prepared this time. "You should've listened to me."

"Been a long time since I took orders from anyone, Doc." I attempt a smile, but I know it's weak.

"If I'm going to be your doctor, you'd better start," he answers with his jaw set.

"I'm not a child," I answer quickly.

"Then stop acting like one," he shoots back, tightening his lips.

When he cleans my wound this time, it doesn't hurt as much. Just my arm and ribs ache badly tonight. "What happened *here*?" He tears open the sleeve over my cut. "Jaime?"

"He had a knife."

"I can see that." He dabs the blood with a soaked gauze square, making the wound sting.

Collin stands nearby, watching Rick with his brows furrowed. I wonder what's going through his mind, seeing me this way, watching Rick hover over me as if this is an everyday event. What must he be thinking? Is it stirring his crooked mind into imagining what he will do to me next?

"Isn't deep enough for stitches. You got lucky this time."

"Not too lucky. I was thrown against a wall." Rick cocks his head at me and then turns to Collin who holds up his hands defensively.

"In my dream, Rick. In my fight," I clarify. Collin's eyes widen as he hears me explain to Rick. His gaze shoots from me to Rick and back to me again.

Rick glares back at Collin. "While this was happening to her, what were *you* doing?"

He doesn't say anything. Seems speechless. He can't utter the words, *I watched.*

Rick turns back to me and palpates my ribcage, taking my breath away. As I watch his expression of concern, I find a new appreciation for his angled features. The captain who always had my back in that great heavenly battle. Nothing has changed, even here on this forsaken planet, he peers down at me in admiration, willing to die for me if necessary. I swallow back the emotions rising to the surface.

He had been by my side as Satan's followers fought their

way toward Michael and me, intent on ambushing and overcoming the greatest forces in heaven. Rick defended me courageously and selflessly, forging a bond greater than that of mere sibling warriors. Our souls were nearly as entwined as that of mine and Michael's. Our hearts beat in sync.

Being here with him once again, in my bedroom, fills my mind with confusing thoughts and sentiments. I want to reach up and stroke his cheek until the muscles holding it taught release their hold and he finds peace once more. I control the urge to whisper the words that will return his memory of our times in the pre-existence. A time when he would comb his fingers through my long hair while we spoke of strategies. So many moments did we lie beside each other, talking while holding hands and discussing the plan to send our siblings to earth. Although this sentimental practice was common in the pre-life, such sensual contact with another in mortal form is meant to draw out the primal instinct to pair and mate. Wouldn't be fair to lead him to a conclusion that could never be. As much as I long to feel his life force, draw the light in his heart to the surface, I must deny myself the pleasure. If he remembers how deeply he loved me then, it could complicate my life even more.

"Yeah, they shifted." Rick's voice pulls me back to the present, again. "They're not aligned. And there's nothing I can do." He presses lightly, but it is still agonizing. He lets out a heavy sigh as if he'd been holding his breath since he entered the house.

"Am I gonna live?"

"This time. You been vomiting?" I close my eyes and sigh. "Thought so." He pulls out a syringe and fills it with liquid drawn from a small, clear bottle. "Phenergan." He shoots it into a vein in my arm. "Will help the nausea. Also, let you sleep. So another monster can try to kill you again, I guess."

He shakes his head in anger and grabs my arm firmly. "You rest." Then, he turns to Collin. "You. Outside."

They close the door behind them, but I can still hear their voices echo in the hallway.

"Do you know who she is? Do you have any idea?" Rick's barely controlled anger is bubbling over, making me roll my eyes. Now that he knows, he's going overboard to protect me.

"I think I understand more than you." I'm surprised by Collin's answer.

"Do you really? Did she tell you what she goes through?"

"No."

"Didn't think so. She doesn't complain."

There's silence for a moment; then, Collin clears his throat.

"I don't need you to be condescending to me. *Yes.* I understand what she goes through. I know very well what a dark angel endures."

How does he know about dark angels? The only way he could is if he's a rogue or a—

"How do you know about dark angels?"

Thank you, Doc. I hold my breath, waiting for Collin's reply, but he hasn't answered yet and it worries me.

He clears his throat again. "I'm one."

Rick is silent. I'm sure it was an answer he hadn't expected. I wasn't prepared for his reply, either, and I'm anxious to hear what he has to say next.

A minute passes before he speaks again. "How do I know you're telling me the truth?"

"You'll have to trust me. How do you know *she* is?"

"I've seen it."

"How could you—"

"Hard to explain." He's quiet again. No doubt he's remembering last night. "I was trapped in one of her dreams. She saved me at her own expense. I saw this happen to her.

Been treating her for nearly a week now and it keeps getting worse. She finally had to tell me."

"And you believed her?" The surprise in Collin's voice makes me want to chuckle, but I hold back. Ribs.

"No. Had to see it for myself. That's how I ended up in her dream. Foolish. It's horrifying to think she goes through that every night."

"I don't understand it either. What's happening to her…it's much worse than I've seen of any dark angel. She collapsed in my arms, begging me not to call an ambulance. When I took off her clothes and saw the scars, ribs, bloody bandages…You don't see that every day."

"She needs someone to watch over her." Rick hesitates.

"I can do that."

There's silence.

"You're not a doctor." Rick's voice sounds defiant.

"You're not a dark angel. You can't keep her from dreaming. I can."

He can do that? I had no idea. Should I be thrilled? Or should I refuse this offer? I certainly wouldn't mind a night off after all I've been through.

"There's a way to stop her from fighting?" Someone sighs and I think it's Rick. "If you're more capable…She can't do this hunting demons stuff and Lord knows *I* can't stop her. She needs someone to stay with her. You can keep her from dreaming? It's possible?" The hallway grows quiet again and I wait. Then, the silence is broken. "Give me your address and I'll get anything you need, bring it here so you don't have to leave her. Just let me know and…keep her safe."

The conversation ends without another word. The sole other sound is the front door closing. I'm alone in the room with my thoughts. There are too many questions in my mind to fall asleep.

Collin's a dark angel. How can that be? Didn't he try to kill me at my door tonight? Or was that foreplay? When he asked if that was what I wanted then grabbed my throat, it didn't seem like he was asking me to bake a cake or even hunt demons with him. That was a pretty aggressive way to say good night, even with his lips moving toward mine. What kind of angel does he think I am? A rogue?

I think back to the dream in his gallery. If we're both dark angels, then who was the monster? I wish I could remember what happened. Suddenly, I'm disappointed that he isn't a demon and that he won't kill me while I sleep or in some heart-pounding erotic way. I thought he might be the one to send me back home. With a doctor to heal me and another dark angel at my side to let me rest, there's a smidgeon of a chance I might find a reason to want to stay on this earth a little longer.

After several moments, the door opens and Collin comes in, closing it quietly behind him. What took him so long? He goes around to the other side of my bed and climbs up onto the mattress beside me. Laying his head on the pillow next to mine, he reaches for my hand. With his nose nuzzling my cheek, he kisses me softly. I squeeze his hand and close my eyes, too tired to think about why he confuses me so much. The medicine is finally working.

CHAPTER 11

The crispness of my shirt scrapes against my skin and I immediately open my eyes. My breath comes fast and strong. Another dream? Am I ready for another fight? My eyes begin scanning the room. I'm lying in a bed, covers to my waist, and there are curtains surrounding the windows. Familiar curtains. The bed, covers stained with spots of blood, the olive green walls, all familiar. I'm in my own room.

Collin lays next to me, still asleep. The sun is up. There are no demons to fight. I'd slept the rest of the night without hunting. For the first time in decades. The fact leaves me in a blissful state of shock. Taking a deep breath, my body relaxes and so does my heart rate. The simple pleasure of a deep breath makes me smile. My ribs barely hurt any more. So this is what it's like to be normal.

Lying still for a while, I think of last night. The memory of the look in his eyes and his hand on my throat makes me shiver. I'm not sure if it's out of fear or arousal. Most likely it is a toxic mixture of both that I still don't understand. Why would he do that if he wasn't planning to kill me? What did he mean when he asked if it was what I wanted?

Then there was the demon in his kitchen and the familiar feeling of someone studying me while I hunted. Was it because he was sitting in the shadows of my room, watching me sleep and then witnessing my battle? Was there anyone else? I search my memory. No. I'm positive it was only the demon, Collin, and me.

Since the night I killed my father's murderer, I've often felt like someone else was in the shadows watching me. In the beginning, I thought it was my mother. After she died and they were still there, I knew it wasn't. Until now, they never harmed me. Except what happened that one night. The night in the mountains. Just the thought of it brings a cringe. Funny that I never associated the one in the shadows with the attack from that night after I took down my father's killer, the memory leaving a deep scar I can't forget. Was it something I simply chose to ignore, pretend it wasn't the same soul? Am I really that short-sighted? At times, I wanted to believe it was the soul of my father, watching over me, even if he couldn't be here with me. Now I fear I know exactly who has lurked in the shadows, watching me, for so long. And he's lying next to me.

I'd turned fifteen a month before that day. A freshman in high school, I was still trying to adjust. Not an introvert, but not as boisterous as the others. No one really tried to get to know me. They had no idea what my life was like. All they knew was that I was different. Nobody realized the tape still playing over in my mind; my father's bloody body lying still in his bed. They had no idea I ended the lives of killers who could do the same to them. I couldn't tell anyone why I had so much anger and resentment. School counselors automatically assumed I was your typical rebellious kid. Soon everything changed for the worst.

That horrible night had been lit by a three-quarter moon when I'd opened my eyes and found myself wandering close to the university campus on Austin Bluffs, dreaming. The streetlights were dim.

Two teenagers, barely a couple years older than me, appeared beside me in a sedan. The odor of alcohol smoldering wood was so strong I caught the scent from where I stood. The stench had been carried with them in their sleep. I'd approached them casually, not considering they were the ones I was sent to kill. I worried they were the prey, not believing they could be the demons. Before I could think about what was happening, they pulled me into the backseat. One fought to hold me down while the car sped away. In mortal fear, I'd scratched his face, gave him a bloody nose and lip, left him rubbing his swollen jaw by the time we reached the mountains. Then, his buddy turned off a dirt road to a hidden campsite. The two of them pulled me from the car.

They threw me to the ground in front of the headlights and I was instantly overcome by the scent of death. Before crawling into their tents for the night, they'd drug another girl to this very location, not in her sleep, in reality. She'd clawed at the same ground beneath me in my dream. A full moon illuminated the blood-stained dirt, the pattern still dark in the glaring lights. The stench of her fear called to me from the location where they'd tossed her lifeless body, mere feet from where I was.

The first boy knelt beside me and pulled my head backward with his fingers tangled in my hair. Fury glared in his eyes, nearly hiding the lust as the fingers of his other hand trailed down my cheek. Gritting my teeth, I lunged for him, but the two of them caught me off balance, throwing me to my back in the dirt.

Ripping my shirt open, his nails dug into my skin as if it were cloth. The bite marks he left in my flesh stung from the salt of his sweat dripping down on me as I fought. After tearing at me with his teeth and hands, he penetrated me as if he were an animal. My screams echoed into the night. I can hear them even now. Then, it was the driver's turn. Throughout the whole horrifying event, someone in the shadows helped, holding my arms, bruising my wrists.

With visions of death consuming my thoughts, I finally dug my nails deep into the one in the shadows. A voice shrieked as the hands in the darkness released me, allowing an opportunity to turn on the two boys. I knew them both. They went to my school. I felt so much rage.

The rest of the night, I spent drawing out the kill, showing them pain they'd never experienced before. When their bodies were found by hunters a week later, authorities had a difficult time identifying them. They'd concluded a wild animal had pulled them from their tents.

Immediately upon rising the morning it'd happened, I rushed to the shower. The memory of them tearing me, violating me while laughing the whole time, tortured my thoughts as I scrubbed my body until my flesh bled again and the hot water turned ice cold. Somehow I couldn't remove the filth they'd left on me or the hatred that stained my soul. My life changed after that night. I became more withdrawn than ever.

My mother asked, but I couldn't begin to explain it to her, what had happened. The old Jaime Connor had died, lying amongst the rocks and pine needles that tore at her body and her spirit. I've hunted differently ever since.

In the following days, I'd distanced myself even more from everyone around me, didn't react like the others when the deaths of our two classmates were announced at school. I couldn't pretend I was sad for them.

The covers pull tight against my hips as Collin stirs beside me, snuggling closer. But I lay still, staring up at the ceiling.

His arm snakes across my chest and his hand brushes the opposite side of my face. The feel of his touch turns me cold. I can't stop thinking about last night. His reaction when I asked about his cuts at the restaurant, the thought of his hand to my throat moments later, still haunts me. I wonder if it had something to do with that night in his gallery. What isn't he telling me and why is he sensitive about his scars to the point of being dangerous?

All I remember of that night is staring into his soul and being immediately drawn to him. Then, he whispered in my ear and circled me to lock the door. What does that mean? On Friday he said the same as in my dream. Was it to get a reaction, find out who I was? Am I fooling myself to believe he's a dark angel when he's really not? I might believe him if it's what I want to hear. *Wait.*

At the gallery on Friday, when we were getting ready to leave, when I was standing next to his new receptionist, she unlocked the door for the departing guests. She turned the mechanism the same direction Collin had in my dream.

He didn't lock the door that night. He was trying to *unlock* it. That changes everything. The intention wasn't to trap me inside. Was he trying to release me before the fight, thinking I was an innocent bystander, yet unable to do so because it had been locked by another? If so, who locked the door? And if Collin wasn't the demon, does he know who is?

If the fight had started before he turned back, he might not know the aggressor. Maybe he thought it was me. And all this time I thought it was him. I was so focused on him, wondering if he was the one, that I didn't pay attention to the room. I'm still not paying attention. What am I missing?

His reaction at the restaurant when he brought me home doesn't fit with this theory. Then, a sickening thought crosses my mind. Assuming Collin lied to Doc last night, imagining for a moment his inner demons control his thoughts, is it possible for something so full of evil to fall in love with a dark angel? Is he trying to save me, knowing I might kill him someday, hoping to change my mind? He certainly acts as if he's torn between killing me and seducing me. Is that what I saw last night? Maybe that's what I missed in his gallery, also.

I can't escape the feeling that Collin is the one who's been watching me all this time. I can't help but entertain the thought he's an angel killer, not unlike the one who killed my father. Could be he also intended to kill me, that I was his prey, but he fell in love instead. Was I sent into his dream last week to kill him before he destroyed me? Is he capable of holding the arms of a girl being attacked by two boys?

Although his sleeves were rolled to his elbows last night, I never looked at the inside of his wrists. I didn't even consider he could be the one.

If he is, I doubt I could find a way to overlook what he did, what he helped those boys do to me. I don't think the desire I feel for him will be enough to keep me from slitting his throat while he sleeps, or torturing him to death in his dream as I had with them. His attraction to my dark side may be insufficient to keep him here long enough for me to finish planning my revenge. He might even kill me first to preserve himself. If so, I'd rather he do it now and get it over with. It would be more humane, because I've already fallen for him.

I'm not attracted to demons, never have been. That's why I can't articulate the way I feel when I'm around him. When I look into his eyes, there's something deep I can't explain. I don't understand it because I've never felt it before. Haven't felt that for anyone, ever. No crushes in high school. Nobody could make me feel giddy like a schoolgirl. I often wished they could. No one has made me tingle all over, not even Rick when we were so close in the pre-existence, no one except

Collin. And that's the trouble.

His effect on me blurs my focus. I can't see him the way I should. I can't feel his darkness and repel it the way I must. *Damn!* Why didn't I kill him last night when I had the chance? Why did I hesitate?

Hesitate. That's what my grandma did. Dad said she hesitated. She always warned me against it. Since we're part human we'd have no choice if our hearts are involved. Maybe Grandma had a demon she was unsure of and it made her stop for a second. That second could kill her, could kill me. I saw how Collin used it to his advantage last night. Now I'm interested in studying his body with a different perspective.

I shift a bit in bed, turning toward him to get a closer look. His forearm is marked with scars from elbow to fingertips. Left shoulder has a three-inch mark. None on his chest, though. A respectable scar on his side. Wonder if there are others on his back. I also wonder if he received any of them fighting me from the shadows. I more than suspect the one in the palm of his right hand was my doing. How many more did I give him? Why am I so excited to see them?

My mind returns to that night in the mountains, unable to get my thoughts off the hands holding me as I screamed and cried, pleading for them to stop. Could Collin Leary be evil enough to do something so terrible? There's just one way to know if he was there.

My hand slips on top of his to turn it over, unsure if I want to know. Staring up at the ceiling, I take several deep breaths. His wrist is exposed. I could have my answer. But I can't look. If the scars are there, my hatred would consume me. Chances are I'd kill him where he lay. My stomach is sick again. I'd rather not know than find out he was the one.

Looking over at Collin, I see his eyes are open and he's watching me. Does he know what I'm thinking? Quickly looking down at his wrist, I see a long scar intersecting the rise of his tendons. No scratch marks from a desperate girl being attacked in the woods. I'm relieved, but still nauseous. Turning back to Collin, I cringe as his expression turns cold once more. The next moment I'm kneeling in front of the toilet again, vomiting. My body must be reacting to the abuse I've received over the past several days.

When I look up, Collin is standing by the sink with a wet washcloth in hand. Taking it, I thank him in a whisper, too low for him to notice. Then, I hear Rick at the front door, letting himself in.

"You hungry?" Collin's voice is frigid.

I shake my head and he turns to leave the bathroom. Rick's voice echoes as he tells Collin he brought a change of clothes. There's no gracious reply, only silence followed by footsteps. Quickly brushing my teeth and rinsing with mouthwash, I move toward the room, attempting to look casual.

Hopefully, Collin wasn't reading my mind as I lay in bed. Maybe he was remembering my fight with the demon and how I let the monster kiss me before I killed him. God, why did I do that? Or, perhaps he can sense that I suspect he's not really a dark angel.

While I wait in the bathroom doorway for what seems like too long a duration, Rick finally enters the room.

"You look better. Little more color in your cheeks." He tries not to sound too chipper, though. He's still mad at me for whatever he thinks I did last night. "I assume you didn't fight demons anymore after I left."

I shake my head.

"Good. Let's take a look."

I start unbuttoning my shirt before lying on the bed. When Rick looks up at me, I can see more in his eyes than concern for his patient. He watches me like he has feelings of attraction and much more. *Oh, Lord*. What have I done?

"You know…" He takes a deep breath. "If he wasn't helping protect you while you're healing, I'd tell you to get rid of him."

He doesn't look at me. I can sense his animosity toward Collin, even jealousy. I also sense his desire for me. And I don't know how I feel toward either of them now. Should I get rid of Collin? Will I also need to tell Rick to go?

When he lifts the bandage, he has a puzzled look on his face.

"What?"

"Your stomach, it's nearly healed. I expected it to be raw and still seeping, but your skin is already fused as if it happened more than a week ago."

A weak smile creases my lips. "I heal fast."

"When you told me, I didn't believe you. Amazing." He palpates my abdomen. "Ribs are back in line, too. What did you do last night?"

"Slept. First time in decades."

After briefly shaking his head in disbelief, he turns serious. "How do you know this man in the other room?" he asks in almost a whisper.

"I don't..." I can't say it. I can't tell him I don't really know him at all. My heart won't let me admit I have suspicions he's the one doing this to me.

"As soon as you're better you say good bye to him. I don't trust him."

"You're jealous, Rick."

He stares back at me for a minute, surprised at my candor. "Maybe I am, but there's something more. I'll say it again I don't trust—"

"I know."

"You're more than a patient to me, Jaime. I'm guessing

you've already realized that. I don't know how you feel about me, if you have similar emotions..." He waits for a response from me.

How do I answer his confession? I'm caught in the middle. I *hate* this.

At this moment, I don't want to think about either of them. I don't want to recall the desire I have for Collin Leary or how I fear him at the same time. I don't want to think about the loyalty I feel toward Rick. The only thing I want at this moment is to be left alone.

Rick's eyes turn downward before he reaches over to button my shirt. Then, he gathers his alcohol and gauze, returning them to his bag without a word, not looking me in the eyes again. When he stands, he leans over and kisses me on the cheek and leaves.

I'm tired of being here, in this damned house, on this forsaken planet. Damn it! After burying my face in the pillow, I punch the bed beside me until I feel the sheet tear beneath my fist. I hate being a girl, having these human emotions.

After a while, I feel restless again. Collin hasn't returned and I wonder if he left. Then, I smell bacon and eggs. Slipping carefully from the covers, I head for the kitchen.

Immediately upon rounding the corner, the aroma of crisp bacon and scrambled eggs fills the air. I want some badly, but my stomach is still weak. What I need is something warm and soothing to drink.

"Can I make you some?" He gestures toward his plate, but I shake my head and scrunch my nose.

He can't look me in the eyes, either. Two men in one day, afraid to see what's in my soul. Or maybe they're afraid of what I'll see in theirs. Maybe *I'm* afraid of what I'll learn also. There's one answer, however, I'm curious to know. First, I need some tea to calm my spirit.

Reaching into the cupboard, I find my favorite cup. When I turn, I find Collin buttering a piece of toast in front of the jar of teabags. I'm not in the mood to ask him to move or hand me the jar. Instead, I reach in front of him for the container. He doesn't move to give me an inch of room and I wonder if it's intentional, to show I have no power over him, or maybe to posture himself as the dominant asshole he is. *God!* Why am I so attracted to this frustrating man? After last night, he must know my physical strength, that I'm much stronger than him, so he challenges me with stubbornness. *Testosterone.*

His breath on my neck makes me hold mine, and I'm suddenly wishing his hands were moving over my body with the same care as he coats his bread. *Shit!* What am I thinking? I need to stop right now. *Get your hand back in the tea jar and get away from him.*

When I have what I'm searching for, I close the lid and move to the other side of the kitchen. Filling the cup with water then placing it in the microwave, I push the minute plus button twice, and wait. My back to the fridge, I yawn and stretch while watching Collin butter his toast. He uses long, slow strokes. His movements are deliberate as if he feels my eyes on him. Then, he turns and reaches for the refrigerator door, his hand grasping my breast instead, forcing a gasp from me. Stunned, I don't move, staring into his eyes as they grow wide and his cheeks turn red, I assume with embarrassment, and he quickly removes his hand.

When the shock wears off, I can't stop watching his face, searching for a sliver of caring in those deep green irises, or a glint of evil that spurs his hatred. Either way I have to know, but he's turned away before I could see into his soul.

The microwave rings and the light turns off inside. Reluctantly, I move out of his way, retrieving my cup to head for the table. Normally, I would toss the bag into the steaming water and let it steep while I accomplish another task. Today, however, I want to play with it.

Sitting quietly at the table, I enjoy surrendering the teabag, dipping it into the water for a moment then tugging on the string, over and over, until the liquid in the cup is a deep olive. It helps me think of something other than the monsters haunting my subconscious.

Soon, Collin sits in front of me as I finally rescue the soaked teabag from my cup and place it on the saucer. I've decided I don't want to know what's in his eyes anymore, at least not at this point. But I still have that matter to clear up.

"What happened that night?"

At my question, Collin looks up with confusion in his eyes.

"The nightmare. The night before we met in person at my bank. What happened in your gallery?"

"You don't know?"

"I don't remember."

Suddenly, his tone grows sarcastic. "How convenient. Why are you playing with me like this?"

I hadn't expected this reaction. "I don't understand."

"You don't?" His reply is more of a taunt than a question.

"I have no idea what you're talking about."

"Unbelievable. For someone with such a damned good memory you seem to have forgotten something pretty important, don't you think? And you know damned well what I'm talking about. You're supposedly a dark angel, but you bring demons to kill me in my sleep."

"What in the *hell* are you talking about?"

While I study his expression, his eyes set on me like a hawk. "That's *exactly* what I'm talking about. *Hell*. You've made your pact and now you're paying for it with your own life. The demons you've partnered with to protect you are the same ones slowly killing you in your own dreams. I saw them watching you and I've seen them watching me. Do you think they only want to take down one when they can have us both? Seems you didn't save yourself after all."

I'm flabbergasted, can't even speak. After such a ludicrous revelation, I have trouble collecting my thoughts.

"Don't look at me like that. I had my suspicions until last night. When I saw you with the demon in my kitchen I had no doubt. Surprised you didn't let him live also, you seemed to enjoy the way he *touched* you. The only reason I'm still here in your house is because of Doc."

Now I'm fuming. I can't believe what he's accusing me of. Partnering with demons? And his sole reason for being here is for Rick? To hell with that. I don't need anybody in my life, especially him. "If that's your only reason then don't waste your time."

He grits his teeth and turns sarcastic. "Don't you need someone to *stay* and save you from your *nightmares*?"

"You think that's the reason you're here is to *save me*? You arrogant *prick*. When you figure out that the world isn't about *you*, maybe you'll realize *I don't need your help*. I don't need anyone to save me, especially not *you*. So if that's your reason for being here, I'd rather you take your *bullshit* and get out." I point toward the door and wait for him to turn.

Instead, his voice turns deep in disgust. "Why am I wasting my time with you?"

"I keep asking myself that same question."

I can tell my words bite him hard. His eyes narrow on me as he grits his teeth. "Screw you."

"*That's* real mature. Why are you afraid to tell me what happened in that gallery?" I'm standing now with my palms on the table.

"Okay, I'll dance, before I could unlock the door, your *friend* attacked me. When I went to kill her, you stepped in my way. When I tried to toss you out of the way, your *friend* swung the vase." He shows me his right hand. "I caught it to keep her from breaking your jaw. The impact sent my hand into your mouth anyway, splitting your lip while the pattern on the vase tore my hand. That's what happened to my palm."

The blood on the vase wasn't mine. It was *his*. Now I'm more confused than ever. "Why can't I remember?"

"Yeah, that's what I keep asking myself!" His voice is so loud it echoes through my kitchen.

"Keep it down. I have neighbors."

"I don't give a *damn* about your neighbors!"

"Collin, I have no idea what you're talking about. The only other one in your dream with me was Sarah. I didn't see any demons in the room. I thought *you* were the demon."

Suddenly, his expression changes to utter shock. "You thought *I* was the demon?" He stares at the table, possibly trying to sort it out in his mind. "You went out with me thinking I was a..."

I can't answer him. No matter what he is, angel or demon, I can't say I went out with him half hoping he'd kill me. The look of betrayal on his face is painful enough. My hands begin to shake.

"Do you still think I'm a monster?" His eyes turn to mine and I can see the hurt in them.

"The way you've been acting it's hard to think you're anything but." I say it more calmly and he can see it wasn't an emotional response, simply an honest one. A shock shoots through my heart and my head begins to spin.

"Have you forgotten where you came from?"

"What? No." I'm offended at the insinuation.

"Have you forgotten you opposed Lucifer? That you were one of *us*?"

Now *I'm* gritting my teeth in anger. "No. Stop it. I haven't forgotten and I haven't turned."

"If you haven't forgotten and you haven't turned, then why would you go out with someone you thought was a demon? And if your intentions are still *pure,* then why is your *friend* trying to kill me?"

"For the last time. I. Don't. Know. What. You're. *Talking* about!"

The fury in his eyes frightens me. I know what he's capable of. Worse than any demon, a dark angel with hatred in their heart is dangerous. He thinks I'm a traitor. His eyes show that his hatred toward me is greater than his revulsion for Lucifer at this moment. And he used seduction to get close enough for revenge. He wants retribution for something I never did. The room starts to spin and before I can sit, my knees buckle under me.

CHAPTER 12

When I open my eyes again, I'm in my room. Again. I'm getting real tired of being here. Rick is hovering over me with his stethoscope on my chest. When I smile up at him, he doesn't smile back.

The silence is getting to me. "Maybe you should move into the guest room. You've been here enough."

"Jaime, this isn't a joke. You've lost a lot of blood over the past few days. Your body may be able to heal rapidly, but it obviously can't replace your volume as fast. You need to take care of yourself." He says it like a scolding father or a concerned friend. "What happened?"

I shake my head, unable to talk about it. He wouldn't understand anyway.

"He called me on your cell to come check on you and then left. Can't say I'm disappointed. Expected as much from him. Assume you two got into one."

"Misunderstanding, that's all."

"Can't he wait until you're better to pick a fight?"

I shake my head. "He thinks I'm trying to kill him."

Rick is visibly stunned. "What? Why would he think

something as ludicrous as that?"

"It's a long story. Can't really blame him. Thought he was trying to kill me, too."

"Well, there you go. A match made in heaven." He shoves his stethoscope in his bag and I roll my eyes at him.

"Don't get attached to me, Rick. As you can see, I'm not your typical girl next door. And I'm not the angel I was. Suppose I never will be again."

"Too late."

His comment is concerning. How do I show him I'm not worth the effort? "Rick, what do you think life would be like being married to someone like me? You think it's all rosy? What would happen on our wedding night when you wake to me being slashed by a psychotic killer in my dream, in *our* bed? Can you handle stepping out of the way while I battle to the death, watching my blood stain our sheets, coat the walls? Can you stand by and watch when I finally meet the one who takes my life?"

He closes his eyes, his body shaking all over. "I can try to do something. I could try to protect you. At least I'd be here for you instead of leaving when you need me most."

"This isn't the life of a mortal. I chose to be a dark angel, you chose to be a human. If I allow myself to get too close to you, one day the demons I hunt could find you too. Could I live with myself knowing you died because of me? Because you fell in love with me? I can't permit myself to fall in love with you for that purpose alone."

"Yet, you let yourself love that immortal who doesn't deserve you?"

I catch my breath at his frankness. My voice is barely a whisper, barely audible, as I avoid the true meaning of his comment. "He's not really immortal. We both can die. You should know that by now."

He's silent. Unable to look me in the eyes. Several minutes go by without a word. A thought pulls at my subconscious and I decide to break the silence.

"Rick?"

"Yes, Jaime?"

"If someone had done something that hurt you, something devastating, could you forget? Do people, you know, mortals, do they forgive easily? Or do they hold their pain inside, letting it destroy them for the rest of their lives?"

"I'm not sure what you're getting at, Jaime. I guess some forgive and some hold onto their anger forever. Why?"

"Something happened once, a long time ago." I can't say that this 'something' happened to me. I guess if I don't say it out loud, then I can pretend for a minute it wasn't me. "A tragedy that tore a girl apart made her two incomplete people, one who wants to save the world, but can't and another who wants revenge, but may never realize her wish. Is there something wrong with wanting two contradictory things? How can one person be so strong and weak at the same time?"

Concern shows in his eyes. "Jaime, what happened to you?"

My eyes close as I shake my head, hoping to hold back the tears. I feel his hand brush my cheek to dry a drop that escapes.

"I don't know how to answer you, Jaime. All I can think to say is that love sometimes heals. Sometimes it's enough to get rid of hatred and bring a torn girl back together again. First, however, she has to learn to love herself. I sense she hasn't allowed herself an opportunity to do that yet."

The inside of my cheek is raw from biting it to keep from crying. I can't let go of my emotions. They're the only part of my life I can control.

"I'm sorry, Jaime. I wish I could help you, but I don't know what happened to cause this split. Maybe if you change your mind, decide to share, it'll help… Promise I'll listen and not say a word. I promise."

I nod in reply, knowing I'm not ready to share with anyone, yet.

"I'm giving you an IV. Help replace your fluids so your body can start making more red blood cells. I'm staying with you until it's done, can't leave you alone. I'll give you a slight sedative so you can relax, make you feel better."

"A sedative?" I ask, wondering if he's forgotten everything I've told him.

"Don't worry," he answers, placing his hand lightly on my shoulder. "It should relax you, not put you to sleep."

Before he turns away, I reach for his hand. He stares me in the eyes and I see kindness toward me. If I were a normal mortal, I would probably allow myself to fall in love with him.

"I care about you more than you think. Not just because you take care of me."

"I understand why you can't love me more. You don't have to pretend."

"I don't pretend about something like that. But I can't be the reason you die. I couldn't live with that."

"Sometimes it's worth taking the chance if you truly love someone. Someday I'd like to heal more than your body." He ties the tourniquet around my arm and searches for a vein.

"It's never worth risking another person's life for selfish reasons."

He cleans a patch of skin with an alcohol swab and sticks the needle into my vein. "Sometimes I'm selfish."

My mind wanders, recalling the feel of Collin's kiss and how it made my heart race. "Yeah. We're all selfish sometimes."

As soon as he shoots the sedative into the line, my cells

begin to wake. My whole body is flooded in warmth and I feel so light.

"This is great, Doc. If I'm not careful, I might like this too much." My speech is slurred, but I have no control and I don't care. I've become so relaxed I can't lift my hand from the bed although I keep trying. "Rick? Are you sure this is the right amount? Because…I'm so…sleepy."

"It's okay, Jaime. Relax," I hear him whisper in the distance and I feel his lips press against my cheek, my mouth, his hand sliding over my shoulder. I can't move a muscle and my mind drifts off into a dark shadow of nothingness.

***

A heavy pressure on my body causes my mind to stir. Before my eyes can open I note the smell of white board markers, industrial laundered sheets, rubbing alcohol and blood. I'm no longer in my home.

My eyes open to see a small room with plain walls. A heart monitor and IV pump rest to the right of me as I lay in a bed with metal railings on both sides. I'm in a hospital. My room is private and empty. Rick betrayed me. He sedated me and brought me here.

Furious, I turn to reach for the railing, but my arms won't move. Searching my body, I discover that I'm restrained, both my arms and my legs. *That bastard!* I'll never forgive him.

Yanking on my wrists, I notice my arms feel weaker than usual. I can't break the ties holding me down. What did he put in my IV? Focusing my energy, I pull again and feel progress as the fabric begins to rip. The restraints slowly tear from the bed. First one arm is free, then the other. I reach down to my legs and pull on them until, one at a time, they finally break free.

In the midst of trying to liberate myself, I hadn't noticed

the aid enter my room. Realizing what I'm doing, he tries to pull me back on the bed, but I easily shove him off me. Reaching for the needle in my arm, I pull it and toss the tubing to the floor. Then, the hospital worker decides to rush me again. Big mistake. I've had it with this guy.

With my fist doubled, I knock him to the wall near the front of the bed so I have a clear pathway to the hall. As soon as my feet hit the floor, however, my legs give way beneath me like they're made of rubber. My sense of balance is impaired and the room seems to be spinning. What's happening to me?

The guy on the floor is stirring again and I have no choice but to continue on. Waiting for him to recover would be *my* mistake.

Finally reaching the doorway, I have to stop and steady myself. My vision is cloudy, making it difficult to focus. Holding onto the frame and peering out through the door, I shudder at what I find. The nurse's station and the surrounding area are completely empty of souls. I should be grateful there's no one to get in my way, but something about this situation seems wrong. What kind of hospital leaves the patients of an entire ward attended by one person?

My feet are cold on the sterile floor as I step into the hallway, fighting to see everything surrounding me. My reflection shines and distorts in the waxed black and white tiles as I stagger down the corridor. Each room I pass is dark. Every bed is bare. Where did everyone go? My body shivers as I move from door to door, holding tightly to the wall, peering into empty rooms. How could it be I was their sole patient? What's going on here?

The hallway is eerily quiet except for footsteps behind me. Someone is following. I don't want to take a chance it's the man I'd knocked out, the one trying to hold me to the bed. If I run, he won't be able to keep up with me. My legs are still unsure, but I have no choice except force them to move, hoping I don't fall to the floor. I need to find someone with commonsense who realizes they can't hold me here against my will.

Racing down the corridor, I hope to lose them. If they're successful in pinning me to the bed, I won't be able to defend myself when I sleep. They don't realize that in their attempt to heal me they'll help a demon kill me instead. There's no way to tell them this without sounding insane. I can't believe Rick would do this, knowing what he knows about me. Asshole.

Standing at an intersection of hallways, I see three corridors headed in different directions. I feel like a drunk in an unfamiliar city. I've never been here before so I have no idea how to get out. A rustling sound in the shadows catches my attention. I'm too confused to make a sound choice, but I have to. Desperate to leave, I hastily decide on the corridor to my left.

When I reach another intersecting hallway I head left again, hoping to shake the one on my tail. These corridors are more like a maze than a hospital. How can anyone find their way in this building? Finally, I reach a set of large double doors. I'm hoping they lead to the hospital lobby and a way out of here. When I rush through, however, I realize I'm in the cafeteria, the one room that seems to have life. Unfortunately, the soft whisper of footsteps still follows.

Slipping into the shadows, I search for another exit. The walls are plain, no artwork or patterns, just old, textured white paint. The carpeted floor is teal with burgundy specks. A serving area on one side of the room is empty of food. Wrong time of day to be here if you're hungry, I guess. No trays, cups, plates or flatware. There's nothing that makes me assume this is a cafeteria other than the tables and chairs and a small sign indicating it is so.

An illuminated green sign on the other side of the room suddenly attracts my attention. Finally, a way out. Between me and that exit, however, are two people having a tense discussion, fairly close to my destination. Although they aren't animated in their gestures, their posture says they're much less than friends. Fortunately, neither has seen me so I slip along the shadows, clinging to the wall while keeping my focus on them and the open door on the other side.

When I'm close enough, I can see that one of them has dark hair, much like Collin's. His posture is similar, also. He's wearing a white t-shirt and a pair of jeans, what he wore when he left my house. His body language seems protective while preparing for an advance. I know that stance. He's so deeply focused on the other person that he doesn't hear me. He didn't even notice when I burst into the room. Their conversation doesn't appear to be going well, either.

The other man has lighter hair, slightly longer than the first. He's wearing a brown, leather jacket and a pair of Levi's, but I'm more curious about the man with dark hair.

I continue to circle the room until I can see his eyes. They're deep green, nearly glowing in the hospital light. *Collin*. What is he doing here? Was he working with Richard Stanton to get me committed? Is it possible that's what the two are in disagreement over? How could he do something so foolish and irresponsible? If he's truly a dark angel he'd know as well as me the danger in having me admitted to a hospital. Even a demon would be able to realize this. Shows how much he really cares. Makes me wonder even more who he really is. *Jerk*.

As much as Collin tries to look casual, the gleam in his eye tells me different. He seems ready for something. I'd say he was preparing to attack. But that would be ridiculous in a public place, in the middle of the afternoon. Maybe he always looks angry unless he's trying to seduce someone. Or maybe something else is going on.

Suddenly, I realize I've made a huge error. There are no windows, no handles on the doors, the lack of dinnerware, cutlery, even a counter to purchase the non-existent food. The rooms are dark, much unlike a typical patient room. And there's no staff, no doctors or nurses. Only the one who tried to pin me to the bed, Collin and this guy. Rick didn't send me to any hospital.

I'm dreaming. I'm here to take out a demon. But which one do I kill?

My first impulse is to protect Collin. I can't explain why I want to place myself between him and the one he's facing down, even if *he's* the defective soul. How can I fight another angel, even kill them, to protect a monster I don't trust? Will I damn my soul to darkness if I save the wrong person?

From my vantage point I can see the whole room; round tables, sensible chairs, Collin, the other man. The smell of pine and wintergreen causes me to turn my eyes to the shadows. There seems to be another person standing off to the side, unseen like me. No, wait. There are *two*. And they're interested in Collin's conversation, as well. Are they with him or just watching? Could they be the demons he accused me of sending after him? My heart begins to pound and I wait to see what happens next.

The unidentified man has his hands in his coat pocket. He begins to circle Collin while the ones in the shadows start to circle as well. What are they doing? As the man in the leather coat pulls out his hand, the blade in his fist reflects the fluorescent lighting. My heart starts pulsing quickly.

Collin waits for the light-haired man to attack, unaware of the presence behind him. The air is heavy, as if the tension has created an invisible fog weighing down my body. Or maybe it's the drug Rick shot into my line. I've never been affected in my dreams by alcohol or anything, so why is Rick's sedative interfering with me now?

Slipping quietly around the room until I'm near enough to hear them, I carefully watch them both, trying to decide which one I should save. They're too focused on each other to notice the ones lurking in the shadow. They don't seem to notice me, either. I hope to discover who the demon is before the battle begins. Collin is cool, waiting for his opponent to lurch forward. When he finally does, the ones in the shadows also move.

"Collin!" I shout and dart forward. My voice echoes through the cafeteria and all eyes turn on me. *Crap!* What did I do?

"Shit!" He's as surprised as I am.

"Collin! Behind you!"

As he turns to the shadows, the other man lunges with his knife, grazing his right side. Collin turns back with a right fist to the other man's jaw. The sight of Collin's blood seeping through his shirt propels me forward, and I run as hard as I possibly can. I have to reach him before the killers in the shadows strike.

A long piece of cloth dangles from the hand of one of the shadow killers. Before I can make it to the center of the battle, he slips the fabric around Collin's throat, pulling him backward. My chest burns with strained breaths, my heart beats loudly in my ear. As hard as I run, I feel as if the room has become the length of a football field and I'm nowhere near to the goal. The harder I run, it seems, the further they are from me.

Collin is thrown off balance by the noose around his neck and falls backward. His foe prepares to strike again while

Collin struggles on the floor, gasping for air. My sole chance of saving him is to reach them before Collin's opponent slashes again.

The man in the leather jacket brings his arm back. The blade slices the air, on an arc toward Collin's throat. My heart skips several beats as I leap forward, my body seeming to hang in the heavy air. In the seconds before reaching them, my eyes remain focused on the position of the two men and the distance between their bodies. As my hand catches the knife, it barely nicks the thin flesh of Collin's neck before the blade is knocked backward. When I slip between them, I twist the knife from the killer's grasp. Sliding across the floor, I roll to my side and prepare for the next attack. I close my eyes and shake the fog from my brain. I need my full faculties to have a solid footing in this dream, as I do in all of my others.

Collin recovers and kicks the other guy in the teeth, sending him flying, while I've turned the blade around in my hands, heading back to the one with the necktie. They've messed with my life long enough.

My jaw is set as I run toward the shadows with the blade in hand, startling the ones who are hidden there with my attack. As I slash the air, the attackers back away and vanish into the night. Before they've completely disappeared, however, I feel metal connect with flesh. I've hit one of them.

When I turn to Collin, he's standing over the body of the man with light hair. I pray he isn't another angel sent to kill Collin and finish the job I couldn't. As his foe takes his last breath, I hold mine, afraid I may have sealed my fate. I'll never be able to go home again.

When Collin turns to me, his head cocks to the side. An inquisitive look crosses his face and his eyes grow wide. As I turn the direction he's gaping, I hear him shout my name. By the time I smell the pine and wintergreen, it's too late. A sudden sharp pain takes my breath away and everything goes black.

CHAPTER 13

I sit up, gasping for air, in my bed in my own room. The pain is too much when I lay back down. *Shit*! My lung.

Searching my surroundings for Rick, I find my room completely empty. IV tubing hangs loosely from a clear bag suspended from the highest post of my headboard with fluid spilling to the floor. Drops of fresh blood are being washed away by the saline. What did I do to this room in my sleep?

My hands find a deep hole in my upper back between my shoulder blades. My fingers come away wet and red. Falling out of bed, I stumble toward the open door and into the dark hallway. I pray I'm awake and that the ones who attack me in the shadows aren't still in my home.

"Doc?" My voice echoes back. What could have happened to him? He said he wouldn't leave.

Not far into the hallway, my foot snags on something large in my path, tripping me to the floor. My hand lands on a soft object covered in fabric and what feels like the sole of a shoe. A body. Panic creeps under my skin and through the marrow of my bones. I don't recall screaming, but I'm positive I have. When I crawl over the still form and touch his face, I note subtle features in the dim light. Not Collin, Rick.

"Breathe. Please, breathe." Coughing from my deflated lung, I put my hand on his chest that doesn't seem to be rising as it should. "No, Rick!"

After pounding my fists on his chest I put a finger under his nose, searching for a sign of breathing. A quick puff of air tickles my skin and I lay my head on him to hear his heart beating. My tears dampen his shirt as I gasp for air above him.

The room is quiet except for my strangled breathing. The floor beneath my foot is wet and there's a dark streak on Rick's sleeve. Did I cut him when I was fighting in my room? Or did the shadow killer attack him while trying to get to me? When I reach for his sleeve, the front door suddenly flies open and I turn to face the intruder. Their silhouette against the lit streetlights outside casts an intimidating image.

My heart is pounding again. Am I finally facing the killer from my shadows? There's no possible way I could fight in this condition, even to protect Rick. As my eyes close, I prepare to be slashed to death by this demon, praying it'll be quick.

As I brace myself for pain, the light switch at the door is flipped and I open my eyes, suddenly wanting to know who will end my life. When I see Collin's pale face, blood streaking his throat where the knife had nicked him, my body shudders violently. His eyes are wild as he rushes toward me, causing me to flinch in fear.

This is it. He must think I brought the ones in the shadows again, planning to kill him. He's finally going to take revenge on me, murder me right here. Maybe he'll make it look like Rick was the one who took my life. I close my eyes, waiting for it to be over, unwilling to look into his eyes.

My body jolts again when he grabs hold of my shoulders. "Are you all right?" He stares back at me, worry creasing his brows.

What? Is that concern? He isn't here to kill me?

While gasping for air, I nod. He reaches up and wipes a strand of hair from my face, kissing my forehead and confusing me even more. Then, he turns to Rick.

Collin puts his hand on Rick's chest to feel for a pulse. "His heart's beating. I think he's okay. What happened?"

I shake my head. I can only guess what might have happened to him while I was sleeping.

Relief helps dull some of my pain. I'm not sure how to interpret his actions to the part of my soul that fears him and sometimes hates him. I startle again as he moves behind me and tears open the back of my shirt to examine my wound.

"This one's deep. You need help." I shake my head in protest. "Jaime, you're already weak from your other wounds. I don't think Doc can help you this time." Still in agony, I shake my head again, having more difficulty breathing.

"No hospital. I go, I'll die. You know that." Each word is difficult to speak, but I have to get it out.

Rick starts to move, still dazed like he's been drinking. I'm still trying to figure out what happened. He's alive, but could've been killed. But, most importantly, Collin doesn't hate me anymore.

The sedative Rick gave me must not have worn off. I can't believe my most pressing thought revolves around how a man feels about me rather than the hole in my back.

Collin pats Rick on the shoulder. "Don't move, Doc. Stay here and rest a moment." He leaves for the bathroom and returns with a washcloth, pressing it against my back. "*Damn it!* I shouldn't have left you. I'm such an ass."

I don't say a word.

Several minutes pass before Rick begins to realize his whereabouts as I fuss over him, fighting back tears. So much is tearing at my emotions.

"Jaime," he whispers softly. "Honey, are you all right?"

"Yes." I whisper, barely audible.

Collin leans over him, examining his face. "What happened, Doc?"

"I was so stupid. I was giving her fluids through an IV and put a light sedative in it to relax her. Didn't think it'd make her sleep. She warned me once before, but I didn't listen. When she started dreaming, she went nuts. Pulled the needle from her arm and when I tried to hold her down she fought me and ran. Didn't realize she was so strong. I followed her through the house until she ended up back in the room."

He stops, taking a couple of deep breaths and shaking his head before going on. "It was the most unbelievable thing I've ever seen. Then, she called out your name and the next thing I know there's someone standing in her room, holding my scalpel. She stabbed Jaime in the back then ran when she saw me."

"Wait a second," Collin interrupts him. "You said 'she?'"

"That's right. It was a woman. I chased after her, but she was too strong. Jumped in the air and kicked me square in the chest. Next thing I know, I'm lying here, staring up at you two."

Collin turns to me, studying my face and thinking about what Rick said. "Did you recognize her?"

Rick shakes his head. "No. Never seen her before."

Suddenly, Collin notices I'm wheezing. "Rick, are you clear enough to help Jaime?"

"No. He needs rest." As I speak, I'm trying not to pass out again, feeling as if I'm drowning.

"Jaime, you need help *now*. He'll have to rest later."

Collin lifts me in his arms and heads toward the bedroom. I grab the door jamb to stop him, shaking my head and fighting for air. He seems confused so I point to the kitchen.

Now standing beside us, Rick grabs Collin's arm. "Don't lay her in there. Take her to the table." His expression has changed from regret to concern. "Damn it, Jaime."

Collin takes me to the dining room while Rick rushes to grab his bag from the bedroom. I seriously doubt he's prepared for this.

When Rick returns, he lays a pillow on the table. "Sit her in that chair and let her lean forward on this."

Raising my arms is painful, but I do it anyway, to place them on the surface in front of me. Rick tears the shirt to expose more of my back; then, Collin unlatches my bra while Rick pulls his stethoscope from the bag.

"Why are we doing this out here? Shouldn't she be in her bed?"

Rick shakes his head. "No. Her lung will collapse if she lays flat. She's better like this."

I see his reflection in the window in front of me as he places the cold stethoscope on my back and listens, moving to one section then another and waiting quietly. He pulls the ends from his ears and turns to Collin.

"My worry is her chest cavity may be filling with fluid. If that happens, her other lung will collapse also and she'll suffocate. I can't take care of her here. She needs to be in a hospital."

I shake my head and try to plead with him, but I can't get enough air to speak.

"The problem, Doc, is they'll ask about her, wonder why she has so many scars she can't explain. There's too much danger they'll contact the police. Once they're involved, they'll wonder what she's doing to cause so many injuries to her body, especially this puncture wound that looks more like she's been stabbed by a knife. We can't explain how she got this."

"I could come up with some kind of excuse."

"None that'll be good enough to appease them. You know that. Then, there's the question of safety. How do we protect her from a demon that roams in the shadows that even armed security can't control? If she's sedated in a hospital, she'll dream and they'll come for her. One of the reasons so many of us have died in hospitals. They can't get away from the demons tracking them in the night."

"So we just let her die?" Rick sounds sarcastic.

"No. We do our best to take care of her here. If she goes to the hospital, she *will* die."

"And if the demons come for her here when she sleeps? I can't fight for her."

Collin takes a deep breath and lets it out slowly. "I'll protect her."

Right. Isn't that what you said yesterday?

"That sounds all fine, but how will you do that when she dreams and you're not here?"

"I'll stay and do what I did before, take her dreams. I'll fight for her until she's strong enough to do it again on her own."

"And what happens when you two have another disagreement? Are you gonna desert her, leave her to fight all alone?"

Good question, Doc.

"No. I won't do that again." I can hear the regret in Collin's voice.

Rick sighs. I can imagine he's shaking his head again. "I'm gonna lose my license for this, you know that, don't you? I've already done enough to be barred from medicine for life. I don't feel good about this at all."

"Don't worry, Doc. We'll both be by her side. And you'll be

well compensated for taking care of her."

"Is that what you think she is to me? Money? You selfish bastard. I care more for her than you can begin to understand. The only reason she prefers you is that you're like her and she doesn't have to worry that her demons will kill you."

Oh, crap! What just happened?

"Don't start, Doc. You don't know where I've walked."

"I know you left her when she needed you. She could've been dead by the time I arrived and *you* would've been off brooding over her. That's not what she needs."

"And she needs you? You don't understand a person like her and you'll never be able to, no matter how hard you try. She told you not to give her a sedative, but you gave it to her anyway. She could've been killed in her dream if I hadn't been there. How can she trust you when you don't even listen to her? And besides that, you're right. You can't fight her demons for her no matter how badly you want to."

I look up at their reflections in the window. They both look furious, but Collin seems like he's preparing to fight.

"At least I'll try. You're so self-absorbed you don't even meet her half-way when she needs someone most."

Collin's jaw tightens at Rick's reprimand.

Bloody Hell. I'm bleeding to death and they're arguing over which one of them is better for me and which is worse. I take a deep breath and shout as loud as I can. "Stop it!" The sound is more like a whimper than a yell. Coughing from the pain, I wish I hadn't tried yelling so loud. My deflated lung doesn't actually allow me to shout, either. Yet, I was loud enough to get their attention.

"Stop or I'm leaving." I gasp for air between words.

The room is finally silent. *Hallelujah.* If I could move, I'd stand up and slap them both then leave the house and let them kill each other. Unfortunately, I'm stuck here with them.

"I need you both."

They hate each other. This won't be easy.

Collin's features soften and he's the first to speak. "I'm sorry. I'm grateful you've been here for her. I don't think she would've made it without you. I owe you more than I can possibly repay." He says it grudgingly, but there's a hint of sincerity in his voice.

Rick appears rightly embarrassed. "Me too. I'll always be jealous that I can't be you. Once, long ago, she and I fought side by side."

If rolling my eyes could make a sound...*Sigh.* Why did I tell him about our past?

"I can't do that for her anymore. I can only fix her when she's done fighting. She needs you by her side where I can't be anymore. And I'll always hate you for that."

Collin chuckles. "I'll keep that in mind."

I see their reflection in the window. They're reluctantly shaking hands. *Progress.*

"You know; I have a large syringe in my bag. I can draw off some of the fluid in her chest, give her lungs room to expand, might keep them from collapsing completely. I'll need something to hold what I drain from her, though, a jar or bowl." Without looking his direction, I point to the cupboard. He continues to talk while he searches for a suitable container. "That's what they'd do if she was in the hospital. I don't do this kind of stuff anymore, though, being a practitioner. And it's been a long time since I did my internship. This'll have to work."

Collin is apprehensive but seems to recognize this may be the lone way to save me from suffocating or drowning in blood. "Whatever you can do will be an improvement. I'm sure you'll do fine." His face turns grim with anticipation. Of what? My demise?

As Rick pulls items from his bag, he holds up a syringe with a tube the size of two of my fingers, causing me to gasp. Noting the size of his needle, I've decided I don't want to see anything else he's preparing to do to me. Instead, I rest my chin on the pillow and pretend I'm somewhere else. Right now I'm imagining myself sitting atop one of the red rocks jutting up from the earth at Garden of the Gods, a favorite place to purge my mind of the demons haunting my thoughts by day.

When I feel the sharp jab between the ribs, I jolt in response and my mind returns to my body at the table in my kitchen. When he sees me wince, Collin slips into a chair across from me and holds my hand. The look on his face is grave. Seems he can't hide the regret he feels for our fight earlier today.

Holding my hand, he lets his eyes drill into my soul as I agree to allow him past the thick barriers I've built. Persistent in his intent to understand my motivations, he reads me as if I'm written on parchment paper, able to see everything in my memory, at least as much as I allow. But first, he opens his mind to me. I suppose the gesture is meant to gain my trust by helping me understand him.

There are scars deep inside him I hadn't expected to uncover. A painful loss had cut him in the heart. Many years before, he fell in love with another dark angel. She was his world. They fought demons together in their dreams. That's how he's learned to enter mine. So he's a dark angel after all. What do you know? But, why does he have so much anger toward me? Sensing my confusion, he continues to show me more.

Shortly after they married, she died in her sleep and Collin was there. He tried to save her, but there was nothing he could do. A demon in the shadows with the sound of the wind and the smell of wintergreen and pine, the same one in his gallery with me that night, had slit her throat. That's why he didn't trust me.

He thought I had something to do with her death. But why does he think I brought the demon? Her death happened long before I met him and he knows I'm being stalked by them as well. After showing me these events, he shifts to reading *my* soul.

The first memory he sees is the night my father was killed. He can feel my pain and fear as we flee to Colorado. He watches me teach myself to fight and experiences the night I kill my father's murderer. I'm afraid to let him see what happens next, but I'd silently agreed to reveal everything. In apprehension, I close my eyes for a moment and take a deep breath before opening them once again. My hands shake as I hold tight to his, anxious about showing him that terrible nightmare.

As he watches what happened to me at the hidden campground, his expression changes, at first showing disbelief then anger. I'm startled to see a tear trickle down his cheek. I'm not the only one crying.

From that point, he insists on watching all of my fights, reviewing them in his mind as if strategizing for a battle. Who did I fight and what happened? He's obsessed with finding the one who's done this to me, the one in the shadows.

When we reach the memory of the gallery dream, he feels my emotions and suspicions of him, but also my deep attraction. The memory ends at him walking to the door and he can't go further. Finally, he feels my frustration for not remembering and understands.

The demon that stalked his bride and now him has followed me most of my life, watching in the shadows and finally turning toward torturing me. The one with the same sound, the same scent. They tried to kill him tonight, another attempt to hurt me. Why are they doing this to us?

"Sarah's the shadow killer," he says and stares at me without emotion.

I shake my head. "No. You're wrong."

Rick lifts his head and cocks it in our direction.

Collin seems determined to convince me. "She's the one who attacked you that night. Everything that happened—" he shakes his head in frustration. "—it was so surreal, Jaime. You weren't yourself, almost like you were awake but drugged. You didn't see her grab the vase. That's why I stepped in. She could have killed you when she swung it at you. She has to be the one doing this to you."

"It's not possible. I'd have smelled her."

"I've noticed she wears a lot of cologne."

He's right. If a demon wanted to hide their scent, cologne would be the perfect way to do so. If Sarah wanted to disguise her smell, she would have to wear enough perfume to repel me. If he's right, she did a great job. She knows I hate her perfume, yet always wears enough to make me sick. Mulling over the possibility, I still come to the same conclusion. There's no way she could pull off something so elaborate. Sarah isn't intelligent enough to carry out a plan so evil.

"She's intelligent enough to take over the bank while you're out sick." He's reading my thoughts. "She's intelligent enough to know to steal my deposit and split it up into several accounts so I'd come into the bank and you'd have to help me get it resolved. She's also intelligent enough to know she could get you to my gallery and replicate the dream."

"Why?"

"Bring us together hoping we'd fall in love? She did everything she could to push us on each other, remember? That way she can torture us at the same time. Or, better yet, get us to kill one another. Me thinking you helped the demon that killed my wife, you thinking I'm the demon who held you down." I feel his heart stop at his words. Two painful events. Hurts him just to think of them. Sensing his pain as well as my own is almost too much. I fight the impulse to pull from his mind and distance myself.

"But why would she care? Why would she want to do this to us?"

"Maybe we've killed too many of her friends. And this is her way of weakening us so she can get us out of her way."

Rick watches us for a moment and clears his throat. "I've taken nearly two pints of fluid from your chest. Does that feel better?"

I realize now that my ability to speak had only become possible because my lung had finally filled with air. "I can breathe again."

Rick pats my arm and smiles before rising to his feet. He slips into the chair at my side, facing me. "I've stitched the hole so you won't bleed out, at least. We need to keep an eye on you through the night, though. You won't be able to lay flat for a few days."

Collin shakes his head. "She'll be better by tomorrow."

With my mind still on our conversation, I turn to Collin. "I can go to work. Take a closer look at Sarah than I ever had before."

"No!" Both men shout it in unison, startling me.

"Collin, you said it. You know we heal fast. I'll be better by then."

Rick grabs my hand. "Jaime, you've had your ribs broken, been stabbed, impaled—"

"Eviscerated, I know, thanks for enumerating my ills, Rick."

Collin reaches for my other hand. "He's right. You won't have the strength you'll need for at least a couple days."

"Now you're both ganging up on me?"

Rick sighs. "No, Jaime. We care about you. Us normal people take weeks to heal, sometimes months." He shakes his head. "I may never get used to this."

"You'll get used to it." When I squeeze his hand, his tired eyes smile back at me. "I'll have to be back by Tuesday. We'll see how she reacts to me."

"Jaime…" Rick still has concern in his eyes.

"I'll be better by then, rested, nearly healed. It's not like I lift heavy objects when I'm there. And I can see what's happened since I've been gone."

Collin stares at my hand in Rick's. "We'll see."

"What I still don't understand is why she'd do it."

His eyes drilling into mine, Collin momentarily takes his mind off Rick. "Will we ever be able to explain the motivation of demons?"

No matter how hard I've tried over the many years, I've failed to find an answer to that question. Sometimes they revel in the torture of another. Other times there's deeper a purpose.

Rick is paying close attention to our conversation, trying to understand more about what's happened, I suppose. I can't read him quite like I can Collin. But then, I wasn't just inside Rick's head.

"Jaime, remember when I asked if one of your demons could still be alive?"

"Only if she didn't kill them." Collin interjects, turning to me.

Staring him in the eyes, I take a breath, but no words come to me.

"Jaime?"

"I never made sure they were dead before I left, always assumed they were when I woke."

"All of them? You've never made sure any of your demons were dead before you left?" Collin studies me.

I wonder what's on his mind. "I couldn't, I...I only waited for one to die, my father's demon. It's not him. I know he's dead. The shadow killer's been there since that night."

"Sarah isn't the only one. She has help. Someone else is fighting with her in the shadows. We're looking for someone who knows how you stopped your father's demon. Someone who was there the night you killed him."

Collin's right, but I've decided I don't want to talk about it anymore. There's far too much to think about and I'm exhausted. "I want some sleep. Can we talk about this in the morning?"

Rick puts his other hand on my arm. "We'll need to put cushions in your bed to prop you up. I'll give you another IV to help replace your fluids. I can give you light medicine, not as powerful, to help you rest."

I smile in agreement.

"I'm going to get some chest tubes just in case." He must see the concern on my face because he shakes his head. "Don't worry. I don't think I'll need them. With you, though, I have to be prepared for everything."

He turns to Collin. "You stay with her until I return. I don't care if you two want to gouge each other's eyes out. She needs your protection."

Collin turns to me with his mouth tight as if he's biting his lip. Apparently, he doesn't like being scolded by the doctor who's in love with me. There's no escaping the tension starting to build again.

To fend off an all-out battle in my kitchen I decide to speak my mind. "Can I say something? I know you both have your own thoughts and feelings. Well, I have mine, too. This is *my life*, you know. I still have control over what I say, what I do and the choices I make. It's pretty obvious you two want to rip the other apart over me. You may even want me to choose between you. Truth is, I care for you both. Each of you gives me the one thing I want and need that the other can't. So hear me well, if you fight each other, you'll lose me. I'm not in a position to choose between you, so don't make me do it right now or you may not like my decision."

When I stand I reach for Rick. With my hands on each side of his face, I kiss him on the lips. "Thank you."

Still in a daze, he takes a while before opening his eyes again. "Thank *you*..." He smirks at Collin and squeezes my hand before leaving.

Collin is studying me again. When the front door closes he finally speaks up. "You shouldn't lead him on like that."

"Who said I was leading him on?" Turning, I head toward the living room to pull the tall pillows from the sofa.

When I turn back, Collin is directly behind me, staring down at me with pinched eyebrows. "What're you doing?"

"Setting up cushions in my bed." Without further elaboration, I pass him, headed toward my room. Moving is much easier now that I can breathe again.

"No. Why are you playing with me and your *friend?*"

"Collin, do you want me to lie? I have feelings for you both and I'm not one to hold back the truth."

When I look over my shoulder I see him throw his hand through the air like he's angry. "Not true. You're *very* good at holding back your feelings." When I don't hesitate to watch him fume, he follows me down the hall to my bedroom.

"To people I don't trust. Can I trust you?" I throw the pillows at the headboard as I speak, growing angry with his interrogation. The movement hurts, but I don't care. I'm too mad.

"Can *I* trust *you*?" He looks hurt.

This is draining. Now I know why I didn't do this in high school.

Sighing, I sit on the edge of the bed, easing carefully down. "I care about Rick because he's kind and gentle. He cares deeply about people, something I saw in him the moment I met him. I fell in love with that. The only mortal I've ever cared about in that way."

"What about me? Am I just the one who protects you from monsters in the night? Is that all I am to you?"

"Until a couple hours ago you scared the hell out of me. I didn't know if you were going to seduce me, then murder me in my sleep or if you were gonna skip the formalities and go straight to bludgeoning me to death. When I move beyond the minor concern that you might want to end my life, I can't stop thinking about you."

His expression changes, his features softening as he stares into my eyes and I fight the urge to pull him closer, to crush my lips into his. "You're so much more to me than someone who fights my demons. If that's all you were, I wouldn't waste your time or mine. Truth is, I can't look at you without feeling the passion I once feared. I've known mostly hatred in my life. You take that hate and bend it to something I can live with. When I look in your eyes, I want you to possess me, to kiss me like it hurts, in a way you've never kissed another woman. It's as if I wanna suffocate in you."

He reaches for my chin and turns my face up to his. His fingers tremble as his lips lower to my mouth. As I hold my breath, he hesitates, unsure, a hair away from touching me. The gentle brush of air on my mouth makes me shudder in anticipation. Closing my eyes, I breathe in his scent, wanting him to go the rest of the way. He steps back, lifting my feet to the mattress and turning me until my back presses into the cushions.

The fire in his eyes captivates me and I want more. Reading my yearning, he climbs up on the bed and straddles me, his lips lightly touching mine, kissing my cheek then moving down to my throat. My back arches and I can barely breathe, not just because of the aching in my chest but also from the yearning for him to do more than kiss me. My heart pounds painfully fast and I love it.

He whispers in my ear, "Are you saying Doc can't give you this?"

As the lock on the front entrance turns, my eyes snap wide. When the door to the bedroom opens, Collin is climbing off the bed, brushing the front of his pants with his hands. Rick's tight expression shows his suspicion of what we've been up to.

"Just getting our girl tucked in." Collin still watches me, clearly enjoying the blood flushing my cheeks.

"Stop tucking her in and get some ice water in this." Rick shoves a huge hospital mug into Collin's chest, the kind that looks like a big gulp with a handle.

"Aye, aye, Captain," Collin tells him, flashing a teasing smile at me before leaving the room.

His eyes narrowed, Rick turns to me. "What did you tell him?" Attempting to hide the smirk on my lips, I shake my head. "Does he know about what you said, you know, the battle in heaven? Is that silly for me to…"

I watch him, slightly amused at his loss for words.

"I don't know what he remembers about the pre-existence, Rick."

"Are you enjoying this? Two men falling all over you?"

"I find it…confusing. I've never felt this way before about anyone. Now I'm torn in two. If you knew my past, you'd understand why."

"Does *he* know your past?"

"My mortal past."

"I understand." With that, he goes quiet.

I'm not sure he does understand. Fairly soon I may find

neither of them will and instead of having the best of two kinds of love, once again I'll have none.

When Collin returns with the water, Rick takes it from him and sets it on the nightstand near me. Watching their interaction, I shake my head with a slight amount of amusement.

"Although I'm giving you an IV, I want you to drink as much as you can. I don't have much tubing so you'll need help getting up and going to the bathroom at night. Don't hesitate to wake me."

The expression on Collin's face shows his distaste for the idea. "There's no need to wake him. I'll be right beside you."

As Rick fumes, I roll my eyes. "I think I can figure out how to do it myself. I like my privacy, you know."

But Rick isn't convinced. "What if you pass out while you're—?"

"I'll figure it out."

"Okay. Fair enough. So, what about sleeping arrangements?" Rick asks, suspiciously eyeing Collin.

I've decided I'd better take control of the conversation quickly before it turns ugly again. "Rick, Collin is right. Without him beside me, I'll hunt again. They're waiting for me. They always are." I can see he understands even if he doesn't like it. "You have to work tomorrow. You won't sleep in that chair watching me."

"I'm not leaving you tonight."

"I know." I can't help but smile at him. His loyalty is warming. "There's a guest bedroom next to my room. You'll have your own bathroom and you can come in to check on me anytime. Trust me, we'll call if there's any trouble."

Rick takes a deep breath, possibly holding back what he would like to say. His lips are still pressed tightly together. "Let me get this IV in you." He pulls the chair to my bedside and searches for a usable vein. The moment seems awkward for him. I can see it in how he's fumbling while searching. "You're dehydrated. None of 'em wanna pop for me."

Gently taking his hand, I look deep into his eyes. "It's all right. Take your time."

Suddenly, I see something in his irises I hadn't noticed before. Something dark and dangerous comes through before he pulls his hand from mine. Jealousy, maybe? Before I can understand what it is, he turns away and starts working on finding a vein again. The harshness of his actions startles me. Did it have something to do with Collin? There almost seemed to be intent to harm someone. Has this competition between the two created a monster I hadn't foreseen?

With the tourniquet still tight around my bicep, he slaps the inside of my arm until his fingers find a strong enough vein. "Too bad you blew the other one earlier when you were thrashing about. Was an easy stick."

He pulls the needle out of the packaging and slides it easily into my flesh. After pulling it back a bit and sweeping it into my arm a couple more times, he hits and draws back blood.

Without looking at me, he mumbles to himself, "Good. Finally."

After setting the saline to dripping, he tosses the wrapped leftovers into his bag. The sense of his mounting frustration makes me uncomfortable and causes confusion. I'm not sure why I feel this way. He shoots a glance at Collin on the other side of the bed. There's something there, more than simple animosity.

Before leaving, he leans over me with an arm on each side. "You sleep tonight. No fighting, okay?"

I give a strained smile. He presses his lips against mine for a long, almost aggressive kiss.

My heart speeds up again and I hold my breath once more.

My body's reaction to him surprises me and I find myself reminiscing on our times together in the pre-existence. Although it was Michael who would typically pull at my sense of longing, it was Raph who would comfort me after the battle. Rick, my loving captain and angel, Raph. I can see by the confidence in his eyes he knows how he's made me feel.

Did my response to his kiss have anything to do with what I saw in his eyes? I don't understand this feeling. I've never had it before, not even with Collin. Am I suddenly attracted to the dangerous side of Richard Stanton? Is that what I felt? How can two men have such unusual and completely different effects on me? Oh, man, am I in trouble.

When Rick reaches the door, he turns and nods good night to Collin. I can feel Collin's smoldering eyes on me as the door closes, leaving us alone.

Trying to diffuse the situation, I narrow my eyes back at him. "Are you two enjoying yourselves?"

A playful smile crosses his face. "I think I'm enjoying the competition."

"I don't know if I'll survive this."

"What's the matter?" He moves closer to the bed, watching me like he's stalking his prey. "Too much passion? Remember, we're being honest now."

My heart may not be able to handle the constant increase in blood pressure from these two men. I feel as if I've been working out instead of lying in bed while they play tag team.

Before I know it, Collin crawls over me like a cat eyeing a mouse.

"Shouldn't we get some rest?" I ask, but he doesn't answer.

Instead, he nuzzles my ear with his nose before moving to the nape of my neck. Oh. My. Hell.

CHAPTER 14

An uneasiness in my soul stirs me awake to the dim light of night. Still lying in bed with Collin asleep next to me, I feel the presence of another nearby. Someone is close, practically hovering over me. Their warm breath tickles my shoulder. My mind races through the possibilities. My first thought: is it Sarah?

Slowly, my hand reaches for Collin, but he doesn't move. He must be in the hunt, maybe preparing to battle one of my demons. I might as well be completely alone.

Am I ready to fight if they attack? My body feels better, perhaps healed enough. If I had to, I could defend myself, even protect Collin if it becomes necessary. First, I'll have to get this IV out of my arm. As my hand reaches over to pull the needle, the person standing over me reaches for my shoulder, causing me to startle and gasp.

"It's okay, Jaime. Just me. Came in to check on you."

Doc?

He turns away and searches for something in his bag. When he returns, he has a stethoscope in his hands. Taking a moment to listen to my chest, he grins and puts his hand on the side of my face.

"You sound better. How are you feeling?"

My heart is still pounding as I stare up at him and manage a tight smile. Rick leans over and kisses me on the lips then lifts his head slightly. He's staring into my eyes and I'm not sure why. His actions are so unusual as if it's not really him. Then, he leans over and kisses me again, longer this time, and my body starts to shudder. After one more glance into my eyes, he rises to his feet and leaves the room. Remaining still, I listen to the thump of my heartbeat pulsing in my chest, wondering why his kiss bothered me so much when it had the opposite effect just hours before. More than an hour passes before I fall asleep again.

The next time I open my eyes, morning light is shining through my curtains and Rick is once again at my side, the stethoscope in his hands. He smiles down at me while warming the metal rim before placing it on my chest.

"Your lungs sound almost healed, amazing. There's only a slight wisp. I think the excess fluid will be absorbed. By tomorrow, you could be back to normal, if it's possible to use that term for you." He smiles at me playfully. "But you need to stay down all day." Then, he turns to glare at Collin. "Don't do *anything* physical."

Collin smirks back. "Thanks, *Rick*." There's obvious sarcasm in his voice. I don't have to see his expression to know there's a mischievous glint in his eyes.

Rick pulls the needle from my arm and immediately tapes a folded gauze square in its place. "Keep it there for an hour. You don't need to bleed anymore."

Before leaving, he leans over and kisses me softly, but passionately, on the mouth. This time, my body doesn't react as it had either time before. In fact, there's no reaction at all. When he pulls back, I lick my lips and he smiles again. "I have to go. Call if you need *anything*."

One more quick peck and he pushes himself to his feet, turns and leaves. As his car rolls down the drive, I lean forward to slip off to the kitchen.

Before I can roll out of bed, Collin's hand catches my arm. "Where are *you* going?" He still has that look on his face, like he's a cat that caught a moth in his teeth.

My eyes narrow back at him. "I'm getting something to eat. I'm starving."

"Didn't you hear *Rick*? You need to stay down."

He accents Rick's name like a bully on the playground. I sigh and shake my head at his childish game.

The grin spreads across his face as he reaches for my ankles and gently eases me flat on the bed, causing my body to tremble with excitement. I almost expect to see a smirk on his face, but his expression has turned serious and intense. The glint in his eyes reflects a hidden fire. His passion is nearly feral and I shiver in anticipation and fear. Once again, he's crawling over me like I'm his prey and he's playing with me before the kill. My body aches for him to do more than tease me, more than nip behind my ear. I want him to touch me and satisfy the burning between my thighs. My arousal makes me want to hunt again, this time kill more than simply some worthless demon.

The tremors racking my body are out of control as I peer into his eyes. As much as I fear what I see, I can't help but want more. Must be the dark angel in me. Or maybe my sick obsession with danger. *Oh, God, forgive me*, I want him to make me scream.

I'm startled when he grabs the front of my shirt and rips it open, laying the halves over my arms. His hand traces a line down the center of my abdomen to my navel. He touches the wide scar in my side with his fingertips as if he's admiring it.

The flesh is all but healed like it happened weeks ago. My breathing grows deep when he slowly lowers his lips to my stitches. I catch my breath when his hand brushes my panties, admiring the texture of the lace before running up my tummy to my ribs. Then, he slides his fingers along my ribcage to my side, taking my hands and pulling them slowly over my head. My heart beats faster as I wonder what he's doing and what he has planned for me, intently watching him as if I'm paralyzed.

Blood surges through my veins like when I sense a demon hiding in a nearby shadow, but it isn't a killer I'm detecting. Though Collin's desire makes him nearly as dangerous in different ways. Reaching over my chest, his hands slide across my collarbone to the neck of his shirt. He grabs the collar, careful not to catch my hair. With one quick motion, the shirt is freed and I'm holding my breath, lying on the bed, vulnerable in my bra and panties.

"Collin, no," I whisper.

He touches my lips with the tip of his finger and slowly shakes his head. "Shh."

I know he won't go much further. *Or will he?* No, he can't. Dark angels aren't allowed to consummate until their union is ordained. But he could drive me mad if he doesn't stop soon. Is this what my mother tried to prepare me for? This animalistic passion that drives me to want this man in a way that I know is wrong. Is this what she meant when she said we make love like we hunt?

Before backing away from me, his lips brush my neck and my tummy to let me know he'll return. Eager to know what he'll do next, I let my eyes follow him to the edge of the bed and soon I realize he's unbuttoning his jeans. *Oh, my God*, he just might do this. To think he'd actually defy the order because he wants me so much excites me in a way I hadn't expected.

Anxiety rises from the pit of my gut, making me unsure if I want to see what happens next. I lower my hands to my eyes and close them tight before turning away. When I hear heavy cloth slip to the floor, I feel his fingers encircle my wrists and pull my hands over my head once again. Oh, God, why do I find it so damned sensual when he dominates me in this way?

"Open your eyes," he whispers, his hands still pinning mine to the bed, and I do as I'm told. He's still wearing his boxer shorts that are pulled tight around his hips by his erection.

With the release of a long-held breath, I'm finally able to breathe, but only until he strips off his t-shirt revealing olive skin pulled taut over sleek muscles. As striking as he appears, I'm more attracted to his scars and work my hand from his grasp. They show his strength and commitment in ways his muscles never could. Reaching for a mark on his abdomen, I want to touch it, trace it with the tips of my fingers. But his hand stops mine, holding it in his palm, his fingers gripping me firmly. From the look in his eyes, his desire is barely contained.

When he releases my hand, his fingers drift below my waist and into my panties, caressing the soft patch hidden within. At the light stroke of his fingers on my moist, sensitive flesh, my body shudders and I draw a sudden, deep breath. I want him to touch me more, stronger, deeper. Sensing my arousal, he continues to hold back to drive my desire for him, yet not long enough to bring me to anger. He clearly understands the female emotions of our kind. Maybe too well.

As his fingers work magic between my thighs, barely slipping into me and starting a fire I've never known before, his mouth finds the flesh my bra barely covers, practically devouring me as I moan in approval. Collin's scent fills my head as my fingers become tangled in his hair and I pull him to me, tearing his lip with my teeth. Suddenly, the gentle stroke of a hidden, sensitive area sends me out of control, and I draw blood with my nails in the taut flesh of his shoulders. His eyes are wild as he clenches his teeth and throws his head back. The sound that rises from his throat is something carnal and thrilling.

While writhing in ecstasy, the muscles in my body grow as tight as his shorts. I want him desperately, but I know I can't have him, not fully. Still, he places my hand on the bulge between his legs, causing my fingers to tremble while discovering the firm, rippled flesh. The smooth rigidity of him makes me gasp, still aching for more.

With my fingers sliding over him, discovering him and longing for him, his body becomes as tense as mine had been moments before. The look on his face is more animalistic than ecstasy as his fingers dig into my hips. The intensity in his eyes stirs fear in me that heightens my arousal as his hips press into mine once again. As soon as his muscles ease, his body forces me into the mattress and his lips find mine, kissing and biting, his blood salty on my tongue.

I've suddenly forgotten about killers hidden in shadows. At this moment, all I can feel is Collin Leary's body on mine as his lips and tongue move over me, owning me. My hands explore him as he explores me, fingers caressing flesh, drawing through creases and coaxing my desire once again to a dangerous level.

I'm not expecting a second release until my voice cries out and the muscles in my groin throb again, causing my body to arch, my head thrown back as if I'm in pain. How can he do this to me with just his tongue or the touch of his fingers? Before the pulsing subsides, he flips me over to my tummy and then grinds his body into mine. A groan escapes his throat and I realize his ecstasy, his body tightening as he bites the back of my neck. A moment later, he collapses on me before rolling gently to my side. His arm and leg drape across my body while he kisses me on the shoulder. I have no idea what happened, but I know I'm dying to do it again. First, my heart needs rest and so does my body. With my mind drifting off to sleep, Collin nuzzles my neck, lightly nipping at my skin.

As I become aware of my room again, I feel Collin's arm still clinging to me. I stare up at the ceiling, unmoving, feeling his breath on my skin. His presence is strong enough without laying a finger on my flesh. With his body tangled in mine, it feels as if the heat has fused him with me.

My mind drifts to the memory of our passion together, his hands on every inch of my skin, his mouth following close behind. Just the memory of his touch takes my breath away. Something has grown between us that I can't explain.

His face is peaceful as he sleeps. The curve of his brows, the long, narrow bridge of his nose, dimpled chin, so familiar are his features. I must have known him in the pre-existence, but I don't remember. There are only few I recall, Michael, Raph, and there were others who were close to me most of the time. My parents, they were always nearby, but Collin wasn't so close. Maybe I noticed him from afar in one of our battles. If he was valiant, I'd have taken note. Maybe that's it. It bothers me that the memory won't come. Not one of his muscles flinches when I reach over and touch the scar on his shoulder, tracing it over the arch to where it ends on his upper bicep. The softness of his marred flesh, so warm, nearly hot, makes me crave him more. I caress the wound on his ribs. When he opened his memories to me, I saw it all. I didn't give him these scars. He earned them in battles with demons. Some happened when he tried to save his wife. The deep one on his side was from that fight. He almost didn't survive, trying to protect her. There were too many rogues for two angels. They were surrounded. His heart was broken as he cradled her body when he woke. Devastating.

My feelings seem to be evolving into something deeper than desire for Collin. Even though he's a formidable warrior, he also seems so vulnerable. When he touched my body, I recognized a hesitation from him. He almost faltered when I cried out as if the sound of my ecstasy made him weak. Then, he turned to beast. A deliciously brutal creature. And I devoured what he gave me. Every. Succulent. Moment.

Running my fingers through his hair, the tresses are nearly black against my skin and feel like silk. The locks slip easily through my fingers to his forehead where fat curls lie on his smooth skin. His dark lashes are long and thick. Aside from his nose and chin, Collin's other prominent features are soft, almost childlike in the filtered light of the room. His lips are full and scrumptious, making me want to lean over and kiss them, and so I do. They're so warm and my lips ache from his teeth tearing at them, drawing my own blood as I had his. The memory arouses my passion and blood surges to my groin.

Even at the feel of my touch, he still doesn't stir so I press my lips to his again, feeling the wet flesh against mine. I lift his palm in mine and touch my lips gently with the tips of his fingers as he had early today. The sensation is indescribable and I kiss them one by one. Am I falling in love with him?

I'm not sure if I'm capable of submitting myself to another, definitely not the submissive type. I wouldn't even know how to ask for a union to be ordained. Doubt he'd ask anyway. He was deeply in love with his wife. Can't imagine he'd be ready to unite with another so easily. *Sigh*. I'm getting way ahead of myself.

As much as I'm enjoying exploring his body while he sleeps, I'm starving and in desperate need of a shower. Placing another kiss on his lips, I slip from the covers and head to the kitchen. A slice of toast and glass of juice will have to do until after I'm clean. I've come to the point where I can't stand myself.

The hot spray of water feels so healing falling over my scalp and running down the rest of my body. The thick lather feels luxurious in my filthy hair. The stitches from a few nights ago stand out in the back of my head. I'll have Rick pull those when he returns. From the feel of it, the gash is completely healed.

My mind wanders to Collin again, the feel of him on my skin, his breath tickling the hairs on the back of my neck. I wonder what it would be like to make love to him; fully give myself to him and claim him as mine. An experience I may never know. Now that I understand more about him, I'm not sure how this story will end. The most important revelation: he's an angel like me.

I'm not alone.

Hopefully, he'll contain his hunger long enough to continue respecting me. His desire overpowers my senses. If it wasn't for the problem of ordaining in advance of uniting, I might have let him take all of me. Drawing my fingers across my mouth, I imagine his lips in their place. I want his hands on my flesh once more, brushing lightly against me, claiming me until I can no longer control my urges. Will I always feel this way?

With a thick, soapy puff I clean the blood from my abdomen. I slowly scrub the top of my shoulders and allow the suds to slide down my back, removing remnants of yesterday's attack. The water flowing down my legs and surrounding my feet is brown for a moment, turning clear as it's replaced with the fresh, the clean, everything toxic being rushed over my body and far away.

As I clean the crease between my breasts, the puff softly

grazes my nipple, making it tighten and I close my eyes. The memory of his fingers between my thighs floods my mind and I reach for the same spot that had sent me soaring beneath his caress. I'd never touched myself this way before. No one had. The desire, the yearning he drew out in me was like the driving energy of Niagara Falls. My fingers search my flesh, gently stroking as he did. When my fingertip brushes a soft fold, a slight thrill shoots through my body and a tiny, erect pearl protrudes. *I had no idea.* Spilling a drop of soap on the tip of my finger, I reach down and stroke again. *Oh, God!* If I'd known about this before, I'd have never left my house. With my back against the cold tile of my shower, I continue, gliding in and out until reaching the climax of my desire and am sent over the edge. When the shudders of ecstasy cease to rack my body, I slip down the wall to sit on the floor, water raining over me and sluicing down the drain.

When I'm finished, I wrap a towel around me and go into the room to check on Collin. As I leave behind the steam of the bathroom, I immediately feel his energy nearby, but that's not all. I also feel the presence of another. We're not the only ones in the room.

When I reach for him, he doesn't stir. He's in a deep sleep, his eyes wide open. When I search his pupils, I see past the veil that shrouds his dream and realize he is caught in a fight. As I turn, I catch the movement of a hidden form leaving the room. I usually don't fare as well in a chase, which is why I typically let the killer come to me. In this instance, however, I see no alternative. They're loose in my home and there's a chance Rick will walk through the door at any moment. They've already attacked him once.

Outside the bedroom, the hallway is empty. There are no sounds of footsteps anywhere throughout my house. Although it's late afternoon, the rooms seem dark. Am I dreaming? Collin said he wouldn't let me fight until I was better. Did he forget?

The floorboard creaks beneath my foot, betraying my presence. The demon has an advantage, knowing my location while I have no knowledge of his. As I leave the darkened hall for the open living room, a searing pain traces my cheek. Spinning to confront the attacker, I find no one there. Reaching up to my face, I feel hot blood on my fingers.

They could be anywhere. Backing up to the wall, I search the room. Starting from my far right, visually moving to the next corner, I search the bookcases, around the overstuffed chair, past the sofa, beneath the table, curio cabinets and the kitchen island. Moving carefully past the next doorway, I keep sufficient distance between me and the shadows. If they're hiding in the darkness they will have the advantage, should I draw too near.

Inside the kitchen, on the breakfast bar, there's the stainless steel knife set. All are intact. The pantry door is open. Nothing seems out of place. Then, I hear a crash coming from the bedroom.

When I reach the room, I see the lamp knocked to the floor. A dark figure stands over Collin. Before I can reach the bed the figure slips off and disappears in the corner shadows while Collin gasps for air, a royal blue necktie wrapped tightly around his throat.

"Collin. Collin, do you hear me?"

After unraveling the cloth, I lift his head. His eyes grow dark and he bolts upright. Blood runs down the front of his chest from a deep cut.

"Collin!"

The sound of him gasping for air paralyzes me. He's still in the fight. I can do nothing for him, only watch, try to keep him safe and stay out of his reach. As I back away, his arm swings forward, barely missing my face. Better to move further backward.

His head finally turns downward, eyes fixed on a target. My heart skips a beat. I know that look, similar to the one he gave while climbing over me this morning, but this time there's fury on his face, not passion. He's in the last throw. One of them is about to die and I hold my breath, waiting for him to finish. Let it not be Collin.

My head turns downward with his, my eyes fixed on him as if it will help. His concentration is precise, eyes moving across the room, tracking the demon. I watch through his eyes, tracking them as well. Then, he reaches forward and pulls his arms around in front of him, ripping the monster through the air and snapping his neck before bringing his hands to his side. With his eyes closed in victory, I move closer to him, releasing the air I've kept trapped in my lungs. When Collin recognizes my face, he reaches for me and pulls me to his chest. I almost thought I heard a sob escape his throat. What happened in his dream?

CHAPTER 15

Before I can pull the answer from Collin, the bedroom door flies open. Leaping from the bed, I hold my breath, preparing to kill. Arms raised, my muscles tense, preparing to attack as Rick bursts into the room.

Collin sprints toward the door, fury showing in eyes and the curve of his brow. When he recognizes Rick, he tries to slow his forward progression before tackling him to the floor. He comes to a jerking halt that almost appears painful.

Rick regards us as if we're crazy. "What're you two up to?" His eyes flick across my towel and Collin's boxers. "Well, at least you still have *something* on. Should I count myself lucky?"

I peer down at myself, realizing what he's reacting to. *Awkward*. I'm not actually embarrassed, but it isn't fair to Rick. So I pull a pair of jeans and a t-shirt from my drawer, slipping into them as quickly as possible.

Rick stars at my jaw and I shoot him a questioning glance. "You're bleeding. What in the hell have you two being doing while I've been gone?"

Reaching up to wipe my face, I find the blood is dry. "Just

a scratch. Rick. Look, whatever you're thinking…"

My explanation ends there. The truth is much worse.

"What am I thinking, Jaime? What I'm seeing is bad enough."

I freeze in place, staring into his eyes. No sense in denying it.

I turn back to Collin. "What happened? What did you see in your dream?"

He shakes his head, unwilling to say. *That explains a lot.*

"If you know something then tell me. Does it have to do with the demons who're stalking us?"

He closes his eyes, I assume, to keep me from seeing what he's thinking. Perhaps it's for fear I'll learn what he's trying to hide. Sitting on the edge of the bed with a worried look on his face, he runs his hands through his hair. Rick watches us, unsure what to say, but my patience has run dry.

"Collin!"

His eyes snap up to mine.

Rick grows impatient also. "What happened?"

"That's what I'm trying to find out. He had a dream."

"In the day?"

"Yes, we have them whenever we sleep. But there's more. When I returned from my shower, there was someone in the house. They lured me out of the room, circled back, and attacked him."

"It's all my fault, Jaime," Collin finally opens up.

"What? What are you talking about?"

"I know who they are, now." He looks up at Rick. "You're in serious danger. You have to stay away from us until this is over."

"Do you mean stay away from *Jaime,* or stay away from *you*?" Rick's voice is sharp, biting.

"Look, this isn't a game! These are killers we're dealing

with and as long as we're alive or they're alive, they'll hunt everyone we care about until they're all dead. You're in the spotlight, Doc."

I can't believe what I'm hearing. My mind is still hung on the words, *it's all my fault*. "What are you saying; it's all your fault? What happened, Collin? What did you see?"

Without answering, he closes his eyes again, trying not to face what he knows. "The ones in the shadows, I know who they are and I know why they're after you."

My growing impatience gets the better of me. "You said that already."

Abruptly, he stands and paces the room. "I messed up. I really messed up. My union to Elizabeth wasn't ordained."

"What're you talking about? You were married, weren't you?"

He looks me in the eyes and nods.

"You didn't get your union ordained before you married?"

He shakes his head in reply.

"A civil wedding. And you consummated on your wedding night, of course."

Collin sighs and runs his fingers through his hair.

"Oh, my hell." My heart feels as if it's been torn from my chest.

Rick appears confused. "What're you two talking about?"

I stare straight ahead at nothing, my mind unable to apprehend what he had said. "We aren't allowed to consummate unless we're ordained."

Rick shakes his head, still confused. "In plain English, Jaime."

"We aren't allowed to…unite…make love unless it's ordained from above. It's mainly an issue with dark angels."

He looks at me sideways as if he's trying unsuccessfully to understand. Then, he seems to comprehend. "So this is a…really *bad* thing?"

I sigh and shake my head. "A *very* bad thing. But I don't understand why you wouldn't take care of that before…you know."

Rick interrupts us. "So you mean you two haven't…" He draws a line between us with his finger.

I give a weak smile and shake my head to let him know we didn't do what he thinks. "It would be too dangerous. We're already dealing with enough."

"And it'll get worse. Jaime, the reason I wasn't ordained to Elizabeth is because I wasn't able to. I'm already preordained to another."

I don't understand, and from his reaction, I know he can see it in my eyes.

"I was preordained to you."

My mind goes blank for a moment. Did he really say what I thought he said? "What? What do you mean? How is that possible?"

"Jaime—"

Anger burns away my shock. "How! How can you be preordained to me without my consent? How do you even *do* that?"

"Jaime—"

Rick's patience is suddenly at an end. "I'm lost. Jaime, what're you two talking about, 'preordained?'"

Looking solely at me, Collin ignores him. "Jaime, I knew you in the preexistence. You were admired by so many, especially me. I saw you with Doc, how close you were then. I was afraid you'd be with him in the future here on earth." He stops and takes a breath.

"Collin. What did you do?" I already know I won't like what he's about to say, but I have to hear it.

"I wanted to be with you so I…well, I guess you would say

I pulled strings to get the blessings. If I hadn't, I worried they'd make Doc a dark angel also and the two of you—"

"You selfish bastard!" Rick's eyes are dark with anger, suddenly realizing what Collin is saying.

"How many more times will you call me that today, *Rick*?" Collin's eyes narrow on him.

"How many more times will you give me a good reason, *Collin*?" Rick's fury is palpable, but we don't have time for this.

I shove my way between them. "How can you preordain without my approval, Collin? Answer me!"

"It was on a contingency."

"What was the contingency?"

"That you accepted. Jaime, I didn't expect this to turn so badly. I lost track of you in the resultant tumult. If I would've found you as soon as you were of age, I could've protected you. I've made a total mess of your life." He takes a deep breath but doesn't go on quickly enough for me.

I can't breathe I'm so angry. "Collin, please go on because I'm seething right now and I'm afraid this is going to get much worse."

"Worse doesn't come close to describing it. I had no idea it would put you in so much danger."

"How, Collin? How does your *little mistake* affect *me*? Other than assuming it was okay for *you* to decide who I'd want to marry?"

"When it was approved and sealed, you became vulnerable. Until you accepted. Or declined."

I want him to spill it all at once, but I can tell he's afraid of what I'll do when I've learned everything. He's wise to be afraid of me. "Collin. *Go on*."

"In order to help me recognize you when we met here on earth, you had to have an open seal. As soon as it happened they knew you, knew who you were."

Rick finally finds the words to jump into the conversation. "Who? What did you unleash on her?"

"As long as I *tracked* Jaime, they knew where she was and tracked her, too."

I close my eyes and sigh. "Rogue angels." How could he?

"Jaime, I had no idea. All I knew was that I loved you and wanted to be with you forever. I thought I'd be here in time."

"What's a rogue angel?" Rick is still trying to catch up to us.

I take a deep breath before turning to him. "A rogue angel is a dark angel that changes allegiance. They no longer align with God but follow Lucifer instead."

"How can that be?"

"Being a dark angel is…challenging," Collin jumps in.

"No kidding."

"Sarcasm noted, *Rick*. There are some who can't deal with what comes with all the killing, seeing what the demons have done. It's devastating to weaker souls."

"So they start killing?"

I nod in answer to his question, unable to speak in my utter shock.

"Who do they kill?"

"Dark angels. Rogues have been around since evil took over the earth again, after the crucifixion. When the earth fell into darkness again and scores of mortals were dying, they were angry for being sent to do a job they felt they could never accomplish. There's always more evil. It never ends."

"If they're killing other angels, that can't be a good thing? I mean, if they're fighting you, doesn't that sort of lose their place in, you know, the afterworld?"

"It's worse for them than for a normal mortal, or a demon. Rogues know the truth and reject it. When they die, they go to a place that's pure darkness. Nothing. Black. And that's their hell. A bleak eternity."

Rick notices the fear in my eyes at discussing the blackness.

"So, why would they go after dark angels, especially if they're one of you, already knowing the truth?"

Collin stands, walking toward the door, and then turns back toward the bed. "They carry animosity toward us for continuing the fight. They think if we join them they can take over earth, win the battle that was already lost in the pre-existence. If we won't join them, they dispose of us. Our fight isn't just against the demons, now, it's against them, our own kind. They'll kill as many of us as they can. Because of that, there's a protective cloak that keeps them from recognizing us. It'll always be there as long as we obey the covenants."

He paces the room again before stopping in front of me. "Jaime is one of the more well-known angels. When she was born to earth with the open seal over her head, the one I put there, her protection was compromised."

Collin puts his hand on my cheek and I flinch at his touch. "You were born in Dublin. You're Irish, like me. Rogue angels tried killing you several times as a baby, so your parents left and I couldn't track you anymore. I had to lose you among the other mortals to keep you safe."

I can't believe what I've heard. "That's not possible. My parents never had the accent. I would've known, at least I would've noticed the scent."

"They were able to cover their scent and ultimately change it with exposure to the woods of the upper west coast. It's why you're so attracted to the way I smell. You're thinking of home, the one you barely knew for a brief and kinder period in your life. They also had to learn the new accent immediately in order to hide. They had it perfected before you were old enough to notice. I followed you to America when I was still young, but I was afraid to search for you. In time, I gave up and fell in love again. Elizabeth."

"And you couldn't get ordained because of me."

Collin sighs. "I couldn't undue the ordinance. It had already been sealed. The only person who could undo it was you."

"And I was lost." My mind spins, wondering what he's about to tell me next. I don't want to interrupt for fear I'll miss something.

"When Elizabeth and I married, when we consummated, I lost my security, so did she. Everyone I loved became vulnerable, open to the evils of this world. My family, Elizabeth's family, yours. Your grandmother, father, and then your mother, all died shielding you."

His eyes are turning red and I can tell he's fighting back his anguish. But I don't care. I want him to feel so much more. How many people have died over his selfishness? I've endured something greater than mere anguish.

"Everything that happened to you has been my fault. These are rogue angels doing this to you, not demons. They know who you are and they won't stop until they've killed everyone you love."

Suddenly, he stops and closes his eyes tightly, trying to obliterate some vision from his mind, I assume. "They sent a demon to show me their plan, said that after they kill me they're planning to torture you until you join them or beg for an end. If you don't become rogue, they'll kill *everything* you love, then make you wish *you* were dead."

I'm numb. I have so much anger in me I can't speak. My grandmother didn't hesitate. They just said that to keep the truth from me. My father's killer had help from a rogue. That's why he pleaded for my life. They didn't want *him*. They wanted *me*.

"I doubt they could make me suffer more than they already have. They haven't broken me yet." My voice is a whisper as I fight the tears flooding my eyes.

"Jaime, everything you've been through is *nothing* compared to what they intend. They *will* break you."

Rick clears his throat to be heard. "What does this mean?"

"She's too powerful to be their enemy so they need her on their side. If she doesn't turn, they'll kill her as well, but not before they have their way with her. They'll tear her apart, bit by bit, and enjoy every moment of it. They'll tear *you* apart, small pieces of flesh at a time, and make her watch. Anyone, even a dark angel, would go mad."

"How could you do this, Collin?" My voice is so soft I can barely hear it myself.

"I'm so sorry. I know there's no apology that'll make this better."

"You're right. So stop apologizing."

I turn to Rick and see something in his eyes. There's something he isn't telling me. What now? "Rick?"

He takes a deep breath, but no words come out and he shakes his head.

"Tell me!" From the corner of my eye, I see Collin startle at my raised voice.

"They found a girl this morning. Fifteen. Died in her sleep."

Rising to my feet, my eyes are still on him, questioning. Why is he telling me this? I'm unsure if I want to press him for the rest, but I do anyway. "And?"

"She had a blue necktie wrapped around her throat, bruises on her wrists."

The age I was on that night. They're reminding me. Taunting me. Calling me to come find them. They killed a young girl to get to me? My breathing grows heavy and my blood surges through my veins. In a rage, I turn and punch Collin in the jaw, practically knocking him to the floor. "I *hate* you." Hesitating for a moment, I turn and leave the room.

His footsteps follow after me into the hall. "Jaime, wait."

Roaring, I grab him by the shoulders and slam him into the wall. Sheetrock dust tumbles down onto my hands. My face is nearly pressed into his. "How could you?"

His eyes grow huge. I can see his fear that I might end his life right there. "I loved you. I wanted to spend an eternity with you. It was the only way I thought I could do it. I'm a selfish bastard."

"Yes. Yes, you are. How *dare* you drop into my life and suddenly accuse me of turning after you've done something like *this?*"

I throw another punch but redirect at the last minute to penetrate the wall beside his face, causing him to flinch. My fist shatters the drywall through to the next room. If I had hit him, I might have killed him. Part of me wishes I had. The desire to hurt someone remains, making my heart pound.

"Doc, put me in a deep sleep."

"No, Doc. It's what they want." Collin grabs me by the shoulders, but I knock his hands away.

"Don't touch me." The words seethe like poison through my gritted teeth. Collin knows I'm too dangerous now to get in my way.

"Jaime. Don't you see? They want you to rush toward them in your weakened state. That's what they're hoping for, what they've planned all along. And they know I'll be there beside you. They'll torture me right in front of you then turn toward anyone else you know. I swear this is the wrong approach. You have to think with your head, not your anger."

"What? Trying to save your ass again? Doc, give me an IV and put me to sleep. Then, you pull the needle and get out."

Sighing in exasperation, Collin sits on the arm of the sofa. "Jaime." He looks up at me with pained eyes. "I'll die for you to make this end."

Rick stands nearby, trying to stay out of my way, but clearly not wanting to leave. "Wait, there's a way to end this?"

"There are two ways to end this." Collin stares into my eyes, searching for an ounce of compassion. I have so much hate right now that there's nothing but fury painting my soul and I want him to see it. "The first way is for Jaime to deny the ordinance. Then, I'll go into a deep sleep and let them kill me. Take as many rogue angels as I can before I go, but ultimately, I'd have to die at the hands of a demon. Jaime will regain her protection and she can go somewhere safe where no one knows her."

"That doesn't sound like a great option." Rick looks over at me and stiffens, reaches out to me, but his hand halts halfway there. "You said there's another option."

Collin shakes his head. "Deny it, Jaime and I'll have Doc put me to sleep. It's the best way."

Rick turns back to Collin. "What's the second option, Collin?"

He still won't answer. "Do it now, Jaime, so we can get this over with."

"Jaime, what's the second option?"

"The second option is I deny the ordinance and sacrifice myself to the demon. Collin will still likely die the next time he hunts, but, at least, he won't be tortured in front of me."

"That's an even *worse* option."

Collin's eyes follow me as I move toward the table. "Jaime, you know they won't let any demon kill you. They'd kill him before he had a chance. Then, they'd follow through with their plan. There's only one way."

I close my eyes and turn away, unable to see his face

anymore. He did this to me, yet I don't want to see him tortured. I would die inside. Tears flow down my cheeks and I can't stop them. Another reason to hate Collin Leary.

Rick starts pacing the room. "There has to be another way." Neither of us answers him. "Collin? There's another option, isn't there? What happens if Jaime accepts the ordination?"

"She's stuck throughout eternity with a selfish bastard. I'd rather die than *force* her to marry me."

"That's a better option. Jaime, that's a much better option than the one of you having to die."

"Doc, she has to feel it in her heart. If she doesn't love me, it won't stick. She hates me right now, there's no room in there for love. It'd be a waste of time, as if she hadn't made a choice at all and we haven't gone anywhere."

I don't have to read minds to know Rick doesn't want to talk me into falling in love with Collin. But he can't see another person suffer, even if they brought their troubles on themselves. I love that about him—probably always will—no matter what choice I make. Unfortunately, Rick understands my stubborn streak. He knows I would rather kill myself, taking with me as many rogue angels as I can.

He comes to me and wraps his arms around my shoulders, resting my head against his chest. With my eyes closed and my sense of smell heightened, I notice something I hadn't recognized before. His scent has changed, but I'm too tired and upset to recognize what it is. All I can think is Collin betrayed me. *He's* the traitor, after all. I could've forgiven him if he would've been a demon I'd fallen in love with by accident. That would have been my fault. Now I can't see any future other than one that realizes my total destruction at the hands of deceitful angels.

"You're not safe here, Rick." I whisper to keep from

betraying my emotions. Collin doesn't deserve to know I'm crying.

"I don't care." Rick gently strokes my hair. The feeling is soothing, but I know what has to be done and Rick can't be anywhere near.

"I do. You have to go now. Not your home, either. Stay at a hotel, with a friend, anyplace somewhat unfamiliar. They'll have difficulty finding you there. Don't go back to your house until you know the final outcome. It won't happen tonight. I need more time to prepare. Probably be tomorrow, so plan for at least two nights. Watch the news. You know what to look for."

He holds me for a while, his hand pressed against my cheek, holding my head against his chest. His heartbeat is rapid and strong with a hint of a wisp of cold wind. Is this the sound of a broken heart? I wonder what mine sounds like. Wish there was someone who could tell me.

Rick kisses me on the forehead and releases me to stand alone. I suddenly feel empty. The room no longer reflects the souls of three people. As the front door closes, the house feels completely devoid of life.

CHAPTER 16

The clock on the wall ticks off seconds. A car passes. My neighbor chats on the phone as she walks to her front door. The sound of her voice startles me. The wind rustles leaves in nearby trees.

Anger is a temporary—and very damaging—emotion. I can choose to hold it and let it devour me or release it to the wind. Right now I want to hold it and nurture it. I want to use it against Collin Leary for his selfishness. But neither of us would win. In that instance, we would all be consumed and I would be the foolish one. Selfish and dead.

Collin is right. My weakness is their strength. I need at least one more night to grow stronger and to plan. The fight will be greater than any other I've known. I'll have to wait for the right moment. Strategize for an angel, not a demon. They fight differently. The demon is secondary. My main focus will be the ones in the shadows.

First, I'll go to work, find out if Sarah is truly one of them. If she is, the strategy will differ. She knows me better than any other rogue. Doesn't matter who the others are. It only matters what *she* does.

"Jaime." Collin stands beside me now. He reaches, hesitantly, for my shoulder, but I don't strike at him or pull away this time. "Deny it now. It's the only way." He can see the determination in my eyes. Too bad he can't read me as easily as he thinks. At least not tonight. Right now he can't read me at all, I'm so closed off.

"If I could deny it for you, I would. If I could kill myself, I'd be dead by now. But you know that's not possible. Don't take this on by yourself. I brought this on both our heads and I have to redeem it for you."

His eyes reflect the soul of a beaten man. There's also a stubbornness reflected in me. I'm confident he won't take 'no' for an answer. That's why I have to execute my plan before he can stop me.

"Why're you waiting, Jaime? Decline the ordinance."

"I can't."

"Yes, you can. Just say it out loud."

"I can't deny what I've already accepted. I accept the ordinance to covenant with you."

"No!"

"It's too late, Collin. You're stuck with me for an eternity."

He immediately stumbles backward at my resolution, reaching for the breakfast bar to steady his weakened body. My own strength is fading as well, as I practically fall to the floor.

"Jaime. It's your acceptance of the marital bond. Damn it! Until we consummate, our strength will be lost."

I hadn't realized how powerful the covenant would be. Mother never told me about the debilitating effect of this covenant. Why wouldn't she feel it vitally important to for me to know?

We're not finished. Until we complete the circle, we'll both be more vulnerable than ever. Had the rogues foreseen this?

Did they know I could take the vow and wouldn't be able to finish due to my anger, or my past? Did they plan this back when I was only fifteen? Hoping I would react like a frightened victim, too traumatized to consummate my marriage? If we go to sleep before completion, they'll have us. What have I done?

The idea of them tearing him to pieces while I watch is more than I want to imagine, angry or not. What could they show him more frightening than that? I now know he could care less what they do to him. What do they have planned for me? What could be worse than what I've already endured?

Collin must sense my fear. "No. They won't win. I won't let them touch you."

His words give minor consolation. In his weakened state he won't be able to stop them. He wouldn't even be able to hold off a demon. Will they make him watch as they torture me? Make his last moments horrific as well? My heart begins to race.

"Jaime. Stop. Don't think about it. That's what they want. Fear can't control your thoughts now or they win. They've underestimated your strength. Focus on that."

The truth of his words aren't lost on me, but my heart won't slow. I try taking deep breaths, but it's not helping. Inhaling deeply once more, I close my eyes.

Once again, I focus on the clock as it ticks off the seconds. The motor on the freezer kicks in with a subtle gasp. The wind is still ruffling leaves in my yard. A lemon scented candle sits unlit on a nearby shelf. The musky smell of the moors of Ireland soon overpowers the sweet smelling wax. And in that sweet and bitter moment, there's nothing that captures my attention other than Collin, his scent, his sound and the feel of his passion for me.

The aroma I noticed the first time we met, his lips brushing my cheek as he whispered in my ear, the roll of his words in the back of his throat, all drew me toward him. I wanted him from that moment. But I held back, fearing my past, also knowing an angel shouldn't covenant with a mortal for the very reasons I enunciated to Rick. Had I only known Collin was far from ordinary.

When I search his face now, I notice his deep green eyes studying mine. His scent is drawing me, calling me. Those eyes stir my desire. I want to touch his skin, explore his flesh again, allow him to discover mine. Will we have the strength?

When he moves toward me, I close the gap between us, my hand slipping over his shoulder, the other sliding across his chest. Reaching for my shirt, he pulls it over my head and my hair flows past the middle of my back, tickling the skin above my pants. His fingers glide up my forearms, biceps and shoulders before drifting down my sternum to the center of my belly. His eyes stare into mine with constrained desire. I can feel that he's fighting the urge to play with me like a wild cat with his prey. The longing he sees in me makes it difficult to hold back.

He runs his fingers along the waistline of my jeans before hesitating over the top button. The quaking of his body has a weakening effect. Like a nervous teenager, he can't open the buttons. I reach down to release it and then slide them over my hips. He kisses my lips before moving around to my back, lifting my hair to lay it over my shoulder. His fingers lightly caress my arms as he kisses the nape of my neck. My breathing is labored, my hands are trembling and a fire is igniting between my thighs.

His hands slide down to the middle of my back and the tension of my bra is released, making me startle. He holds me tightly until my trembling subsides, laying gentle kisses on my brow until I'm ready to proceed. His fingers slowly rise to my shoulders again and slip the straps down my arms as he kisses and nips at my flesh.

My eyes are closed so I can't see a thing. No more can I hear the clock ticking or the wind in the trees. The lone sound is my heart beating in my ears and Collin breathing heavily as he slowly touches my body. The smell of Ireland excites my senses and makes me long for a home I don't remember.

Collin's hands slip around my hips, appreciating my lacy boy-shorts, the sole piece of clothing left on my body. His hands rise up my ribcage and my breath catches when they cup around my breasts. He pulls my back into his chest with my buttocks pressed against his groin and I feel the anxiety he keeps under control. When he tugs at the lower lace of my shorts, they slip down my legs to the floor at my feet.

Clinging tightly to me, he lowers to his knees and I go with him, his legs straddling mine. He holds his breath, reaching around and taking me the rest of the way to the floor. While the heat of my back is cooled by the ceramic tiles, he hovers over me, staring into my eyes as his hands move, barely touching, tickling my body. When his fingers reach my breasts he hesitates then grasps them firmly. The air catches in my throat as he kneads and rolls the flesh, admiring them as if playing a fine instrument. One of his hands trails down the center of my abdomen, leaving my skin burning where he traces. Reaching my groin, his palm lays flat and his finger slips gently between the soft flesh at the summit of my thighs. Still watching me, he delicately strokes, each pass penetrating deeper until reaching that tender pearl that shoots pleasure through my groin. My fingers reflexively curl into a fist and my back arches under his touch. *Oh, my God,* I can't hold back.

My hand reaches for his and slides his finger deeper into me as the muscles begin to contract. The groan in the back of his throat tells me he's barely able to hold on and he covers my mouth with his. As his lips hungrily consume me, both his hands glide over my hips to my behind. When his lips release me once again, I moan in disapproval, but his eyes never leave mine and I'm sedated by his hungry glare. Drops of sweat trickle down my tummy and over my sides, distracting me momentarily from the hands drifting to the backs of my knees. He tugs gently upward, folding my legs until my feet are flat on the cool floor. He separates them to kneel between my ankles and his mouth lowers to my throat.

My breathing grows heavy as he trails his lips over my collar bone to my breast, sucking and teasing with his tongue. My fingers weave through his hair, curling into a fist, and pulling his mouth into me. The tender skin fills his mouth as he sucks and grazes my flesh while his fingers discover my other breast and nipple. Soon, his mouth loosens its hold on me and slinks up my nipple, lightly sucking and tugging then kissing and nipping. Releasing my damp skin to cool in the air, his tongue slithers slowly and longingly to the mound of flesh at the top of my thighs. Again, his eyes turn to mine, flashing the yearning he barely contains. His fingers tremble as he spreads my thighs wider, lowering his head. The silky caress of his tongue through the creased flesh forces my muscles to contract and my back to arch again. His eyes raise instantly to mine, nearly glowing in the darkened room. I pant with desire.

Crawling carefully up my body until his lips find mine and his erection presses into my groin, he reaches between his legs and centers himself at the moist aperture. My body shudders in fear and anticipation.

"Collin," I gasp, my body quivering.

He places his fingertip on my lips and traces them slowly. Apprehension and fierce longing betray him with an unsteady touch. I take a deep breath the moment his lips fall over mine.

His body covers me as his hands hold the sides of my head and my fingers clutch his shoulders. A rush of pain and excitement tells me he's entered me as he takes a shuddered breath and pushes deeper inside. My nails dig into his shoulders forcing a moan from his throat. The feel of this man gliding snuggly toward my core brings the voracity of my passion to the surface, the pain and passion driving the hunter in me. The desire is so deep I only want to devour him.

While his body moves with mine, I feel another, stronger rise making me cry out in ecstasy. Pulling deep inside, this time he releases with me, cradling my head in his palms and staring into my eyes, his lust feeding my soul until we can move no more. When we're finished, I lay still in his arms, naked and vulnerable on my kitchen floor, with tears flooding my cheeks and Collin kissing my wet face, telling me he loves me. We're now joined, but my heart still aches for the loss of my family, the ones torn from my life by the man lying beside me. In this moment, the moment of our joining, I try my best to forgive him.

Feeling my desire still burning in spite of my tears, Collin gathers me in his arms and carries me to the bedroom where we continue exploring each other. His prideful nature humbles beneath my touch and I find myself aching to take advantage. I assume the huntress position over him this time, my mouth and tongue discovering him, coaxing him to the summit then driving him over the peak. Moments later, I allow him to take me again, and we continue in this way, making love throughout the evening, strengthening our bond, forcing me to love him deeper and crave him even more. Our new union puts a protective shield around us for the night, unable to be penetrated by dreams or demons, even rogue angels, while we rest for the final battle.

Chapter 17

We sleep deeply with our bodies woven together. Occasionally, one of us stirs, kissing and touching until we drift off again. In time, the sun rises and I peel Collin from my body so I can prepare for work. We will have one more opportunity to strengthen our bond before sleep this evening. I'm strong and I'm ready.

Almost fully healed, I decide to go out for a morning run and release the weight on my shoulders. First mile, I go through last night in my mind. I think of the morning passion between Collin and me, a hot shower, the shadow killer in my room. The look in Collin's eyes when finishing the kill. I saw something there other than concentration. To call it fury would minimize the intensity. I understand it a little better, now.

Mile two, I replay Rick returning, Collin pacing the floor, telling me about the mistake he'd made in the preexistence. A preordained union put my life in danger and my family on the run. Ultimately, his selfishness leads to the death of all I love as well as others I've never met. He might as well have killed them himself. He takes the blame for my torment at the hands of turned angels intent on destroying me. A sharp pain strikes my heart as I learn of a fifteen-year-old girl killed in her sleep. A senseless act of violence perpetrated to cause me fear and make me want immediate revenge. They're calling me to them, wanting me to make a mistake, bringing my demise. I reach deep into my soul to find the strength to forgive Collin.

Mile three, I think of how I said good bye to Rick last night, knowing I'll probably never see him again. He has no idea how the night ended, with Collin agreeing to die and my willingness to allow him, or my stubborn intent on destroying myself. He knows I long for this life to be over. His secret hope is to save me while allowing Collin the chivalrous death.

Mile four, the wind picks up again. The leaves rustle and I smell fresh pine in the air, similar to last night. So much different from Washington. A drier smell, no ferns. The smell…the feel. I stop mid-stride. Wet pine and ferns, I smelled it. I heard it. Last night. Not where I would've expected either. Then, I remember a watch, one I've seen before. How could I be so blind? It was there all along.

I've been betrayed by the one I trusted most.

The four miles back to my house are spent clearing everything I thought I already knew from my mind. My plan has changed. I'll have to correct for a new contingency. This night will be even more difficult than previously imagined. The rogue angels trying to kill us will die tonight or they'll hunt us for the rest of our lives. I need the fortitude and unbreakable courage to face them, hoping it will be enough to sustain me. If not, and should I fail, may I be strong enough to endure what I face without compromise. My eternal soul depends on it.

After I shower, while brushing my hair in the bathroom, Collin steps in behind me and circles my waist with his arms. "Are you ready for this?"

Looking at his reflection in the mirror, I nod. I'm ready for the fight, but I'm not a fool. There's still a chance I'll die. Or, even worse, I'll be kept alive for days of torture while the ones I care about are ripped apart. They know what I did to those boys in the woods. Would my fate be any less?

Before leaving for the bank, Collin ties a braided band around the finger on my left hand. The symbol links our souls. We're tied together for an eternity regardless of the number of hours, days or years we pass here on earth. Our lips find each other once more, hungry and longing before I head to the car. This may be the last time I'll feel his kiss and because of it, my heart aches.

The neighborhood is uniquely quiet. The birds don't sing this day. Lesser angels, birds always seem to know when one of their own is in danger.

I take the long way to work, watching sunlight caressing flowers in the freeway median. Gliders float through the sky above the academy. Pikes Peak is nearly melted. The campfire-like odor of charred trees on the west side brings the hint of a memory I push from my mind. I wonder if I'll always think of that night.

When I arrive, Sarah is already there, working away at her computer, barely acknowledging my presence. Tension seems to hang in the air like the smoke from this summer's wildfires. I don't lock myself in my office, though. Leaving the door wide open, I want Sarah to come to me. My hope is she'll make a mistake that betrays her. I prefer to be as prepared as possible. Oddly, she avoids my office and when I speak to her, she doesn't react as she normally would. Not a hint of perkiness in her tone today. Perhaps she's preparing herself as well. I've no doubt she's already been made aware that I know.

Toward the end of the day, she comes into my office,

cradling a newspaper. "Such sad news." She says it with a less than sad expression, laying the paper on my desk.

Today, she doesn't wear a jacket as she usually does. Her sleeves are rolled to her elbows as if she wants me to see her arms. I oblige her by searching her wrists for thick, long scars but there are none. She wasn't there that night. There are several other long-healed scars up and down her arms. She'd fought demons many years before. Now she hunts me. I'm surprised at the boldness of the gesture to expose her past, especially the fresh scar just a few days old.

That night in the alley, I swung into the darkness at the one who broke my ribs. With the demon's knife in my hand, I cut the shadow killer, ending their assault on me. Had to be Sarah. She bears the fresh scar. No wonder she sounded tired the next day. And I had felt guilty for leaving so much on her shoulders. I look for another fresh scar from the night at the hospital. The one I'd inflicted while Collin was finishing off the demon, right before I was stabbed in the back with Rick's scalpel. I'd swiped the air and hit someone. But that wound isn't there. I wonder if I'll recognize it on one of the rogues I'll meet tonight.

When a smile crosses my face, she realizes I'm studying the mark I'd given her. Her feigned pity disappears as her eyes glare into mine. She feels my satisfaction over having wounded her, I can see it on her face, feel it in her aura.

Picking up the paper, I scan the front page until finding the article. A family killed in their sleep. The father was murdered in his bed, his flesh shredded like cheese. 'Unrecognizable' they reported. The mother was tied to a chair and tortured. They believe she had been repeatedly violated by the intruders. Wouldn't say how they knew. Their ten-year-old daughter was found strangled in her room, a royal blue necktie wrapped around her throat, similar to the one tied to the fifteen-year-old found the day before. They're guessing the two incidents are connected. The fifteen-year-old girl is the same age I was when my father died in a somewhat similar way. The woman also died similar to my mother. I was seventeen then.

Sarah waits as I turn away and close my eyes. "They said there was no forced entry. Hmm. Who do you think could do something like that?" I open my eyes as she crosses in front of my desk and picks up the paper. "I wonder if they pleaded for their lives. I can tell you, if it was me, I'd beg them to kill me." Her voice is flat and unemotional.

She stares me in the eyes so I glare back to show the message was received. The fury in my eyes is enough to satisfy her and she smiles wryly, sauntering out of the room. She tipped her hand trying to scare me. What she doesn't realize is that I know more than she thinks and I won't make a mistake. Instead of being scared, I'm angry for the family I was unable to save.

For the next two hours, I run through the past week in my mind with new information to help put the events into perspective. Every moment I can force myself to remember from the dream in Collin's gallery, all the way up to the second Sarah walked out of my office this afternoon. Then, I go further back, to my earliest memories.

Everything my parents told me, every fight Grandma shared, is imprinted in my mind. I know they worried for me. I have no doubt they understood they wouldn't be here for this. What they taught me was meant to help in this moment. They had faith. They knew my potential and educated me to that end. My father taught me to fight like a man. My mother taught me how to throw them off guard using my femininity. Grandma sharpened my ability to focus on finer details. I can't let them down any longer by entertaining suicidal thoughts and death wishes. Now it's time to fight like I've never fought before.

All of those particulars are in the forefront of my memory, ready to be accessed as needed. I'll use them each moment of the fight, reaching into the past as was meant to be. My legacy. Knowing which mistakes they're expecting me to make.

Using my cell to call Collin, I ask him to meet me at his house. "I'm working late tonight. Will you have dinner ready when I arrive?"

After a short and sweet conversation that feels a little too domestic for my comfort, I make a call to Rick. I decide to leave work slightly early to meet Rick at his office in the clinic. He has a sleeping pill ready for me to take. I shoot Sarah a promising look filled with vehemence as I leave. While at Rick's, I slip a scalpel from the drawer into my purse without his knowledge. He won't miss it. I'm sure he has plenty.

Oddly enough, he doesn't ask my intentions as far as Collin and our situation is concerned. Perhaps he's distracted with an overload of patients today. His waiting room is rather full. Before leaving, I ask him to meet me in twenty minutes for drinks at the micro-brew around the corner. He eagerly agrees.

After leaving the clinic, I stop at a nearby grocery store. There are items I need to purchase before going home tonight. Then, I can relax with Rick and have a last drink.

At exactly twenty minutes after five he shows up at the bar. I've traded my conservative clothing for something more revealing. I want his last memory of me to be exciting, one he'll remember until *his* last moments. My clingy shirt is unbuttoned to just below my bust. A short, tight skirt the color of deep blue falls less than six inches below my behind. Being well-tanned, I don't need stockings. A pair of pumps that match my skirt elongate my legs.

I've taken the liberty of ordering apple martinis for us. Two each.

When Rick enters the bar, his eyes lock on me immediately, smiling while heading to where I'm seated. Once he's at my side, he reaches for my chin and pulls me toward him, giving me a long, passionate kiss, his teeth scraping my lips, and nearly knocking me off my stool. He makes it apparent he appreciates what he sees.

"My, my, I didn't anticipate this. Did you change your mind and decide to toss Collin to the rogues he exposed you to?"

"No. I've decided to go in on my own. Tonight's my last night and I thought I'd spend some of that time with the man I love, drinking martinis. To hell with Collin." I hold up my glass in a toast.

He smiles at my comment. "Jaime, is there anything I can do to change your mind?"

"No." I take a long sip of my appletini and set it down. "Drink up. I don't wanna drink alone and I *don't* wanna talk about anything depressing. This is my last night." I throw back the last of my drink. "You need to catch up." I smile at him again.

"Well, this is a treat. I've never had apple martinis before."

"Real name is appletini. See the seeds in the bottom? Try not to swallow them."

Smiling again, I remove the sliver of apple from the edge of my glass. After dipping it into my drink, I lift the slice to my lips and suck cool drops of alcohol from the green skin and pale flesh. Rick watches every movement with his mouth open, practically drooling.

"Get ready, they have a kick, but once you get past the tartness you'll enjoy the resulting buzz." My smile makes him grin.

I can hear his pulse pick up so I cross my legs slowly. Both by his slack expression and the spike in his emotions, I can tell he notices I'm not wearing panties. He takes a long drink of his martini while still trying to see up my skirt. Suddenly, his face puckers as he shakes off the sharp after-taste.

"Good, huh?"

He smiles back at me and nods, unable to say a word.

"Say, Rick, why don't you wear a watch?"

He looks down at his wrist. "Oh, I usually do when I go out. They bother me when I'm at work, though, my hands always getting wet. I worry I'll ruin it." He gives me an appreciative smile.

"You know, I *love* Breitling. Such a masculine timepiece. You should get one," I tell him and watch his reaction.

His face lights up. "I already have one. You have great taste in watches, among so many other things." Staring down at my legs again, he runs his hand up my thigh and over to the back of my skirt coming to rest on the roundness of my behind. "I love this color on you."

"I had no doubt you would." Finishing off the second martini, I order another round of four. "They're on me tonight," I tell him and give my sultry look. "Finish up. The next round is almost here."

"Jaime, have I told you how beautiful you are?" He's admiring my legs again by tracing my thigh with his fingertips. "You know, I fell in love the first time I saw you. I've loved you for years, literally centuries, you know that? Do you know that?"

"Doc? Are you a light drinker?" I smile at him and he begins to laugh.

"I don't ever drink." His speech is starting to slur. *How cute.*

"Since this is my going away party, you'll drink for me,

though, right?"

He grins and hick-ups.

"And then you'll go home and sleep and not tell Collin I'm at home dreaming, right?"

He smiles again.

"I knew I could count on you. Here's our next round. Drink up."

The bartender is studying us. "You know I can't let him leave if he drinks these. He's already looped."

"Don't worry, we're friends, celebrating a new beginning, right, *Ricky*?"

He burps and raises his glass to me before taking a sip.

"I'll give him a ride."

The bartender looks at me sideways. "How do I know you can handle your liquor better than he can?"

I down the third drink and set the glass on the bar. "Do I look like I can't handle my drink?"

He chuckles and smiles at me. "Don't get me in trouble. Get yourselves home in one piece, okay?"

Leaning on the bar so that my shirt opens enough to flash him a peek, I smile and flirt back. "I wouldn't think of getting you in trouble."

"Hey, don't flirt with my girl. She's mine tonight." Rick waves his arm across the surface of the bar to shoo the bartender away. "Give me one more a those apple things. They're better the more you have."

"I knew you'd like 'em." I smile and shove the next glass in front of him. "Drink up."

Before he can down the martini, nearly half of it spills in his lap then down his shirt as he slurps the last drops and sets his glass on the bar. "Delicious!"

Reaching for Rick's hands, I caress his fingers with mine while staring deep into his eyes. In his drunken state he opens his mind freely to me. I don't have to go too far back into his memory before having the information I need. Releasing his hands, I turn back to the drinks on the bar.

"Look! We both have only one more." I pick mine up and hold it in the air. He lifts his and I clink the edge of his glass with mine. "Salute!"

Before a drop reaches my lips, Rick stops me, waving his hand in the air. "Wait, what're we toasting to?" His speech is sloppy.

"Here's to…finding truth in the darkness, to drinking the poison that kills the evil lurking in corners and shadows."

"That's a rather odd toast, but here, here!" After spilling more alcohol in his lap, he swigs his drink as I watch, assessing his sobriety, or lack thereof. Satisfied he's well inebriated, I throw mine back and set my glass down.

Rick notices me watching with an empty glass in front of me. "How, how do you jrink those so fass?" His speech is more slurred, can barely get the words out. *Perfect.*

"Let's go, Doc. You're gonna need to sleep this off. Sorry for the headache you'll have later." I wink at the bartender and lead Doc to the door by the royal blue tie around his neck. I can feel the varying sets of eyes on my legs as we cross the room.

For most of the ride, his hand caresses my thigh and I allow it, trying to be patient with his drunkenness. Half a mile from his home, however, he turns to me and slides his right hand up my skirt. Before he reaches anything of significance, I make a hard left then a hard right to pass another car on the freeway, throwing him back into his seat.

Alcohol can bring out the worst in people. The part of their personality they're most ashamed of is usually the side that takes over when their defenses are numbed. I'm patient with Rick as he displays his hidden qualities, though. This is all part of my plan. He unwittingly played along.

At his home, I help him inside and to his room.

"Stay with me, Jaime. Sleep with me. I promise I'll be a gettl, gettleman." He pulls me onto his bed and tries to kiss me while his hand slips into my shirt.

"Oho, kay, drunk man. I'd love to stay, but I have a date with an angel." Pulling the covers over his body, I leave his suit and dress shoes on. "A nasty little rogue angel. Oh, and I'm gonna borrow some butterfly needles and a bit of tape, okay? Don't forget, I have those butterfly needles on me. Do you have any cyanide?" He grins and starts to mumble so I put a finger to my lips.

"What do you want with butter…butter…fly needles and cy…nide?" His voice fades as he falls asleep, a smile still caught on his face.

"That's my man."

I kneel down and slip a small box, lid lifted, under his bed. Before rising to my feet, I cover my fingers and lips with powder, and then reach for his hands and kiss him good night, leaving residue on his fingers and lips. Immediately going into the bathroom, I scrub my hands and mouth; then, I set to searching his home.

His massive living room has a large fireplace with mortared rock from floor to ceiling as a centerpiece. Not even the vaulted ceilings can diminish the impact. Impressive. The scent of burnt wood still lingers. As I reach out and touch the rough surface, I push away painful thoughts. That memory ends tonight. My fingers reach under the lip, feeling for the flue and the placement of the lever. It'll do.

There are several bedrooms as well as an expansive study with overloaded bookshelves, small bronze statues here and there, very similar to another room I've seen in my not too distant past. Pedestals throughout his home prop up larger marble and bronze pieces, a Cervantes' Don Quixote bronze in mid joust, Icarus in black marble, many more. Each of them is worth more than I make in a year. He has an interesting taste in décor. Tells a lot about the man.

One of Collin's vases, the one I recognize well, sits on a high shelf. I know Collin's pieces aren't cheap either. I had no idea Doc made so much in his small family practice. No wonder he was offended at Collin's offer of money for his assistance. That's definitely not what he was after.

Finding what I need, I leave, keeping his front door unlocked behind me. I have to get home and to sleep before Collin becomes suspicious. The fight has to be over before he tries to find me. Popping the sleeping pill in my mouth as I travel, I swallow it dry. The sedative effect should be acting on my body by the time I arrive.

When my head hits the pillow, my mind is clear. I know what to do. There will be no mistakes made this evening.

Tonight, I don't hunt demons. I hunt angels.

CHAPTER 18

When my eyes fully open, I find myself in a dim room. Someone's house, but whose? As dark as it is, the room still seems familiar. Not my bedroom. Doctor Stanton's. I look to his bed and see he's still asleep. They know me too well. Hopefully, I understand *them* even better.

The pair of pajama pants and sleeveless top I put on before going to sleep no longer cling to me. Instead, I'm wearing a thin, snug night-top that falls just below my bottom. Wonder whose idea this was? But then, that's the question of the night. Who is the one controlling this dream, for now? The anticipation speeds my heart.

Careful not to wake Doc, I exit to the hall, lock the front door, and feel my way to the living room where it all will take place. I have the advantage they hadn't expected. I'd searched and prepared the hunting ground before heading off to bed. Whether or not they had chosen this place for our final battle, I would have found a way to lead them here regardless.

I'll be watching the shadows tonight, remembering my grandmother's teachings. I focus on the surroundings, what has changed, what remains constant. Every curve, every sharp edge, is committed to my photographic memory. *Take it slow and remember everything. Don't rush a resolution this time. We have all night.* I'm not afraid, something I may need to remind myself of throughout the night.

The hallway spills into an enormous living room with vaulted ceilings and the fireplace with heavy rock. All still the same. I turn the Don Quixote bronze on its pedestal. *Wait.*

A new art piece sits against the opposite wall. Appears to be a large…cross. I remember my conversation with Rick about Jesus and being unable to imagine the pain He endured. Remembering those words, my skin turns cold and I begin to shiver. Surely, I hadn't anticipated this. My breathing has turned shallow and my pulse rate has increased. *I'm not afraid. Take a deep breath and relax.*

The room smells like the ocean. So far inland? Wind rustles nearby trees. There's movement in the shadows. Following the surge with my eyes, I remain still. Soon my gaze falls on a chair set in the middle of the room, in front of the fireplace. That wasn't there before either. Neither was the demon sitting in it. I shoot him a sideways glance, knowing he's not the one I'm searching for. He hasn't killed yet. Tonight is meant to be his first. I can see it in the tension of his body, the eagerness written all over his face. If I'm to survive this evening, I can't allow him to distract me. That's what they want.

"Didn't expect ya ta be so lovely." I hate how demons always think they're slick in their dream state. My stomach turns.

Instead of responding in kind, I ignore him, reminding myself again he's not the one. If I kill him now, the dream would finish and we'd have to wait for another night and start all over again. I've prepared too well to finish before the planned outcome. The attacks from these rogue angels will end tonight.

More movement in the shadows. A presence in the kitchen, one near the fireplace, behind the sofa. Demon standing behind me. I can feel others, not exactly sure how many or if they're demon or angel, but the ones I'm looking for and most concerned about haven't yet shown.

The demon rises from the chair and reaches for me. "Hey, I'm talking to you." He turns me to face him. "I was promised my time with you," he sputters and pulls me into him, pressing his mouth hard against mine.

Shoving him backward in disgust, I turn away. "I don't have time for you tonight. You, I'll kill another time."

"What makes you think I won't kill *you*?"

When he reaches for my arm, his rage is evident. As he pulls me toward him again, the ones in the shadows move, descending upon us in a whirlwind of motion. Drawing up my strength, I throw the demon across the room as hard as I can. He slams into a wall, head snapping back to dent the sheetrock. Good, it will keep him away from me for a moment. Hopefully, a moment is long enough. I reach into the darkness, tangling my fingers in a tassel of hair. My arm yanks backward and suddenly I'm whipped around. Something sharp slices my cheek, but I don't allow it to faze me. My focus is on the one I have trapped by the hair in my clutches and the others circling around me. The angel caught in my fingers shrieks in fear—a very feminine shriek—as I slam her against the wall.

With her body pinned, I move in closer to see her face. She isn't Sarah, but she *is* familiar. The blond woman in the gallery who kept hanging on Collin. *Ha!* I wondered if I'd see her again. Didn't place her as an angel, though. I wonder how many rogues Collin and I had surrounding us.

The confident smirk leaves her face and I can't help but smile. "This'll be easy."

Her eyes grow huge, knowing she's about to die and my hands quickly snap her neck. No time to play with my prey tonight. Besides, this is different. These aren't demons.

When her body slips to the floor, the other angels circle me. Two of them will be exceptionally strong. They won't be as simple. There's one in the kitchen, one on each side of the fireplace, one in the hall.

The demon is on the floor near the chair, rising back to his feet. "I'm gonna kill someone."

"That *is* their plan." I say it mostly to myself.

Soon enough, he's recovered and rushing me, but I hold out my hand without looking his direction. Unprepared for my reaction, he skids to a halt.

"I'm *not* the one you want to fight tonight. Like I said, I'm not planning to kill you." My eyes and attention don't leave the shadows.

The energy of the circling angels increases. "You might wanna move," I tell him, still standing an arm's length away.

"Huh?" *Too late.*

The assault is more directed this time, better planned and their patsy is knocked against the wall. This rogue is male, shoulder-length hair, tall with broad shoulders and I know he must be taken out immediately. As I focus on him, another races from the shadows toward me. Some asshole hiding in the shadows so I couldn't see them launching forward. Before I can react, the male rogue knocks me across the face with the back of his hand. *Not bad*. Made my lip bleed. I smile at him and grab his shirt, throw him across the room, my smile increasing as his back slams against the kitchen counter.

While still recovering from the throw, the shadow rogue rushes toward me again. I manage to raise my hands to block him, for the most part, but the impact still drives my own arms into my abdomen. I may be healed, but my wounds are still tender. Doubled over with pain for a second, I've forgotten to watch the next one I intend to kill. My failure is his break.

In a flash he's at my side, reaching for my hair and pulling me into the kitchen. In a moment of panic, I grab his hand and try to plant my feet in the cold tile. As I've mentioned, the kitchen is not my favorite place to fight.

He opens a drawer to retrieve a butcher knife, but I slam the drawer on his hand with my foot. Screaming in agony, he releases me, cradling his broken fingers. Three others track me from the shadows, waiting for an opportunity. This one's too big to snap his neck. I'll need something sharp.

Facing him, my eyes on the ones in the darkness, I step backward and he follows. He wants to be the one to trap me. I let him believe he's good enough, pretending to be afraid. Once past the counter, I turn and run into the living room as fast as my legs allow. Thankfully, he's dumb enough to assume I'm that weak and follows full sprint. When I slow, he gains fast. The other three follow. Reaching the Don Quixote bronze, I step to the side. Fortunately for me, he doesn't see the long, metal staff pointing toward him. The rogue impales himself on the statue all the way up the metal arm, the tip of the staff exiting his back. He blinks in amazement.

The demon watches with respect for my skill, but I also sense his fear of me. "What's your name?" I ask, trying to create a connection.

He seems startled I'd asked. "G-Gilbert."

"Gilbert, stay out of my way, okay?"

He doesn't say a word but slips into the shadows to watch.

Three to go. Weakest ones out of the way. Now the fight becomes interesting. Now I slow the pace. If the fight progresses too quickly, the ones I'm waiting for won't show themselves. They all need to participate. It's the only way I'll truly be free of them.

With my head turned downward, I listen to the soul of the house. The silver brick and wooden slats breathe as I breathe, absorbing the energy of my battle. The ones in the shadows pant, eager to have a piece of me. I taste blood on my tongue. Not mine. One of them has a love for it. Makes it part of the kill. Part of the torture. The scent of perfume fills the air.

Sarah.

I don't kid myself that she wore it by accident. She wanted me to recognize her. Makes me want to kill her more. I always hated her perfume.

I know what's to come and what I'll endure in order to draw out the ones still hiding, and I'm ready. They have to believe I'm weakened, bolstering their confidence and readiness to rush the resolution while I patiently wait. Lowering my guard to commence the next phase of my plan, I brace myself while trying to look casual. I wince as my face suddenly rebounds from a sharp hit.

The strike was greater than I'd expected, forcing me to reach out for something to stop my body from flying to the floor. Abs tensing, I take a swift kick to the stomach and try to look like it hurt more than it did. I want her to think she's hurting me, weakening me. And she's dumb enough to believe it. Her assumption is my gain.

Soon I'm lifted into the air and thrown against the wall. I struggle to breathe as the impact knocks the air from me. Staring into the eyes of my employee, I feel the other two tie rope around my wrists, cinching them together behind my back. The rogues who grabbed me slip back into the shadows while Sarah faces me down. I'm only slightly disappointed she turned out to be a fink. The way she'd grow to annoy me, I look forward to the opportunity to beat the shit out of her before I kill her and bury that fucking perfume with her.

Gritting my teeth, I glare into her eyes. "You're fired."

She laughs and throws me to the floor beside the chair, kicking me again. A deep, cleansing breath clears my mind after the assault. The demon is still watching from the corner. One of the rogue angels watches from the kitchen, the other is missing, maybe the hallway. Not exactly sure where he went.

Sarah lifts me from the ground by my hair and sets me in the seat, securing my tied hands behind the wooden back so I can't move. When my ankles are secured to the two front legs, she kneels in front of me and wraps her hands around my neck, tightening them slowly until I start to choke. My hands struggle with the ropes at my wrists.

"In the preexistence, I was called Sariah. I watched you and Michael fight like warriors, like your very existence depended on our victory. I respected you for that. But you never even glanced in my direction, never even noticed me. Do you see me now?" Her face appears child-like as if she's waiting for a parent's approval. With her fingers tightening around my trachea, I find it hard to give her what she desires and glare back at her.

"Jaime Connor, tainted archangel. All the others fear you. Ha!" She lets go of my throat moments before I lose consciousness. "Now they'll fear me."

In a ridiculously dramatic move, she brings her arm across her body, swinging back toward my face. The blow causes me to bite my tongue and the taste of the iron in my blood fills my mouth, flowing down the back of my throat. My breathing becomes labored and my heart is pounding in my chest. Closing my eyes, I take a deep breath again, clearing my mind, remembering what I was taught. I begin to chuckle.

Sarah walks away and into the kitchen, reaching into a drawer, taking her time returning. A steel blade glints in the moonlight streaming through the window. Soon she's back at my side, crouched in front of me and holding a steak knife where I can see.

"Did you know that serrated edges are duller than flat ones? I know, huh? Who would've thought? That is, if you take good care of your cutlery," she says and rubs the blade against her arm as if such a move would intimidate me. What a putz. "That's why it hurts so much when you get cut by one of these."

Watching her movements while tracking the rogues still waiting in the shadows, I stay silent. Words are wasted on a fool.

"What's the matter? Not talkative today? Never much for conversation, are you? I always hated that about you." She presses the blade against my thigh and then yanks it across, cutting deep into my skin. With my head thrown back, I gasp, trying to hide my pain. The pleasure she feels in seeing me flinch is evident. Her hands are trembling with excitement.

The killers in the shadows grow restless as she lifts my top and lays the knife against my ribs. Without another word, she pulls it quickly away, strafing my skin. I bite the inside of my mouth to keep her from seeing the pain in my eyes.

"You like that, huh? I thought you would. You always seemed to love pain. I've watched you in the shadows for so long. Watched you toy with demons, letting them play with you before taking them down, even letting them cut you. Half expected you'd go all the way one of these days. That's when I realized how much you love pain, how erotic it was for you. Am I right in my assessment, Jaime? You like a little alone time with a demon, don't you? We have one here for you if you like." Sarah licks my blood from the knife.

Really? As if licking blood off a knife would scare me. She was always one for foolish antics. I can't help but laugh, stirring her anger, causing her to backhand me, but I can't stop chuckling.

Furious, she jerks the knife up to my throat. "Do you know how easy it would be to end it right now?" Calming her rage, she hesitates then smiles. "The great dark angel falls."

Silliness. She's wasting my time. Why can't she just get on with it?

As she puts pressure on the blade against my trachea, there's a sound in the hallway. Footsteps. Sarah rises to her feet, putting a finger to her lips.

"Jaime? Is that you?"

"Rick?"

With the help of another, Sarah lunges for him, tackling him to the floor. Rick fights to be free, but they're too strong for him. As I watch, they drag him from the shadows and into the room. He's still wearing the suit he'd worn to bed, black dress shoes still on his feet.

Noticing the rogue impaled on his statue and the blond with a broken neck, he can't take his eyes off them. The two rogues drag him to the cross in the living room and tie his hands to the crossbeam while he fights with them.

"Welcome, Doc. We've been waiting for you to join us. You see, this whole night wouldn't be complete without a spectator."

"Let her go. Do whatever you want with me, but let her go." His eyes show fear, but I'm not overly convinced.

"What d'ya know, Jaime? You got an admirer. You gonna let him sacrifice his life for you?"

I know their game and still won't give her what she wants. "Ha! That's what I thought."

As Sarah raises her knife to his throat, Rick fights against the restraints. "What do you want from her?"

"Well, Doc, I'd love to kill her, but we're better off if she joins us. Our *power* would be *unmatched*." The sarcastic slant of Sarah's words shows the disdain she feels for me and I realize she's not the one calling the shots. Someone else has forced her to restrain the desire to kill me. "And if she refuses to join..." Sarah reaches the knife to his chest and cuts through his shirt, into the flesh beneath, causing him to cry out in pain.

Rick shoots her an angry glare, struggling against the ropes. "Jaime, don't do it."

"I don't intend to." My reply is delivered flat and honest, surprising and confusing him. I can barely control the urge to laugh in his face. His performance is pathetic.

Sarah's head perks up. "She speaks," she quips and allows the hand holding the knife to fall to her side as she saunters over to me. Moving around to the back of the chair, she reaches for my hair, pulling my head back to expose my throat. The knife raised, she presses it against the thin flesh until I feel the trickle of cooled blood running down my neck and into my hair.

"If you don't join us, you'll die. Then, we'll cut your doctor friend to small pieces in his sleep."

"Like you did to that family?"

She smiles. "Exactly the same."

"How're you gonna kill *me, Sariah,* bore me to death? Please, put me out of my misery now so I don't have to watch you embarrass yourself."

Sarah's mouth tightens. Moving the knife from my throat to the top of my shoulder, she slices open the flesh. Then, she leans forward with her lips close to my ear. "Soon. But first, we're gonna let our friend have some fun before it's all over, then I'll wrap it up."

She waves to the demon in the corner and he shakes his head, his eyes wide with dread.

I can't help laughing at her. "You have no idea how lame this is."

Glaring back at me, Sarah slaps me so hard my face stings,

but I still can't stop laughing.

Her lip curls at Gilbert. "What did I bring you for? If you don't do what I say, I'll kill you right here."

"No, she won't, Gilbert. She needs you. At least for now."

"This is the only reason you're here. I swear I'll end you right now if you don't." She revealed something important. I counted on her to be the idiot I knew she would be.

Hunched down in the shadows, Gilbert thinks about what Sarah told him and then starts from the corner, toward me. I see his fear of me, but his desire is slightly greater.

"That's it. She can't stop you. She's tied up."

When Gilbert reaches me, he straddles my legs and grabs hold of my hair, pulling my head back again.

Looking up into his eyes, I make sure my expression is confident in spite of my fear. "Don't do this, Gil."

He leans over my face and whispers to me. "I'm sorry. You know she's making me do this. Please don't kill me." He starts to kiss my cheek, moving down to my throat.

Rick lets out a guttural yell. "No. Don't do it. She'll join you. I'll talk her into it, she'll listen to me. I promise. Just stop." His speech isn't as convincing as I would've anticipated. He'd performed better the past few days.

Sarah turns to me. "Well, what do you say?" She slices Rick's shoulder, still staring at me.

He grits his teeth before crying out. Then, he turns his eyes to mine. "Jaime, please, if not for you, then for me. You're an archangel. You don't feel pain like mortals. If you love me, you won't make me suffer like this."

The traitorous display is appalling and I can only narrow my eyes at him while shaking my head. Sarah can see the answer in my eyes.

She turns to Rick. "Sorry, lover, you're not the prize, just the entertainment." She reaches her hand up to his face and cuts his cheek with the steak knife.

"Stop it, Sarah."

The voice comes from the shadows near the fireplace. I smell the moors of Ireland and hear the slight lilt in his voice, causing my heart to beat faster. He wasn't supposed to be asleep yet. As he appears from the darkness, I shake my head at him, trying to tell him to leave. I have this under control.

Collin notices the demon straddling me, hands on my body and he lowers his head, narrowing his eyes at him.

"Take your hands off her or I'll end you now." His voice is deep with anger, eyes focused directly on him.

Gilbert shudders before letting his hands slip from my body.

"Don't you dare move away from her, Gilbert. I swear I'll kill you right here." Sarah isn't fazed by Collin's appearance. She must've been expecting him.

After silently acknowledging Sarah, Collin turns to the woman beside her. "Mandy." His jaw is tight, the look of a killer in his eyes.

His receptionist. Why didn't I recognize her?

"Sorry, Jaime, I couldn't let you do this alone. When Rick called I got there as fast as I could, but you were already asleep." *Rick*. Jackass.

"You aren't supposed to be here, Collin. I have this handled."

"Yeah, I can see that." He reaches for the ropes, untying one of Rick's hands.

"Collin! No!"

Before he turns to me, Rick has his other hand free and surprises Collin, pulling a necktie around his throat and throwing him off balance. He immediately pulls backward toward the cross and fastens Collin to the upright beam before he can begin to fight back.

CHAPTER 19

"No!" My mind reels and my body quivers. I try to control my panic but am afraid it may be a losing battle. This wasn't supposed to happen.

Mandy has moved behind Collin, holding him by the tie around his throat, while Sarah and Rick struggle to wrap ligatures around his wrists and secure them to the crossbeam. Collin pulls one arm free and punches Rick in the jaw, knocking him to the floor. Then, he reaches for Sarah. Seeing what happened to Rick, she shoves the knife deep into the left side of Collin's abdomen and pulls the blade sideways, making a deep, wide gash. Mandy yanks on the tie again until he chokes.

Collin reaches for his side to remove the knife instead of fighting. I can tell he's in agony, weakened by the injury. This is going terribly wrong. Just his presence here has ruined my plans and may change the outcome. I don't know what I'll do now. We may lose after all.

Rick shakes his head and recovers fairly quickly, rising to his feet and glaring at Collin. He and Sarah finish securing Collin's arms. Then, Sarah and Mandy loop the rope around his ankles and tie them to the base of the wooden plank.

I know pleading for his life won't help. Begging is what they want from me, and I'm not a good beggar.

Rick stares Collin in the eyes for what seems like several minutes but is possibly seconds. My mind won't allow me to track moments, just events as they happen.

"Your girlfriend has a better right hook. Still, you'll pay for that. I'll show you pain you've never felt before, *Collin*. I promise."

"Rick, I swear, if you don't stop…" My words are growled between clenched teeth.

He rubs his jaw where Collin hit him. "Oh, don't swear, lovely Jaime, it's not appropriate."

His movements are deliberate as he crosses the room to a cabinet, pulling open a drawer and removing a long black leather pouch. He returns to stand in front of the cross. Crouching by the ottoman between me and Collin, he stares into my eyes as he opens it to show a line of surgical tools. His motions are measured and cautious as he lays open the contents, wanting me to be keenly aware of what he's doing. One at a time, he lifts different pieces with sharp points or razor edges. Selecting one, he looks up into my eyes and rises to his feet, and then turns to Collin.

"This one is my sharpest I believe. It doesn't hurt as much while it cuts." He makes two parallel incisions—around an eighth of an inch apart—through Collin's clothing and into his chest. Blood immediately soaks his shirt. "But it can facilitate an opportunity to create excruciating pain." He cuts an intersecting incision, marking an open rectangle in his flesh. Then, Rick grabs the cut section of skin and rips it from Collin's body like a piece of cloth.

The room is warm, but my body shudders, feeling ice cold as Collin screams in pain. He works to free his hands of the restraints. Bile rises up my throat at the sight of his torn flesh.

"You know, Jaime, this is a very difficult thing for me right now. Seeing this man hanging here." Doc makes three more incisions in Collin's skin then tears again. "Reminds me of that terrible, terrible day. Do you remember?" He turns to me with a serious expression. "The day they nailed Christ to the cross."

I shake my head 'no' as Sarah hands Rick a nail and he centers it in the middle of Collin's hand. He whispers in Collin's ear, "Don't move, 'cause this is gonna hurt." Then, he turns back to me. "Do you remember, Jaime? We discussed it not too long ago. You expressed concern over how much *pain* He endured." Mandy hands him a hammer and he gives her the scalpel. "Well, I agree. From a doctor's perspective, I can promise you it was painful. Very, *very* painful. Each pound of the spike…" He drives the nail into the hand and Collin throws his head back in agony, trying not to show his suffering.

"Collin! Rick, stop it!"

"Was like they were hammering a spike,"—he hits the nail again, driving it into the wood and my body jolts at the sound—"into my heart. Did you feel the same, Jaime?"

"Stop it! Rick, stop it! Leave him out of this. You want me, not him."

"You're so right, Jaime. I *do* want you." He crosses over to Collin's other side and drives another nail through his other palm into the wood. Collin's blood pours over his hands and drips to the floor.

"Rick! Put the hammer down."

As my voice echoes through the house, Rick turns and smiles, dropping the tool to the floor. "As you wish. See how simple that was?"

My body shakes uncontrollably as Collin coughs, trying to catch his breath. Sarah reaches for his shirt and rips it the rest of the way open and I can clearly see the section of exposed muscle where Rick had torn his skin away. Feeling the bile rising into my throat again, I have to close my eyes and catch my breath.

When I open them, Sarah is running her hands over Collin's chest, digging her nails into the fresh wounds. Collin grits his teeth and closes his eyes, his muscles twitching in pain. For the first time I'm powerless to stop what's happening, unable to save someone who's being tortured in front of me.

Sarah kisses his lips, moves to his neck, turning every now and then to see my expression. She turns his face to hers. "I always found you *hot,*" she says and presses her lips to his.

Although I know she's doing this only to anger me, I still want to rip every hair out of her empty head.

Covering his mouth with hers, she brings the steak knife to his upper arm. With a quick motion, she slices open his skin and blood flows over his bicep as she gasps in appreciation. The sight of his agony is turning her on. She reaches for his face with her right hand, passionately kissing him again as her left hand brings the blade to the other side of his chest and cuts him again. He flinches in pain. Then, she lowers the knife to his ribs.

"Sarah." I say her name as calmly as I am able.

She turns to me and smiles. "Yes, Jaime?"

My head is lowered and my eyes are set on her. "I'm gonna kill you." My body still trembles with anger.

She stops touching Collin for a moment, unable to control a shudder. She knows what I'm capable of. As she said, she's watched me for years. After a moment, a nervous smile returns to her lips. "Not if I kill you first."

"You say that with a lack of confidence." I release a sarcastic breath and glare back, my head still lowered, eyes still on her.

Collin chokes again and takes several deep breaths. "Jaime? Are you okay?" His voice is unsteady as he tries to hide his pain.

"I'm fine, Babe. I have it all under control."

Rick pulls Gilbert off my lap and shoves him toward the sofa. "Why am I not convinced? Why do I think you don't have anything within your control right now, Jaime? Or should I say *Jerrica*? I miss hearing that name. So heavenly. Why in the hell did your parents change it when you were born?"

Gilbert scrambles to his feet and I track his movements into the shadows behind the cross. "To hide me from sick bastards like you, I suppose."

The pale moonlight illuminates the room as I now glare into the eyes of a traitor, my captain, my confidant. Unaffected by my rage toward him, Rick runs his hand across my cheek, wiping away thickening blood. Then, he moves his fingers down to my shoulders, pressing on the cut from Sarah. I feel his fingers, wet and red, slip up to my throat, pressing against my trachea and he breathes heavily as if it brings him pleasure. He closes his eyes for a moment, reveling in the sickness infecting his soul. When his eyes open again, he stares into mine.

Glaring back at him, I grit my teeth. "I'm gonna kill *you*, too."

"Jerrica, Jerrica. No one has to die tonight. Well, except those two." He turns toward the two dead angels. "And maybe *him*." He tilts his head toward Collin then crouches in front of me. "I always hated him, you know. Couldn't understand what you saw in him. But I always loved *you*." He draws his finger down my chest to the first button on my shirt. "And I can't get the picture out of my mind, that tight skirt you wore to the bar tonight. Oh…" Lowering his hands to my thighs, he slips them under the shirt I'm wearing.

"Get away from her, Rick." Collin's jaw is set and I can feel the fury quickening his pulse as he fights the ropes and nails holding him to the cross.

"Can't do that, Collin. You see, I've been waiting for this moment for a real long time."

Sarah runs her fingers over Collin's body, spreading his blood over the sections of skin she hasn't yet set her knife to. Taking a deep breath, I remind myself I'm not afraid. For him or for myself. I clear my mind. Don't forget what I was taught.

Collin grits his teeth. "Rick, I'm gonna kill you."

My eyes are set when I look the doctor in the eyes. "Don't worry, Babe. Got that covered."

But Rick is confident. "Wow, you two are quite the couple, talking about killing people and all." *Sarcastic bastard.* He kneels beside my chair, propping his elbows on my thighs, his chin resting in the palms of his hands. "How long have you known?"

Turning from him, I watch Sarah press her body against Collin's and run the blade over his back. With my teeth grinding together, I narrow my eyes. She reaches down to his jeans, unbuttoning and sliding them to his ankles. Her hand lowers and slices open his thigh.

Grabbing hold of my jaw, Rick turns my head to face him. "How long have you known?"

Controlling the venom in my soul, I glare back at him. Then, I laugh in his face. "You were good, a pretty good actor. That's excluding your awful performance a few minutes ago. You were so brilliant at covering up your true nature until last night." When I hesitate, he nods at me as if to say, *go on*. "But then, you hugged me before you left. *Sloppy*. Your cologne wore off, Rick. I smelled Washington on you. I heard the wind in the forest trees in your breathing. That was your first mistake."

With a smirk on his face, Rick stands, removes his suit jacket, and slowly rolls up his sleeves. A fresh, thin cut marks his forearm. He was in the shadows in my dream in the hospital, trying to kill Collin, maybe the one who stabbed me with his scalpel. More notable, though, are the long, thick scars that mark the insides of his wrists.

My breathing becomes deep and my heart races again. My eyes close, my body trembling as if I'm freezing. *No.* This is what he wants. He needs me to know he was the one. The plan is to frighten me, make me weak enough that when they begin to torture me I won't have my typical resolve and will, in time, give in.

I have to remember their tactic. They know that most minds can't endure continuous torture. Any person will do anything to make it stop, even give in to their attacker. Too many angels have turned under prolonged torment being inflicted by other rogue angels, turning them jaded, angry that they were left ill-equipped to overcome such abuse. I can only guess this will be the plan in their attempt to turn me.

Ignoring the marks on his arms, I take several deep breaths and clear my mind. I won't remember that night. It's not time, not yet.

Maintaining sight of my plan, I keep talking, hoping he'll be the one to make a mistake, give me my opportunity. "After I recognized your scent it all fell in place, the gallery showing was when you bought that."

He looks up to the shelf with Collin's crystal vase, tulips rimming the edge. Then, he smiles and turns back to me.

"You wore your Breitling watch that night. But you were clever enough to keep me from seeing your face, knowing I'd recognize you. I saw that watch when you accidentally wore it to my house last night, however."

He smiles as if he's admiring my attention to detail.

"That night in Phillip Bradley's office was when I first caught your scent. I suppose that was intentional since I never noticed it before when you watched me while I dreamt. Phillip. He was your older brother from a different father, am I right? Thus, the last names that didn't match, but the same blue eyes and similar taste in decor. Not a dark angel, not an angel at all, that one. He liked to strangle the women he violated. You learned a lot from watching him, your *big brother*. He even used some of your neckties." I nod to his chest and he looks down at his blue tie.

His face sets into a smug look. Hell, it radiates off him. I keep playing to it although he repulses me.

"You killed demons, but you couldn't kill him, the brother you've looked up to since you were young. Soon you started enjoying watching him kill, got a cheap thrill out of it. Even better, that night I met up with him, seeing his hands on me like I was his secretary. You wished for more, didn't you? Would've loved to see him go further before I killed him, living out your voyeuristic fantasy. What a disappointment. Regardless, Big Brother finally had to go. You let your own sibling be killed by me because he would've exposed you as an accomplice if he was caught. Even if you were exonerated, it could've interrupted your ability to practice medicine. What woman wants to be examined by the sketchy brother of a serial rapist/murderer? *Pathetic*."

He glares at me for my last comment as he approaches and kneels beside me again. But I'm not done yet.

"The dream about Collin's gallery, you gave Sarah the Versed to slip into my water at work, knowing it wouldn't only put me into a deep sleep, but cause me to forget everything that happened. I was in my office at the end of the day so no one would have known I'd fallen asleep. After everyone had left, except for you and Sarah that is, you drove me to the gallery to create the connection between the two of us, me and Collin. The fight actually took place there, not just in our minds. I don't remember going in and I don't remember you throwing the demon out before Mandy locked the door. After the fight, you dragged me home and threw me in my bed while Sarah trailed with my car. It's as if I'd had a normal evening except for the intervening hours I couldn't explain. By the way, what did you do to me before Sarah arrived, or maybe while she watched? My torn bed sheets don't fit the scenario."

The pleasure in his eyes is abundantly evident. "Oh, he doesn't deserve you. You're way too clever."

I ignore the comment; glad his focus is on me instead of Collin. "My confusion grew because I didn't remember the dream. You brought Collin into the hunt to set us against each other, one thinking the other was a demon or a rogue. To keep us from realizing you and Sarah were the rogues and the demon wasn't even in the fight. They watched from the shadows after locking the door. You planned on me and Collin fighting each other even worked to stoke hatred. But you didn't count on the strong attraction between the two of us. Foolish move when your target was me all along."

Rick's jaw tightens as he quickly glances over to Sarah. I wonder about this subconscious reaction.

"You saved Gilbert for the bigger fight, tonight. What he doesn't realize is that someone has to die—not one of us, a demon—before we can leave this nightmare. You brought him to draw us here and you'll keep him until you're ready for it to be over, I've turned or I'm dead. Then, you'll kill him. It's your only way out."

I turn to Sarah and Collin, his body covered in blood now.

She's slowed her cutting but hasn't stopped.

"The night on Gold Camp Road, when I threw you into the water, I didn't know you were an angel or I'd have known it wouldn't work. You were still there, right behind me, holding me down with one of your coveted neckties while Sarah impaled me with the shower curtain rod. An upright gentleman."

"Jerrica..." Rick sounds condescending, like the first time I met him in his clinic. "All that is past. You know, this never would've happened if it wasn't for *him*." He tilts toward Collin again. "He's right. It *is* his fault, everything."

Circling my chair, he stops behind me, putting his hands on my shoulders. "When I found out they were sending you down to be a dark angel, also..."

He grips my skin firmly and laughs. His hand on the cut flesh sends a sharp pain through my arm. I feel like I can't breathe from the anxiety taking over my body.

"I couldn't believe it. Nobody could. We all thought they'd keep you there with Michael." His hands slide down my arms and he leans over until his lips touch my ear. "I thought you'd be by his side for an eternity. You were both always so cozy." He releases me and moves back in front of me. "But you came to earth instead, with no idea what a big deal that was. Not Jesus Christ big, but still, pretty damned big."

Rick sits on the ottoman and his eyes quickly dart to a shadow, his attention momentarily distracted, and I make note of this subtle, involuntary response. His attention returned to me again, he picks up a scalpel and scrapes beneath his nails, wiping the rest on his pants. "You know, some of us worried Michael would follow you. But when he didn't and we realized you were here alone...I can't even begin to tell you how thrilled I was, how excited we all were." His gaze moves above my head. I assume he's visualizing something from his past, maybe *our* past.

His expression turns dark as his eyes return to mine. "But *he* had to go and screw it all up. Ordaining in advance, snatching you up for his self before even Michael could have any say. If it had been Michael making his claim on you, no one would've batted an eye, but *him*? Just another archangel you didn't even *know*? Even worse, he didn't let you make the choice, didn't tell you what he was up to. And *they* allowed. They *sealed* it!"

"Oh, my God. Shut up. Just shut the hell up. There was nothing between Michael and me. We fought together. Nothing more."

Rick chuckles at me. "You're still oblivious. Every male angel wanted you, even Michael."

"*If* I believed that, maybe the only reason I'm *oblivious*, as you say, is because I don't care. You minimize everything we did like it was some sort of heavenly dating service rather than a battle for our free agency. My loyalty isn't to an angel. And my allegiance isn't to the one who was fighting beside me in the pre-existence."

"Then, who are you aligned with, Jerrica? Lucifer? Ah ha, I know *he's* not the one. But, God? The one who deserted you here on this planet like a bundle of rotting flesh? Who left you to be soiled by demons and destroyed by rogue angels? Not much better than what you'd expect from Lucifer, wouldn't you say? You've always made poor choices, Jerrica. You're still on the wrong team."

"Only if I follow someone like you."

Out of the corner of my eye I see his jaw tighten and his eyes flick to a shadow once again. I feel his anger mounting. After a moment, he takes a breath and calms himself. "I know you don't mean that."

Reaching for my jaw again, he turns me toward him. When

his lips meet mine, I tilt my head backward and away from him. The fury over my rejection shows in his eyes. "Oh, you *will* kiss me, Jerrica." He grabs me by the hair at the back of my head and pulls me forward, pressing my lips into his. He slides his hands down my arms and over my body. Now *my* anger is mounting and I bite until he pulls away.

Laughing as if I've told him a joke, he wipes away the blood on his lips. "You see; I *love* that about you. You like it rough. Just like the old days. You've always fought with a fury few others could match. Even Michael admired your strength. And I was right there to witness your intensity. Always there. You were a Goddess to me. *God*, I miss fighting by your side! Can't you see, Jerrica? This is meant to be, the only way for you and me to be together. I know how you feel about me deep down inside, even if you can't see it, yet. Once you do, though, you'll realize how spectacular we can be together. Imagine, you and me, fighting side by side again. I can see by the way you fight demons; you miss those days as much as I."

Brushing my cheek with the back of his fingers, he leans over and kisses it lightly. If he could only see how his touch makes me sick. I may never be able to scrub the feeling of him from my skin.

"I've waited patiently, hoping you'd fall in love with me. And each day I saw you falling deeper for Collin, smelling *Ireland* on him, craving the home where you once felt safe. I smell like the home you ran away from, the place where you're haunted by memories of a murdered father and the fear of death. No way for me to compete."

He looks down at the floor with the look of dejection in his eyes. Then, he stands and walks toward the cross. "If Collin wasn't around, if we could've killed him before you two ever met, you'd have fallen for me instead."

Taking the knife from Sarah, he turns it in his hand and

examines it. Collin's blood drips from the serrated edge to the carpeted floor. "There's no doubt in my mind. I would have convinced you to join us without all this drama." Laying the knife on Collin's arm, Rick grits his teeth and pulls it backward, cutting his flesh while staring him in the eyes. "Tonight would've never happened. I could've saved you from all of this." He turns back to me. "The violence of this past week…avoided. You know, it wasn't *my* strategy to get the two of you together. *Someone* thought it was the only option to get you *both* out of the way." He hands the steak knife back to Sarah, glaring at her for a brief moment. "The two of you kept killing our demons, ruining far too many plans and none of us could kill Collin no matter how hard we tried."

Sarah flashes a wry grin at Rick as he turns his gaze from her and returns to me. The animosity between them is evident. An unusual dynamic. When he reaches my side again, I can still feel his anger toward her and now I wonder who's really in charge.

"Once it happened, you meeting *him,* I was stuck with the outcome." Rick kneels in front of me with his hands on my knees. "Can't you see? If you take Collin from the equation, I'm the one you'd be with. I'm the one you fall in love with. I have the same passion for you but with more of that danger you love so much. Unlike *him,* I'll stand back and watch, even enjoy it, when you allow a demon to touch you. Then, when we kill him together, we'll make passionate love."

His hands glide up my thighs again and I close my eyes, trying to forget he's touching me. "I can only imagine what it'd be like with you. That is, with you enjoying me as much as I'm enjoying you. By the way, did you know that once you've fallen asleep, it takes more than two hours for you to slip into REM?"

My eyes snap open and I glare at him in astonishment.

"That's right. I've timed you on many occasions. Most people take ninety minutes, give or take. More than *two hours*. That's a lot, Jerrica. You're vulnerable that whole time to someone in the shadows, someone who may be watching you sleeping. What do you think could happen in those two, long hours?" His eyes practically glow in the dim light.

My stomach tightens as I absorb what he's insinuating. Did he do more to me in my sleep than I'm aware? I can't look at him anymore and turn to Collin instead.

From my peripheral vision, I see Rick scowl at my reaction. His hand reaches for my hair, forcing me to face him again. "I'm the only one who can save you now! He's the one who put you in this predicament, remember? And I *will* make him pay for what he's done to you. And I'll give you the opportunity to decide how he dies. If you join me, I'll end it quickly, just a little pain. But if you don't, I'll tear his skin from his body, every inch of him. When I'm done you won't recognize him, I promise you won't."

Ill from the thought of all he's revealed, I close my eyes and the vision of my father passes through my mind. He had the same tears on his body. Blood and flesh littered my parents' bed and floor. My body shudders again and I can't stop my knees from shaking. Collin was right. What they have planned is worse than I could have imagined.

Rick strokes my hair, causing me to startle. He kisses my cheek again. "Are you too poisoned by him that you can't find a way to live the rest of your life with me, Jerrica? I know you have feelings for me. We can have a satisfying life together if you'll open your heart to me. Can you try? Do you remember when you told me you loved me? Do you remember it like I do?"

Now is the moment. This scene changes right here. I have

to play it right or it could go terribly wrong. I'm prepared. *I'm not afraid.* Deep breath. My eyes turn to his, flat and honest. "How could I forget? I felt *sick* when I lied to you like that."

He stands, his eyes burning with rage. "No." Pulling his arm across his body, he prepares to backhand me.

Taking another deep breath, I lean forward and stare up into his eyes, ready to accept the blow. "My name isn't Jerrica. It's Jaime, and I'm not afraid of you."

He hesitates for a moment before swinging his arm.

Collin sees him strike me and fights to pull the nails through his hands to free himself. "Stanton! Stop or I swear…"

Fury still dilating his eyes, Rick reaches down to untie my ankles and then moves behind the chair to loosen my hands with my wrists still bound together behind my back. Grabbing me by the shoulders, he lifts me from the seat and throws me to my knees by the ottoman, directly in front of Collin.

Wait. No. This isn't what I'd planned. This isn't my plan at all. It's his. When I look up at Collin, he can see the horror in my eyes and fights even harder to pull free of the nails binding him to the cross. I have to lower my eyes. He can't know what I'm feeling or what I'm thinking at this stage.

Rick drops to his knees behind me and shoves me forward against the cushion. In my arrogance, I'd pushed him too far too fast. I can't believe I've hastened a completion. It wasn't supposed to happen this way.

"I'll break every bone in every one of your fingers, slowly and methodically, until you're screaming in agony. Then, I'll move up your hand until you're begging me to stop." His words are tense like he's gritting his teeth. "I'll cut *him* up to show what you'll endure in your last hours. And if you still can't find it in your heart to love me after that, I'll begin, slowly, tearing *you* apart until you bleed from every inch of your body. That'll take days so I made sure to take some time off from work before entering this dream. I wanted to be prepared." A clink like the rattle of a belt buckle captures my attention. His hands are pulling at something behind me, but I can't see what he's doing while he rants in my ear.

"When you're a bloody mess and you don't think you could possibly feel greater agony, I'll let Sarah pull your hair from your head, one small segment at a time. That's her forte, you know, creating pain you couldn't imagine existed. And by the time she finishes, I won't want you anymore and she might as well kill you to satisfy her own *hatred* for you. But, before we begin with all that, I'll have what *I* want and I'll have you until I don't want it anymore. That alone could take hours. You may be impressed to know I have *amazing* stamina."

One of his hands shoves my face into the padding while he reaches for a surgical instrument. I fight to breathe, terror taking over my mind while Collin shouts at him. I can't listen to his voice, now. In a panic, I begin losing my resolve just hearing him. Before I suffocate, Rick releases my head and I turn my face to the side, gasping for air. I can't do anything with the ropes tying my wrists so tightly behind me. Still, I struggle to get them free.

Leaning over my body with the scalpel in his hand, Rick holds it near my face where I can see a sliver of light reflecting off a sharp edge. He pushes his weight on me further, pressing the air from my lungs as he brings his lips close to my ear. "So, tell me, *Jaime,* are you frightened, *now*?" His teeth are still clenched, his body trembles, barely controlling his anger, but not for long. "Tell me!" He pushes himself back to kneel behind me, waiting for my answer.

Please, body, don't betray me now with a tremor. I can't allow him to see my fear or he'll have me. Stay steady. And it does. Not one shudder racks me and I'm strengthened by that. I turn to see him over my shoulder. I'm not afraid. I'm angry, but I'm not afraid. Take a deep breath.

"No. I'm not frightened of you." The instrument in his hand is lowered to my jaw line and he draws it slowly across my flesh, from below my ear to the edge of my chin. I feel blood trickle over my throat as I grit my teeth to keep them from chattering. At least Collin couldn't see what he had done.

Rick slips a thick strap over my head with a metal buckle digging into my flesh. As the leather encircles my neck, Collin shouts at him again. My head is yanked backward as Rick tightens the belt around my throat.

Instead of being frightened, I begin to laugh. "This is it? This is what you had planned? I really expected worse from you, Rick." As he pulls the leather tighter around my throat, I laugh again and shake my head. Trying to catch my breath, I look over my shoulder again. "I'm just grateful you didn't go the direction I thought you would." My words stop him from pulling on the leather and he glares back at me. "I figured you'd live out your fantasy, follow the path of the demons you'd watched and slam me against a cold wall, taking me there where you can watch my eyes. Isn't that what you prefer to see, the fear and pain you're causing? At least this way I don't have to *look* at you."

He's silent and unmoving, seems to be contemplating what I've said until he loosens the leather around my neck and reaches for my shoulders again. The belt falls to the ottoman as he lifts me to my feet and drags me to the wall. Slamming my back flat, he grabs hold of my shirt. My mind is relieved. The plan is nearly back on the path I'd envisioned. I'm almost where I need to be.

Thrusting his hand into a pocket, he pulls out a pair of scissors.

I shake my head. "I've had more of a weakening effect on

you than I thought. You *have* gone soft. When I saw that enormous fireplace I thought for sure you planned to throw me against the rock. You seem to love the idea of my back being torn while I'm being attacked." I make my voice breathy, almost sultry as if the idea excites me. I know he won't be able to resist that.

He smiles as he raises the scissors to the neck of my shirt, cutting through the collar and tearing the rest open with his hands. I'm still not getting what I'm hoping for. I may have to push him further.

I smirk at him to show I think he's pathetic. "The scissors you used to cut the threads when you tied my sutures. *Classy*."

He cuts the sleeves on both sides and rips the shirt from my back. Then, he brings the point of the scissors to my shoulder. "You don't want to anger me, Jaime." Speaking through gritted teeth again, he shoves the point deep into my muscle. I bite the inside of my cheek to keep from screaming in agony, to keep Collin from knowing what's happening.

Realizing what I've done, Rick looks over his shoulder at Collin, understanding it would hurt more to have him know what was being done to me. "Sarah, I want you to stop cutting up our friend and let him watch the show. He's gonna wanna see this."

Disappointment shows in her eyes as she lowers the knife to her side. She grabs his face and turns it so he's looking our direction.

My skin is wet with sweat and blood. Large drops tickle the sides of my face and neck. Next change to happen…now. "Man, it's hot in here! *Phew*. Are you getting hot, Rick?" At first He looks confused. The room isn't as warm as I want him to think it is. "Will you at least open a window?" I breathe heavier, in a sensual, almost tantalizing way. I can't over play this, though, or he'll know I'm up to something. I've already shown my repulsion for him. Realization suddenly spreads across his face as he raises his hands to my neck.

His eyes pour over my body and he smirks in appreciation. His hands slip down my damp arms, spreading blood from my shoulders to my wrists. His breathing comes quicker. "I don't think so. I like this." Rings of sweat form at his armpits. *Perfect.*

When I look past him to Collin, his sunken eyes find mine, guilt showing on his face as he sees the blood coating my neck and shoulder. I shake my head. There's no time for pity. Hold in there. Just a moment longer.

"Forget him. He'll die soon and we'll be free to unite. You'll remember how much you love me. At least you'd better."

His desire is stoked. Now's the time. Now I remember that night and make him remember it also.

"You think I'll unite with a rogue angel? Someone who held me down, taking delight from watching two boys *ravage* me?" I say the word as if it's filth I can't wash from my hands.

He turns to the fireplace and then back at me with his jaw set. That's it. That's exactly what I want.

The perversion that poisons his mind shows in his eyes. As Rick pulls me by the arm across the room to the fireplace, he slams my back against the jagged rock. He backhands me across the face the same as one of the boys that night in the mountains. I ignore the sting, knowing it'll bruise later. Collin shouts at him again, but I still can't listen to him. His elevated emotions colored with guilt will distract me. A knowing smile crosses my face when I turn back to Rick as if I don't mind the rock cutting my skin.

Inching toward Collin, I move closer to the center of the stone, but Rick grabs my shoulders and throws me once more, against the solid wall. The rocks cut deeper into my flesh, my blood staining the surface. Just what he wanted and what I had anticipated. His distraction gives me the opening I need.

With his eagerness barely under control, he moves closer to my ear and whispers, "I enjoyed every moment, Jaime. Watching your back being torn by the ground. Holding your arms while they took you again and again. All these years, I haven't been able to get it out of my mind."

"Yeah? Me neither." Glaring back at him with my jaw set, I hear their laughter once again. This'll be the last time I remember that night.

He kisses me and runs his hands over my exposed flesh. The disgust I feel at his weight pressing against me, pinning me to the rock wall, causes me to turn away, clenching my teeth in determination. Reaching my hand under the lip of the fireplace, I search for the lever that opens the flue.

Rick's breath is hot against my throat and I cringe at the feel of his lips on my skin. "You know, if I was stronger, I'd have joined them. But I already knew what you were capable of and knew I couldn't match you. Even at fifteen, you could have killed me, too. Ha. Those boys had no idea what they were about to unleash when they threw you in the backseat of that car." The thrill shows in his eyes as he relives the moment.

With one hand at my throat, the other rises up my body, over my ribcage, and to my breast. I stare him in the eyes with the look of a killer—seething—and I want him to know. He loves the challenge, conquering the woman who hates him.

"You know, Rick, I promised myself long ago, if I ever found the one who held my hands that night, I'd kill him in a *sick* and memorable way."

With his hand still on my throat, he looks me deep in the eyes. "I'm waiting."

My expression stays calm. "Don't get choked up."

He appears confused at my reply for a moment before he

lowers his eyes to my bra. "This is adorable on you, but I'm afraid I'll need to remove it if I want to finish this. You don't mind, do you?" He releases my neck, sliding his other hand down and around my back to unlatch my bra.

I smile at him, staring deep into his eyes. "Go for it. But you might watch out for those butterfly needles I taped back there."

"Ouch! What the—" He stops for a moment, feeling around; then, he rips away the needles taped to my bra, pulling them in front of him. "Heh. You thought this would stop me from taking off what little you have left on your body and enjoying you in front of *him*?" He sounds so cocky before putting his fingers in his mouth and sucking off the blood.

Biting my lip and still looking him in the eyes, I smile again. "Yes, Rick, I do." His eyes grow dark as he studies my expression. "Each of those needles is filled with cyanide."

He stops sucking on his fingertips, searching his thoughts. I can see the panic in his eyes, something I've waited years to see.

Then, he forces a half smile. "This is a dream. You can't possibly poison me without my willingness to believe."

My smile grows as I stare back at him, my chin lifted in defiance. "You hold the needles from my imagination in your hands. Your fingers bleed and ache from being stabbed by them. I've already planted the seed. The idea that cyanide is invading your system has already poisoned your thoughts. But I didn't leave it to chance. I spiked your appletini at the bar. Do you remember the seeds in the bottom of your drink?"

He laughs loudly. "Arsenic?" He throws back his head and laughs again. "That wasn't enough to kill me and it takes far too long to take effect, anyway. I'll be two hundred years old before I develop cancer from the arsenic in those apples."

"That's right. But when you add to it the rat poison I also

put in your little cocktail." His eyes shift from me to search his memory. "Consider my actions. If I already knew about you, would I have asked you out, dressed so revealing, without an alternative motive? I crossed my legs and you swallowed the poison." The smile slips from his face. "Now consider the drink I ordered. Do you think my selection was by chance? My drink of choice is gin. Nice and dry. Appletinis are far too sweet for someone like me. Why do you think I drank them so fast? However, even you would have to admit, they *are* memorable." I laugh in his face. "And I can't get the thought out of my head. The doctor being killed by an apple. I find it poetic."

The more I talk the tighter his throat becomes, causing him to gag.

"The super-tart taste you noticed nearly covered up the bitterness of the real poison. Appletinis suck, but they're not bitter, not if they're made correctly. And the arsenic? Not just in the apple seeds, but a little extra sprinkled in. A cross between the two poisons gave it a little extra *punch*, wouldn't you say? I put enough in your glass to kill you by the time you wake. Oh, and when I held your hands before leaving, I spread it over your fingers. When I kissed you, it was on my lips. Can you feel the powder?"

He lifts his hands. They're covered in white and I smile at the impression my words are leaving in his mind.

"I've no doubt you rubbed your face while you were sleeping."

He lifts his arm to his lips and wipes them with his sleeve, spitting and trying to remove the bitter taste from his mouth.

"And in all your excitement over what you'd planned to do to me, you've worked up such a sweat, dilating your veins so your blood could flow more freely than usual. Poison is racing through your sleeping, sweaty body. No matter what happens here and now, you're still gonna die."

"Why would you do that? They saw me leave with you. They'll suspect you poisoned me." I can tell he's in pain and I'm enjoying it more than I can ever articulate.

"You're right. Until they find the open box on the floor under your bed and the dead rat in your trash. I was a busy little girl before I left your house tonight. The traces on your fingers and lips will be enough to show you weren't very cautious with your extermination procedures. Maybe they'll think you were too drunk last night and in your inebriated state, put it there yourself. Who knows what they'll surmise. Maybe they'll find the white on your nose and wonder if you were snorting cocaine."

He wipes his face again with his other sleeve.

"You're sleeping. You can't get rid of it so easily. When they do their toxicology test, they'll find the arsenic and think you've been drinking some bad water. But when they find the rat poison in your system, on your fingers and mouth, they'll think you were careless and may have even poisoned your own patients as well."

His eyes turn away from me now. His hands go to his throat. He licks his lips and gasps for air. Also licking my lips in anticipation, I enjoy watching him suffer.

"Right about now, your heart is speeding up and your bronchial tubes are tightening. That gagging reflex is your esophagus growing thick. The cyanide is working. Soon the rat poison will cause you to bleed out of your eyes. Then, you'll bleed out of every orifice in your body. But you already knew that, didn't you?"

His eyes are so dilated with fear his blue irises have nearly disappeared. I grind my teeth together in anticipation, excited at seeing the horror in them. It's wrong, I know it's wrong, and I may hate myself for it later, but damn it, after all he's done to me I can't help but enjoy his torment.

"So, tell me, *Rick*, are you *frightened*?"

He doesn't need to answer. I already know.

As he starts choking and gagging I feel a long carried weight being lifted from my chest. I'll never again wonder what it would be like to kill my attacker in the shadows. The memory of that night will no longer evoke fear, only satisfaction. Pondering all of his victims, I feel resolution, knowing he will never again torture another the way he tortured me. Not one more rape victim strangled by his blue necktie in their sleep.

Before Rick sinks to his knees, I attract Gilbert's attention, nodding toward Sarah. I've been working the ropes across the scalpel I'd affixed to the flue of the fireplace. When my ropes are free, I turn to unravel the tape around the handle. No need to waste my time on Rick. He's no longer a threat.

As I'm working to free my weapon, I see Sarah moving toward me with the steak knife in her hand. Seeing me notice her, she lunges for me. Suddenly turning on her, I knock her hand away and pull the surgical tool into my fist. Before she can swing her knife again, I stab her in the abdomen, twisting the blade inside her body and jerking it sideways before shoving her backward.

She tumbles over the sofa as I rush to Collin and cut his ligatures on one wrist then turn to Gilbert. "Can I trust you?"

He stares back at me, allowing me to see into his soul. "You saved me from that woman. What do you think?"

In his eyes I see he's a changed man. Whatever brought him to this stage, I don't know and I don't have time to find out. What I do know is he realizes he's dependent on us to wake from this dream alive. That's all I need to know and I hand him the scalpel.

"Help me," I tell him and he nods and begins cutting at the

ligatures.

A hard yank on Collin's hand pulls the nail through. Before I can move to his other, he grabs me and kisses me.

"I love you," he whispers into my lips.

After Gilbert cuts the ropes on his other hand, I yank that one free also and he falls to his knees. I turn from him, knowing he'll be safe for the moment. My emotions cold and attention to detail sharpened, I calculate Sarah's actions in order to end her life as expeditiously as possible.

"I promised to kill you Sarah. And you know I've always kept my promises. So you might as well come out of the corner and get this over with."

She's been standing in the shadows, wounded and unsure while watching Rick suffer. She can't leave. Her choices are to fight or kill Gilbert. In a battle with me she knows she'll lose. Her only chance of survival is to eliminate the demon.

Gathering her strength, she starts toward Gilbert with the steak knife tight in her fist, intent on ending the dream and escaping into the night. When I see her charging toward him I sidestep between them, swing my hand, hitting her in the throat and knocking her backward. The stab wound in my shoulder, however, has made me weaker than I'd thought. That move should've crushed her trachea.

As soon as Sarah regains her balance, she reaches for my hair and I roll past her shoulder, bringing my arm to her neck again, this time throwing her to the floor. She slices the air with the knife, but misses me. A spin and kick to her arm still doesn't cause her to let go. The knife cuts the air again, ripping my calf muscle. As I fall hard to the floor, I clench my teeth to keep from screaming out in pain.

Her hand flies forward, the blade aimed at my throat, but I catch it, holding the knife in mid thrust. Forcing her fist to the floor, I crawl on top of her, holding her arms out to her side.

Out of my peripheral I see Gilbert helping Collin cut the ropes around his ankles. On the other side of the room, Mandy still creeps in the shadows.

"Collin?" My focus is still on Sarah beneath me as I try to assess his condition.

Sarah spits at me and starts kicking her legs to try and flip her body over. "I'm gonna kill you, bitch, then I'm gonna finish your boyfriend." Her voice is strained as she fights to raise the knife to me.

"Good luck with that." I let go of her right arm and punch her in the face. I grab the handle of the knife with both hands. Sarah also reaches for it.

From the corner of my eye, I see Rick sink to his knees, blood leaking from his nose and mouth. His throat seems to be closed and he's struggling to breathe. Soon, he slips to the floor, his body completely still.

My eyes are on Sarah, again, but my mind is in two places now. "Collin? You all right?"

He's on the floor and doesn't answer.

"Gilbert?"

"He's lost a lot of blood."

"Collin, talk to me." I wait for his voice while Sarah smiles up at me as if she's won. She may not have killed me yet, but she's nearly killed him.

"I'm here, Babe," he speaks up, his voice weak and hoarse.

I give Sarah a look of determination with the hint of a grin. "You've already lost, Sarah. You're through."

My hands twist the handle of the knife, turning the tip of the blade to her chest. She struggles to stop me with shaking hands as I plant it in her sternum. Her eyes dilate and her breathing becomes erratic. She's frightened, knowing her inevitable destination, but I'm unwavering.

"This knife may not be as sharp," I tell her, tightening my

grip on the handle. "But it'll do." With both hands, I shove downward, holding the knife in place until her body stops jerking. Knowing she's dead, I call over my shoulder. "Collin?"

When I try to stand, my strength is gone and I collapse to the floor. Blood coats my lower leg and I can't make it to my feet for the cut calf muscle. Crawling on one knee, I'm able to pull myself to Collin's side.

"Talk to me, Collin. Please. Tell me you're all right." I kiss his lips, his cheek, his forehead and then run my fingers through his wet hair.

He opens his eyes and nods. There are so many cuts on his body.

Gilbert is still at my side and I want to be sure his alliance is firm. "Gilbert? Still with me?"

He looks me in the eyes. "Not going anywhere. Thanks…for saving me. Even though I don't deserve—"

I nod, knowing his change of heart is solid. After what he's witnessed he'll think twice before considering doing wrong again.

He turns to Collin, concern for his condition showing. "Is it possible to live after something like this?"

"I hope so. Collin, stay with me. Gilbert, go get some wet towels from the bathroom." He cocks his head at me. "Trust me, just do it." He nods and surveys the room before heading off. "Collin, open your eyes, talk to me."

Seconds later Gilbert has returned with several towels, both wet and dry.

"Thanks. That'll work."

A rolled towel is place under Collin's neck, a second under the back of his knees. The rest are wet and I wipe his face and arms, blotting his chest, stomach and legs to assess his cuts. Nothing *too* deep except the one in his abdomen. This one can be closed with sutures. Blood loss is significant and I'm concerned about his chance for survival, but he's a dark angel. If anyone could survive this, it would be him.

Even with pressure over the deepest cut in the lower part of his abdomen, the bleeding won't stop. "Gilbert, hold your hand here."

Doc's medical bag is somewhere around here. The Lidocaine with Epinephrine, he said it slows the bleeding. A quick visual search of the living room and kitchen area turns up nothing. Maybe his bedroom. The pain in my leg is excruciating, but I rise to my feet anyway, limping down the hallway.

As I ease open the door to Rick's room, my mind grows apprehensive, wondering what I'll find. The room seems darker than the rest of the house, or maybe it's my fear playing tricks on me. As I progress further inside, I realize my eyes haven't adjusted, yet, I'm unsure if I want to see what may be waiting. Moving forward into the darkness, I see his body lying on the bed. My hands tremble once more, remembering what he did and what he'd planned for me. I can't look at him right now, though. There's a medical bag I have to find.

Searching the floor, I finally catch a glimpse of a black bag from the corner of my eye. Grabbing the handle, I immediately head toward the living room. Then, the feeling of a presence behind me stays my feet and holds me in place.

A rush of wind tickles my shoulder and I begin to shudder once again. "Jaime, we're not through."

I immediately spin around to see no one is there. The voice was a whisper. I didn't recognize who spoke. Was it my imagination?

My stomach turns and my body shakes uncontrollably. I'll never rest until I know he's dead. I can't finish my life always searching the shadows, wondering if I'll find him there, waiting. Dropping the bag at my feet, I inch forward, making my way to Rick's bed. The coverings aren't pulled over his body as they were when I left. My mind shifts between the idea I prefer to entertain and the one I fear may be true, that I didn't actually kill Richard Stanton.

While moving slowly to Rick's side, my heart pounds in my chest, my breathing is shallow. In the dim light leaking past the edges of his heavy drapes, I see a stream of black running down his face from his eyes, nose and mouth. Blood.

As I lean over his body, I bring my ear to his nose to see if he's breathing. When my weight presses against the edge of the mattress, his hand comes off the bed and reaches for my leg. I jump backward and my scream echoes throughout the room. The sound of Gilbert's voice is barely audible when he calls to me to see if I'm all right.

Rick's arm dangles limply in the air and I take a deep breath; then, swallow to call back to him. "I'm okay. Startled by a rat."

My heart thumps loudly in my chest. I'm hesitant to touch him, but I have no choice, now. I have to make sure he's dead, that my fight with him is over. Stepping closer to the bed, I lean forward again. My hand shakes as it slides over his throat, feeling for a pulse, carefully watching his extremities. There's no sense of blood pulsing through his arteries. His chest isn't rising or falling either. He isn't breathing and I know his soul has gone to a dark place.

Taking in a deep breath, I release it quickly. My plan worked. Kneeling beside the bed, I pull the open box from beneath, carrying it with me as I limp out to the living room with Doc's med bag in my other hand.

At Collin's side once again, I set the box on the floor and search for the Lidocaine in the bottom of the bag. A bundle of syringes catches my eye and then I see it. The translucent bottle he used for me just days ago, lying next to a sterile set of sutures.

Gilbert is still kneeling next to Collin as I fill the syringe, snap the bubbles to the top and press them through the tip of the needle. "You've done this before?"

"No." I turn to Collin and insert the needle into his wound, starting with the one in his abdomen first. "I have a photographic memory." He looks at me in question. "I've had this done to me before."

As he feels the prick of the needle, Collin flinches and his eyes open. His hand reaches for mine as I work at stopping his bleeding.

"It's all right. Lay down while I do this. There's gonna be a lot of pain, Collin. You're gonna have to hold on while I do this. It's the only way to save you."

He nods.

"Jaime, I'm sorry." He swallows before going on, his voice hoarse with pain. "This never would've happened to you if I hadn't—"

"Shh. Be quiet now."

I'm not ready to talk about what he did. Not yet. And I'm not sure when I will be. His betrayal runs deep beneath my skin. Although I know I love him, I can't find the words to tell him so and I don't know if I ever will.

"Will it make any difference in a dream? I mean, sewing him up."

Thank you, Gilbert, for giving me something else to dwell on. "It'll trick his mind into thinking his wounds were closed. His body will automatically repair itself in his sleep. If we wake and he's still bleeding, he'll die. I won't have a way to save him because I won't have access to these sutures."

He stares back at me, and I can see he understands. "What,

what happened in there?" he asks and nods toward Rick's bedroom.

"I was checking on Doc, making sure he's dead. Saw something that startled me."

"But…I thought he was out here, on the floor over there."

"His soul is over here, but his physical body is still in there. Unlike most dreams, this one takes place in an actual location. I don't know how they do it, but some way they're able to change dreams to physical settings. It's something I've never done and so I don't really understand it myself."

Gilbert looks past me to the box at my side. "Is that the rat poison you gave the Doc?"

"No. It's dryer sheets." Keeping my attention on Collin, I continue shooting Lidocaine into his wounds.

Gilbert stares at me curiously for a moment; a smile spreads across his lips. "You didn't give him rat poison?"

"No."

"No dead rat in the trash, either?"

I shake my head.

"And you didn't give him arsenic."

"Just like the cyanide, I only planted the idea. His mind did the rest."

"Oh, you're slick. I find that *hot* in a woman."

"Don't get too excited, Gilbert. I haven't forgotten what you agreed to do to me."

"Whoa. Wait a minute. I'm giving up those ways. After all, I didn't follow through."

"You touched me after I told you not to." As I work on Collin, my eyes see only him, but I can feel my posture is causing Gilbert concern.

Gilbert swallows loudly. "I did, I did do that and I'm really sorry. If there's any way I can make this right…You *did* tell me you weren't gonna kill me tonight." He sounds more nervous than usual.

"I did promise that, didn't I?" Lifting one of his eyelids, I examine Collin's pupils, searching for signs of shock.

Collin clears his throat and then speaks to me in a weak voice. "You have to kill him, Jaime."

"Don't try to speak right now, just rest."

"What does he mean you have to kill me?" Gilbert rises to his feet and backs away from me. "I helped you."

"I don't have to kill you, Gilbert." My back is to him as I tie off the last suture on Collin. "However, if you really want to make this right, then you'll never, and I do mean *never,* do that to anyone again. Because, if you ever turn back, ever murder anyone in your sleep or awake, I will find you and I *will* kill you. Do you understand?" I look up at him to show I'm serious.

Gilbert studies me, his eyes darting between me and Collin. "I promise."

I'm nearly finished, feeling Gilbert's eyes still on me. "What, Gilbert?"

"I don't know if I should ask this, but, I was thinking about what you said earlier, about them being stuck in the dream until I die? Was that a lie?"

Trimming the ends of the last suture, I wrap what is left in the package and toss it into Doc's bag. "Not really. Sarah showed her hand when she threatened you. They'd planned for me to kill you at some point. At least that was Rick's hope." I look up into his eyes again so he can see I'm telling the truth.

He's definitely scared. "When you turned, when you joined them?"

"Right, that, or if I killed you right away, distracting my focus and allowing them an early advantage."

"But…from the sounds of it, if that happened, then the

dream would end before they had what they wanted, wouldn't it? Seems like ending the dream before they got you to turn would've messed up their plan."

"*If* the dream were to actually end when I killed you. But it wouldn't have. They had a contingency."

"I don't understand."

"Mandy. She's not a rogue angel. She's like you."

"And that means?"

"That means they could kill you and still keep going since you hadn't murdered anyone yet and since there was a demon still left in the dream, one who's killed other mortals. They would've had to kill her, at some point, when they were finished and ready to wake. No matter what, Mandy was going to die tonight. You were a prop."

"That sucks."

"Yep. Either way, in their calculations, *you* were the throw away."

Looking over Collin's body, I see that his bleeding has nearly stopped. Now I have one more thing to do before we can leave.

"But, isn't she gone? Mandy? I saw her run."

Rising to my feet, I hold my breath while putting slight pressure on my aching leg. "Before I came into the living room, before you saw me for the first time, I locked the front door, the only one unlocked when I left earlier this evening. She can't leave until *I* unlock a door. She's been moving around the house, trying to get out since I killed Sarah."

Listening for a moment to know which direction to go, I finally turn back to Gilbert. "If I ever see you again, it had better be on the street, not in a dream."

His eyes widen with fear as I turn my attention toward Mandy. The house is still, yet I feel her presence near the front doorway. My head down, I take a deep breath before moving on.

"You were smart to stay in the shadows as much as you did, Mandy." I continue limping toward the hallway. "If you hadn't, I would've noticed sooner." I listen while slowly making my way, holding onto the wall. "Sarah gave it away earlier when she threatened to kill Gilbert so early. He wasn't in the gallery that night in my dream. You were. The demon they tossed out before locking the door, until the fight was over, saving you for another night."

As I near the sitting room by the front door, I can hear her heart pounding like a trapped animal.

"I didn't let on that my memory returned for a reason," I say.

Her breathing becomes shallow and her heart flutters loud enough for me to hear.

"Rick knew Versed isn't foolproof, doesn't always cause the patient to forget, but he counted on it working perfectly on this occasion. He ignored the fact that people still remember sometimes. Until tonight, I let him believe he was right."

She's pacing. I can feel her anxiety increase with each breath.

"The fight, someone swung the crystal vase at me. Collin caught it before it could hit me, but the momentum caused his fist to split my lip. Once I learned that fact from him, everything else eventually fell into place. I started to remember it all in bits and pieces. Sarah and Doc rushing from the room, leaving the other demon behind; not you, your sister, an identical twin, perhaps. I saw it in Doc's eyes at the bar before I sent him off to sleep with copious amounts of alcohol. Your sister was the one Collin really hired. I could barely tell the difference. Now I can see the slight slant in your left eye that she didn't have."

She's in my line of sight, but unable to see me. "You

despised Collin for killing her. That's what I noticed the night of the gallery showing, your disdain. But you were wrong in your hatred, because he didn't." I hesitate for a moment, letting her digest what I'm telling her. "I did. You should really learn to read people better. It was in Doc's eyes tonight, whenever he peered toward the shadows. Searching for you."

At the moment of my revelation, she stops pacing.

With her body stilled, I move from the shadows, letting her see me. "Unlike Gilbert, you've killed before. You helped Sarah and Doc kill that family. You strangled that girl in her bed, helped Sarah hold the mother while Doc beat her and violated her, all to get back at Collin by helping them hurt me. You helped Sarah cut the husband over and over again until he was pleading for you to kill him. And worst of all, you enjoyed it."

Her eyes narrow as I regard her calmly. "I have no choice. I *will* kill you. You're small. It'll be easy. You were brought here to die tonight anyway. I promise I'll make it fast."

A growl rolls up her throat as she lowers her head, her eyes fixed on me. A second later she lunges. Reaching out before her fingers can wrap around my throat, I snap her neck and let her fall to the floor.

In the seconds before her death and my waking, I feel the presence of another, not a demon, a rogue. How did I miss that before?

My eyes flip open and I'm in my bed next to Collin. He looks over at me and pulls my hand in his. We still have time to rest before deciding where we'll go from here.

CHAPTER 20

Someone once uttered the words, *sweet revenge,* and the world drew a collective gasp at the idea of an untainted soul-killing in pleasure. Since that day, humans have nurtured an obsession with vengeance, romanticizing the idea of seeing someone suffer for the pain they once put another through. An ideology such as this, two words tossed flippantly into the wind, never takes responsibility for the aftermath of such a violent act.

This morning as I wake, after having allowed the demon within me to not just roam but lay waste to all who I have hated, the ones who betrayed me, the feeling is nothing near that sweetness I'd expected. The weight of my captain's death lays heavy on my shoulders. Was there another way I could have ended this? Had I confronted Rick with my suspicions, pleaded with him to find a more sustainable direction, reminded him of who he once was, could I have turned him from the darkness that captured his heart? My fury didn't even consider another option other than devastation. And now I will never know. I will always wonder.

All forms of conversation are practically non-existent

today. Collin moves slowly, protecting his injuries of last night's fight, while bringing food to me as I lay balled up and naked on the covers, staring into the nothingness that has consumed me. He offers, but I'm motionless and unresponsive. The touch of his fingers on my shoulder, neck, ear, gently caressing while showering me with declarations of love and caring thoughts, bring no comfort. I don't want to feel comfort or love. Those are two notions I've come to know as foreign and abhorrent.

The memory of Rick's face haunts me still, his flesh turning blue as he choked to death in front of me, blood streaming from his eyes. These visions eventually mingle with those of him after a ferocious battle with Lucifer and his followers, gently caressing my shoulders just as Collin does now. The tender soul and the dark killer, the trusted friend, a twisted shadow-dweller. Each of them were rolled into one like the many melding pictures in my mind of the varying moods of Doctor Richard Stanton. And I loved then hated him. Now his soul dwells in eternal darkness with the other rogue angels I've sent to their deaths.

Collin rests on the edge of the bed and strokes my hair, exactly as *he* had in the pre-life, my loyal underling, my trusted captain. My husband's touch should assuage me, but it only brings more sorrow as my thoughts drift to the inevitable question: Did I allow Rick to love me too much in the pre-existence? Was that the true cause of his demise?

Had I stayed in heaven, would the outcome have been different? Should I have expected this end result with my mere presence here? Was it entirely my fault?

The answers don't present themselves like sacred papyrus on the walls of my bedroom. I'm fully empty, more so now than ever before. I can't begin to see daylight in this chasm I'd sunken into. I've stumbled into hell without even taking my last breath. My breath. My life. It continues on without effort on my part. If I had a choice, I wouldn't allow my lungs to expand or contract another time. And the hours tick by while I lay here and breathe. There is no way to console me or resurrect me from the type of death I now know. The day seems to draw on for an eternity.

As evening comes, the demons call me to sleep. Collin curls up beside me and I drift off to the blackness I never knew in my dreams before this night. Even God refuses to shed the light of a single star to console me. I must walk this path alone as I await the next damaged soul, the one I will send on to meet our heavenly father.

Before long, a pinprick of light turns to a dim glow in the distance. I trudge forward, knowing it is my duty to meet the monster waiting for his prey. And I remember my conversation with Rick, telling me he would jump into a raging river to save a drowning child, but he would never throw another in to do it for him. Was he trying to tell me I had taken the wrong journey, that I'd been forced into a mission that would one day steal my soul? He must have known these demons God leads me to will someday destroy my will.

"Why not allow the police to handle this?" He had practically begged me to stop hunting. Was it his way of saving us both from a devastating outcome?

The defective soul isn't far from me now. I can feel their anger driving a deep hatred for humanity. Do they sense my self-loathing, as well? Are they attracted to others like me who are damaged goods, worthless spirits?

The silhouette of his enormous form appears to nearly blot out the distant light and I stand, quietly waiting for him. He isn't in a hurry to reach me as he strides casually forward. The faces of those I'd killed before today, flash through my mind as I wait. The two boys in the mountains, torn to shreds. The one I'd impaled in my bathroom the night before. Those I'd turned their own weapons back on them. Snapped their necks, crushed bones, cracked skulls, all of their faces flash before my eyes as I await the demon's assault. I have nearly sixty years of death on my hands. My sole consolation is the number of lives these deaths have saved. As much as I try to reconcile the weight of my actions toward the consequences of theirs, it still becomes a factor that pulls on my soul. Multiplied by three hundred sixty-five, and you have twenty-one thousand, nine hundred spirits. That's practically twenty-two thousand lives I'm responsible for ending. All of them, souls who once knew me. Every single one of them fought with me in a distant past that had never existed on this earth, the great battle in the pre-existence. Could any of them have been like Rick, possibly salvageable if only I had tried? I'll never know.

As he nears, I'm reminded of another I'd killed of equally impressive size. In the mountains. With Rick, watching from a nearby shadow. There is no shower curtain rod at my disposal here. I'm without a weapon and devoid of will to take this monster down. Is this the one who will send me back to atone for my life here on earth?

As he reaches me, I notice the way his shirt pulls tight across his chest. His muscles flex in the dim light when he moves. I study his face, wanting to remember the sharp edge of his jaw, the squared chin below full lips. An angular nose rises to meet dark eyes that drill into mine. His brow curves cynically before his hands reach for my throat. My eyes track his as I involuntarily struggle to breathe, hoping my life will be over soon. In my weakness, I sink to my knees, feeling his fingers tighten, and I wonder if I've turned the same shade as Rick had before he slipped from this earth. And it is then that I hear my husband's voice.

"Jaime!" A blow to my chest sends me careening backward. The monster's tight grasp on my life is broken and before my body sinks to the ground, from the corner of my eye, I see him. His comforting scent fills my mind as I gulp in air, shaking my head. I don't want to be comforted.

"No, Collin! Let me go!" I shriek and lunge forward while he struggles with the hulking mass in front of him. "Let me die!"

My words puncture the thick air and he turns to me in shock. The look in his eyes is wounding as if I had stabbed him in the heart with a dagger, forged from the splinters of our marital bed. His hesitation gives the monster the advantage.

Although I try to force him out of the way, a heavy blow from the demon's fist sends Collin tumbling to the ground. He's still far too weak to effectively fight such a strong foe.

With a quick, backward swipe, he tosses me in the opposite direction like a ragdoll made of sackcloth. Then, he turns on Collin. My blood pulses through me as I push up from the floor and bound toward them. As the monster grabs a handful of Collin's shirt, I land square on his back and weave my fingers through his thick hair. Remembering the way I'd driven the monolith's face into the gravel on Gold Camp Road, I yank backward with every ounce of power that's within me. This time, however, I'm unable to knock him unconscious, merely stunning him momentarily. If I don't act to kill him now, he'll kill Collin instead of me. I can't allow the blood of his death to stain my hands, also.

Desperate for an ending to this night, I scan the surrounding area for anything that could be used as a tool. As if my thoughts had made it so, large splinters, like daggers, litter the ground at my feet, each of them gnawed from the same wood as the headboard of my bed. Some, stained with splattered blood, I would guess, from one of my more violent fights.

As the monster struggles to rise, I lift a piece of fragmented wood into my fist. The size is that of a wooden stake, the kind you are directed to use to kill vampires in ancient books of folklore. I turn the wood over in my palm and note the scar filled with my blood. The one I'd made in my battle with Phillip P. Bradley. My body begins to shake violently.

With the sharpened stake in hand, I turn to see the monster moving toward Collin again. His heavy hand, once again, knocks my husband to the ground. As he kneels over the man I've come to love, the damaged beast wraps his hands around Collin's throat. The anger I'd known a day before that allowed me to kill someone who was once a friend, drives me forward and onto the demon's back. I grit my teeth and raise my hands high above my head. I drive the stake into the back of his neck, severing his spinal cord and ending his life. Collin and I wake before his body collapses to the floor.

When my eyes snap open, I search my hands for the weapon I had used to kill the demon. The splintered wood with traces of my life is no longer in my grasp but reunited with the native grain in the furniture of my bed chambers. As my fingers brush the imperfect surface, I see the face of the killer. I'd finished him with something of my own, drove my blood deep into him with wood constructed from scars of past battles that continue to haunt my memory.

The screams echoing off the walls of my room, sound like my voice. I don't realize at first that it is me who is creating the shrill sound. Collin immediately pulls me into his arms and strokes my hair as he kisses my forehead. An hour passes before my sobs subside and I'm calmed once again. As I stare off in the distance, I clear my throat and take a deep breath.

"Twenty-one thousand, nine hundred and one," I whisper

into the universe.

***

As I stare at my pale features in the mirror, I note the dried blood drawn by Rick's scalpel, smeared from jaw to wrist. The slice Sarah made in my other cheek the day she attacked Collin in his sleep, in my room, is nearly healed. Others she and Rick made in our final meeting, scattered across my body, are nearly the same. The scars will remain for an eternity as a badge of my hatred and deep loss. I once adored Sarah. Once loved Rick, too.

The person I've become is unrecognizable, more determined to end my life here than ever before. Is this my destiny? Am I meant to leave the living with a tormented heart and mind? An angel such as me could never return to my father's presence in such a state. Maybe I will never know the comfort of his love wrapping around my grateful soul ever again. Could I withstand an eternity in torment?

I barely feel Collin's energy as he enters the room and lifts the brush to my hair. His scent is subtler than I've ever known, barely noticeable. Have my emotional struggles drowned my other senses, made me more vulnerable to those who kill?

The severe wounds in his chest are prominent as he stands before me without a shirt. The battle scars I once admired have an opposite effect on me now. I'm repulsed at the sight of what he endured in our battle with Rick and Sarah. I am sickened at the others that were given to him while he, too, killed another defective soul. Will I ever find the strength I once had to continue to fight demons?

Deep lines of worry and pain crease his forehead as he studies my reflection, wondering if I will ever return from the dead. I can't help but wonder myself. The light touch of his hand and his lips pressed against the crown of my head, don't bring me the solace he intends. As much as I yearn to remember the passion we had known, I feel emptiness. I know he wants me to remember how deeply he loves me. His strong arms encircle me, bind me to his chest until I feel his life force radiating through mine. As much as I try, I'm unable to accept the love he extends to me. How much longer can I keep this up? How long will he endure the animosity I feel - toward him and myself? Is it possible to love and despise him without destroying us both? Isn't that what I've done for years? Kill. With one last kiss to my forehead, he leaves me for the kitchen.

The sound of a skillet clinking the stove's surface startles me. The resonant timbre reverberating through my body suddenly awakens a part of my soul I had abandoned as lost. My senses heighten once again as I smell it, hear it, feel it multiplying, growing within me. The sound is ancient Celtic. The scent is that of Irish moorlands. How could it be? In only one night. A life grows within me. Somehow it survived my hatred, the ire I'd cultivated to destroy Rick and Sarah. I'm immediately struck with stunning force. I'm carrying Collin's baby in my womb.

With an unsteady hand, I caress my flat abdomen to sense the life force of the one incubating deep within. Another archangel coming to earth to help with our fight. God hasn't forgotten me after all. But I don't want this child to endure what I had, to become like me.

As I sense this being growing stronger and more viable with each moment that passes, I recognize the irony. If I'd let the monster kill me, I'd have taken another life—that of my own child. This changes everything. A feeling of protectiveness more powerful than anything I've ever felt washes over me. God, to think what I had almost done... But no, I can't think about that. Not now. The self-loathing, self-destruction, it has to stop.

There is no possible way I could remain here. The pain of what I have become, of what Collin drove me to, is too great to stay. He knowingly put me in danger all those years ago and didn't seek me out to keep me safe. What other types of danger might his selfishness bring upon our unborn child? I have to remove myself and this tiny life from my past and hope to give it the peace I've longed for since the death of my father. The only one who matters at this juncture is the child.

Before Collin catches the scent, himself, I must make my move. If he were to realize what is hidden inside of me, he would never allow me to leave. At least for now, I have to go.

As I contemplate my options, my mind is drawn to the place of my birth and the land I've longed to know. He would never think to find me there. First opportunity, I will gather the most necessary of my belongings and make my departure. As much as it will multiply his pain, I must do it for the both of us, but mostly, for our child.

Thank you for reading! Please leave your review. And find more from B. Hughes-Millman and the Dark Angel series at www.facebook.com/ShadowKiller.DarkAngel/

Please sign up for the City Owl Press newsletter for chances to win special subscriber-only contests and giveaways as well as receiving information on upcoming releases and special excerpts.

@ Bobbi_Bobbi

All reviews are welcome and appreciated. Please consider leaving one on your favorite social media and book buying sites.

For books in the world of romance and speculative fiction that embody Innovation, Creativity, and Affordability, check out City Owl Press at www.cityowlpress.com.

ACKNOWLEDGEMENTS

I want to wish a tremendous thanks to my editor, Heather McCorkle, for helping to make loving Purgatory's Angel, for making it a better, cleaner novel and for helping to make it shine. To Tina Moss for taking that great photo of Rafael Mercado Salas' and creating a beautiful cover. And to Gio for the great author pic. Your talent still amazes me. Thank you, Rafael, for allowing me to use your beautiful photo for my cover. You are truly a talented man!

This novel is for anyone who has ever known the sting of loss and forced the tears back down their throat. This novel is for anyone who has ever wept at the misfortune of others. This novel is for anyone who has been told by someone they looked up to that they can't and did anyway. And it is for anyone who has fought demons far greater than so many would dare challenge.

This novel is for those who gave up the fight only to lift the sword once again to battle on. And it is for those who have said "Never again," far too many times.

For it is you who are the Dark Angels of the world. In the end, it is you who will save us all.

ABOUT THE AUTHOR

B. HUGHES-MILLMAN is an award-winning writer of short stories and author of young adult paranormal as well as adult urban fantasy and contemporary romance novels. She spends her time teaching English to professionals in France over the internet while participating as chief entertainer and chauffeur to her two sons along with her husband and partner in crime.

www.facebook.com/bhughesmillman

@bobbi_bobbi

About the Publisher

CITY OWL PRESS is a cutting edge indie publishing company, bringing the world of romance and speculative fiction to discerning readers.

www.cityowlpress.com

Made in the USA
Middletown, DE
01 May 2022

65059254R00170